Books by Julianna Zacleese

Single Titles

Forgotten Love

Forgotten Love

ISBN # 978-1-78686-191-7

©Copyright Julianna Zacleese 2017

Cover Art by Posh Gosh ©Copyright 2017

Interior text design by Claire Siemaszkiewicz

Totally Bound Publishing

FORGOTTEN LOVE

JULIANNA ZACLEESE

Dedication

In loving memory of Anthony Wilson, who bought me
books before I even knew I wanted to read them.

Acknowledgments

Thank you to Justin, JD and Jake for allowing me the time
to pursue my dreams. I love you all.

Chapter One

Hello again

"Hello, wife," a seductive voice echoes in the bedroom behind me as I sit staring at my reflection in the dressing table mirror.

"Hello, husband," I reply, grinning at the impossibly handsome man reflected in the glass. He leans casually against the door, tightening his cufflink, his dark-gray suit accentuating his steely dark-blue eyes and dark, tousled locks that turn up at the ends.

"You look beautiful, as always."

I roll my eyes as Nick closes the gap between us. "Stop saying that."

He leans in behind me, regarding our reflections in the mirror.

"Never," he replies, curling the corners of his lips in an innocent, childlike way. "Are you nearly ready? Our guests are starting to arrive." He leans in close to my ear, sensing my anxiety. "Don't worry. I'll be right by your side."

I turn around to look at him and there, in the lines of his face, in the warmth of his eyes, I find in him the courage I haven't been able to find in myself to make the journey downstairs.

Nick holds out his hand to me. "Shall we?"

I put mine in his and he summons me into his arms, his eyes soft and heady.

"I love you, Mrs. Pierce," he whispers, lowering his lips to mine.

I freeze, unable to respond. I'm not exactly sure how I

feel about my husband, Nick. I married him, so I must love him, right?

Truth is, I really don't know. I really don't know anything since the accident.

As we start down the stairs, the sound of wine-induced laughter and chitchat grows louder, grating my already fraying nerves. I reach out, taking a firm hold of the balustrade. Nick turns to look at me.

"It's okay — it's only close friends and family, and they're all here for you. To reconnect with you. There's nothing to be afraid of."

I arch an eyebrow.

"Besides, you've met them all before," he jokes.

"That's not funny."

"Really? Not even a little bit?"

"Not at all."

"Come on." He takes a step forward and tugs at my hand.

I drift forward, but I still can't let go of the balustrade. He turns back to me, amused.

"Let go."

I nod at him, without any intention of complying.

"Let go, then," he coaxes, tugging me away from the balustrade and tucking me under his arm so I can't do it again. "You know, if memory serves me, I can't recall ever seeing you this nervous."

I glare up at him. "At least someone's memory's serving them."

"I see you haven't lost your sense of humor."

My lips twitch, fighting a smile, his sarcasm producing the desired effect, but it doesn't last long.

I know it's only close friends and family gathering here to see me, but for all intents and purposes, it's a room full of strangers.

People I have no memory of.

It's been six months since the car accident that claimed my memories. Memories of who I was and the twenty-eight years of life I'd lived, replaced by nothing. A void of emptiness and darkness.

My very first memory—waking up in a hospital room, lying damaged and broken, surrounded by people I didn't know and have only now begun to accept. I watched while they rejoiced for a life saved—a life I didn't even know existed—listening as they told me how I'd lost control of my car. How it had spun off the road into icy-cold waters and how a man had rescued me and swum me to safety, risking his life to save mine. I didn't remember it.

Not a single thing.

For a time, University Hospital was my home and doctors' and nurses' faces more familiar to me than my own 'family'. Weeks turned into months, blending together without distinction as I relearned the basics of everyday life. Some things came naturally, of course, while others took time.

Doctors breezed in and out of my room, doing tests, sending me for tests and often testing my patience, offering their best guesses with regard to my recovery, that perhaps one day I would remember something, maybe everything, maybe nothing. In other words, they didn't know. They call my condition Focal Retrograde Amnesia. I like to call it Living in the Moment.

The day I left the hospital with my husband, Nick, a man of whom I had absolutely no recollection, I decided right there and then I would live in the here and now. Nothing had come back to me—maybe nothing ever would. Instead of wasting my energy on what I'd lost, I was determined to focus on my new life…and the intimidatingly beautiful man to whom I happened to be married. The man who sat beside me, driving me away from the only home I'd ever known.

As we reach the bottom of the stairs, people seem to swarm from all directions, with me nectar to the bees. One by one, friends and relatives reintroduce themselves to me, reminding me of places we've been and things we've done. As they speak, I search every line of their faces for something familiar, for one solitary hint of association.

But there's nothing.

Afterward, they stand and stare at me, as though at any moment I'll remember them, followed closely by a look of disappointment when I don't. I cast a fleeting glimpse around the opulent, densely populated room. Here I am, surrounded by friends and family, people I've apparently known all my life.

I've never felt more alone.

Suddenly, a man's face appears in front of me, freeing me from my wayward train of thought. My mother stands beside him, weaving her arm around him.

"Honey, I have someone I want you to meet," she gushes, anticipation glowing in her eyes. "This is Mitchell Morgan."

I shift my gaze to the tall, thirty-something, dark-haired man standing beside her. He looks as anxious as I am. He curves his lips into a warm, friendly smile that creeps slowly into his mysterious dark-brown eyes. He reaches his hand out to me and I look down at it curiously.

"Mitchell's the brave young man who pulled you from the car wreck that night. He saved your life!" she continues.

"Oh!" I blink at him in surprise, extending my hand to his.

"It's just Mitch," he corrects, eyeing me intently, our hands still connected.

I drift toward him, surprising us both when I throw my arms around him, hugging him tightly.

"Thank you," I whisper into his neck, unexpectedly overwhelmed by the bewitching scent of his skin.

"You're welcome," he replies, his body tense, his voice a little disjointed. I glance over his shoulder as he holds me to him to find Nick's brooding dark-blue eyes regarding us closely. I inhale sharply, stepping back out of Mitch's arms.

"So, how are you doing?" he asks. "You look much better than you did the last time I saw you."

I glance at my long, flowing red evening gown. "This dress probably helps."

He raises his eyebrow, amused, but keeps his gaze locked

with mine, as though waiting for a more honest answer.

"I'm much better, thank you."

"That's good to hear."

My mother squeezes Mitch's arm. "We're so lucky you were there. She can't swim, you know."

"Yes, I heard that," he answers.

My mother shakes her head. "I don't know. She can't swim, can't drive, obviously, or she wouldn't have been in the water in the first place. Otherwise she's a very clever girl."

"Mother!" I protest, glancing sideways at Mitch as he presses his curled fist to his mouth in an attempt to conceal his grin.

I steal a glimpse in Nick's direction, but he's nowhere to be seen, leaving me hovering precariously on the brink of panic. Suddenly, the lack of him in the room means more to me than all the people in the room put together.

"Trish!" my father calls from across the room, distracting me. My mother groans.

"Not again!" she complains, turning her attention to him. My father waves her toward him impatiently. "Yes, yes, I'm coming," she snaps, her temper clearly fraying. I glance up at Mitch and he chuckles. My mother turns back to us, slowly winding up the corners of her mouth like two movie theatre curtains parting, suddenly all refined and composed.

"You'll have to excuse me. Mitchell, it was so good of you to come."

"No, thank you for asking me, Mrs. Lawren."

My mother bows her head graciously. "I do hope to see more of you."

"Well, *that's* a bit forward!" Nick's voice interrupts, brazenly, behind us. I flinch, startled by the touch of his cool hands on my shoulders.

"*Nick!*" My mother scolds, swiping at his shoulder before rushing off toward my father. We can't help but laugh, my amusement slowly fading as I realize Nick and Mitch haven't been introduced.

"Nick, this is Mitchell Morgan. Mitchell, this is my husband, Nick."

Nick frowns, as though uncertain what to make of the introduction.

"Mitchell's the man who rescued me from the car that night," I continue.

Nick raises an eyebrow, giving just an inch to the man standing before him.

"Ah, Mr. Morgan. Nick Pierce." He steps forward, extending his hand to Mitch. "It's a pleasure to finally meet you."

"You, too. And it's just Mitch." The two exchange a firm handshake.

"Mitch it is," Nick replies, squaring his shoulders. "I think I just missed you at the hospital that night. I would have contacted you myself, but Scarlet's mother insisted on a more formal meeting. I just didn't know it was tonight. I can't thank you enough for what you did. We're very lucky you were there." Nick snakes his arm around my waist, pulling me tightly to his side like a wild animal staking its claim. "I don't know what I'd do without her."

I blush like a giant beetroot and peek up at Nick, only to meet him bringing his lips down on mine in a surprise attack.

Uncomfortable kissing in front of company, I pull back from him and glance across at Mitch, abashed. He creases his brow, an awkward silence filling the air, as the two regard each other intently.

Mitch turns his attention to me. "So, your mother tells me you can't remember a lot since the accident."

"No. Nothing at all."

Nick shifts his stance, clearly uncomfortable with my response.

"It's frustrating, to say the least."

"I imagine it would be," Mitch replies to me, letting his smoldering brown eyes linger on mine much longer than they should.

A waitress stops to offer drinks. She passes beers to Nick and Mitch.

I swallow hard, glad of the sudden interruption.

"So, what is it that you do, Mr. Morgan?" Nick asks.

Mitch takes a sip of beer, swallowing it hastily. "Uh, boat building. I build boats. I've got a boatyard down by the Coomera River."

Nick raises an eyebrow. "Really? Boat building. That must be *very* fulfilling work."

Mitch nods.

"Exactly what type of boats do you build, Mr. Morgan?"

I look up at Nick, puzzled by his condescending tone.

"Uh, small skiffs mainly. The wooden, hand-sculptured, heart-and-soul-type boats."

"Racing skiffs?"

"Some, yeah."

"So, you race then?" Nick asks.

"I've been known to race, yeah. I've got a traditional forty-five-footer that I take around the block from time to time."

"You built it yourself?"

"My grandfather and I built it, yeah."

"I'd imagine that would be quite time-consuming."

"It was, but it's a labor of love," Mitch replies, resting his gaze on mine.

A second waitress steps in close to Nick, offering appetizers, her tan fingers, with their long red-painted nails, clinging to his biceps as she flashes him a wide, toothy, big-cat smile. Nick barely responds to her at all, but I do, treating her to my most transparent 'what the fuck' look. She closes her lips swiftly, retracting her claws from his arm and flipping her long platinum-blonde locks as she strides off in her ridiculously too-high stilettos like a head on a stick. I only hope she's hired help and not a relative or friend I haven't met yet.

"What is it that *you* do, Mr. Pierce?" Mitch asks.

I almost laugh out loud at the innuendo in Mitch's voice

as they serve *misters* at each other like players in a tennis match.

"I'm a partner at Chase, Patten & Lomax, the global financial firm."

Mitch raises his eyebrow, suitably impressed. "Nice. Difficult times, though, I bet, with all the dramatic plunges in the stock market."

"Yes, well, it's not without its challenges, but at the end of the day it's worth the stress," he replies, casting his gaze upward at the grandiose chandelier hanging above us, its diamond-filtered light dancing in the shadows of the ornate ivory-vaulted ceilings.

Mitch follows his gaze. "Yeah, I can see that," he says, his eyes sparkling luminously, making the diamonds in the chandelier look like cheap imitations. "You certainly have a lovely home."

"Thank you," I reply.

I glance across at Nick, to find him studying Mitch with close scrutiny.

"So, are you here with your wife then or...?"

"Uh, no. No wife. It's just me." He holds up his hand, revealing his naked ring finger.

Nick nods, narrowing his eyes to thin slits. "So, boats. Is that how you came to be down by the water the night of Scarlet's accident?"

"Well, no, actually, I was driving in my car and Scarlet's car spun off the road in front of me."

A deep crevice forms between Nick's brows. "So, you just saw the car go off the road and jumped into freezing-cold water after it?"

"Pretty much, yeah."

"That's pretty heroic. I imagine there wouldn't be too many people out there willing to risk their lives for others like that."

Mitch shrugs. "I didn't really give it a lot of thought."

"Well, I'm certainly glad that you did. If there's ever anything I can do for you..."

"Well, thank you, but just seeing Scarlet here alive, walking and talking is enough for me." He curls his lips, two soft dimples punctuating his cheeks as he settles his gaze on mine again.

All the blood in my body hurtles to my face at warp speed. I blush, again—a ridiculously bright shade of ruby red, I suspect.

"Scarlet!" a female voice interrupts and couldn't have come at a better time. The tension between Nick and Mitch is almost unbearable. I was sure they were just about to strip down to their loincloths and bash each other over the head with their caveman clubs. I look up to find my two best friends, Natasha and Tayla, standing in front of us, martinis in hand.

"Well, hello there," Tayla gushes, squaring her lean, tanned shoulders as she flips her long strawberry-blonde locks. Nick groans.

"Who is this gorgeous man you're talking to?" Tash asks, who I've learned is never shy of saying whatever she feels, regardless of consequence.

Nick steps forward. "Nick Pierce," he quips, holding out his hand.

"Not you, idiot!" she replies, the roar of our laughter cutting through the room.

"Well, aren't you going to introduce us?" Tayla purrs, grinning at Mitch like a Cheshire cat.

"Of course. *Mitch*, these are my good friends, Tayla and Natasha."

"It's Tash," she corrects, only *Natasha* when the mood strikes, as I've been informed.

"*Sorry!* Tash," I revise. "Tash is a curator over at the Living Art Gallery on Bundall Road and Tayla owns her own antique store in Southport."

Mitch dips his chin. "Hello, ladies."

They both smile like movie stars, batting their long black lashes at their would-be prey.

Nick groans, turning to Mitch. "Don't hang around with

these two for too long. They'll suck your brain cells dry."

Tash eyes Nick with mock disgust. "Ugh, I can*not* believe this is the best you could do, Scarlet."

"Yes, it really is scraping the bottom of the barrel," Tayla adds, in a fake noble English accent. They both laugh hysterically, well on their way to Crazy Town, then clang their glasses, making a loud clinking sound.

Nick raises an eyebrow at Mitch. "Run away, run away."

Mitch chuckles, watching helplessly as the girls close in on him.

"And, on that note, I'm going to take my own advice," Nick continues, kissing my forehead before he turns to leave. The second Nick turns his back, the girls pounce, Tayla the tiger first.

"So, *Mitch*, are you single?" she asks, seductively sucking on her martini olive on its stick.

Mitch swallows his drink prematurely.

"Tayla!" I scold.

"What?" she giggles, shrugging at me like a spoiled teenager before turning her attention back to Mitch.

"Uh, I *was* seeing someone, but that's, well, yes, I guess I am single," he replies, rather inarticulately.

Jeez, and I thought I was confused!

"Ah-ha," she replies, drawing the olive farther into her mouth. Mitch shifts his weight awkwardly, visibly fighting a grin.

"And what do you do, Mitch?" Tash asks, twirling her long brown hair around her finger like a shy twelve-year-old girl, though she's anything but.

"I build boats," he replies, taking a sip of his beer.

"*Really?* Boats?" She gazes up and down his body, as though his reply isn't what she expected.

"You work with your hands then?" Tayla asks boldly, taking his hand in hers and inspecting it at great length.

Tash reaches out, running her long, French-manicured nails down his arm. "Are you a Libra? I bet you're a Libra."

Mitch glances up at me, lost for words, and I hang my

head in a bid to stifle my impending belly laugh.

"No. I'm not a Libra," he replies, politely retracting his hand from Tayla's, not offering anything further. He gulps down the last of his beer, then holds up his empty glass, copying Nick's action of earlier. "Time for another, I think. Ladies, if you'll please excuse me?"

They both dip their heads in quick succession like nodding dashboard dogs, ogling him shamelessly as he walks away.

"So, he's the one, huh?" Tayla asks.

I look at her curiously. "The one?"

"The one who saved your life."

I seek Mitch out, studying his profile objectively. "Apparently so." Mitch turns suddenly, catching my stare, and I quickly look away.

Tayla lets out a long, dreamy sigh. "He's a hero!"

"He's a *superhero*!" Tash replies.

"He's a *god*!" Tayla echoes. They both laugh.

Really? I risk another glimpse of him, briefly allowing myself to admire his physique.

"If only there were two. I wonder if he has a brother. Does he have a brother?" Tash queries.

They both turn to me at once and I hold up my hands in surrender. "I only just met the man. I don't know anything about him."

Tash nudges her shoulder against mine. "Well, you know he can *swim*." They both burst into fits of laughter.

Jeez, Louise!

I watch on — with the rest of the room, I suspect — as they snort and giggle. I have to agree with Nick — as much fun as the girls are, I *can* feel my brain cells depleting.

I take a deep breath, scanning the room. It's barely recognizable. My mother's done a superb job setting the mood. A fire flickers in the hearth, its low flames radiating a soft, golden glow, making shadows of our silhouettes dance across the walls surrounding us. The french doors to the terrace stand wide open, letting in the fresh lily- and lilac-scented air from outside, while Nina Simone reminds me, just quietly, that I'm feeling good. Anxiety quickly settles in and I excuse myself from the girls, making a beeline for the terrace, when I notice Mitch walking toward me.

"Scarlet," he says, passing me a glass of champagne, "you look as though you could use one of these."

I exhale loudly "How did you know?"

"Ah, there you are," my mother interrupts, slipping her arms under each of ours. "Come with me. Everyone is wanting to meet the hero." She ushers us around the room, telling tales of Mitch's heroism to everyone she can, while we smile politely as they ooh and aah, firing questions at Mitch and flashing me intermittent expressions of condolence.

I watch him talk, a reluctant hero at best, assuring us all that anyone would have done the same thing, though I'm not so sure. I allow my gaze to drift down his face to his broad shoulders, admiring the way the darkness of his shirt accentuates the depth in his eyes. Every now and then he looks up at me, his gaze holding mine until I look away.

I gaze around the room at all the unfamiliar faces, feeling like a gatecrasher at my own party, finally resting my focus on Nick. He stands by the fireplace, his arm draped over the mantel, talking to my cousins Clay and Tom. He takes a sip of his beer, then throws back his head and laughs, his whole face lighting up, lighting mine. He glances across at me, a look developing on his face, his lips inching up at the corners, one eye narrower than the other. I've never seen anything more mesmerizing. He excuses himself, puts his drink down on the table beside him and strides toward me, his tall, powerful frame towering inches above anyone else in the room.

"Hey, you," he whispers, wrapping his big, strong arm around me before whisking me out onto the terrace.

"Hey." I smile up at him, thankful for the rescue effort.

"How are you doing?"

My smile quickly turns to a scowl.

"*That* good?" he jokes, rubbing my arms. "Whoa, you're

so cold." He takes off his jacket, to drape it around my shoulders. "Here, put this on." The smell of his cologne fills my nostrils. I close my eyes, nuzzling my nose into the collar, taking a deep breath of his magnificent, manly scent. It takes my breath away, in all the right ways. "Better?"

"Yes. Thank you."

The girls giggle loudly behind us and we turn, looking over in their direction as they swoop in on either side of Mitch, both slipping an arm under his, Tash's plunging neckline seemingly lower and Tayla's light sheath mini clinging to her body so tightly it's growing shorter by the minute.

"Looks as if the girls have a shiny new toy." Nick snickers, turning his attention back to me. "I'm glad. He's been practically glued to your side all night. I was going to ask if you needed something to get him off, but I think you're already doing that."

I gape at him and swipe at his arm. "You're terrible!"

He laughs heartily and pulls me tightly to his chest, before taking my hand in his and swaying slowly to the music in the background. I stare up at him, awestruck, the silver flecks of the moonlight catching in his eyes, making them sparkle with a devilish gleam.

"I'm very proud of you, you know," he whispers, his voice like a thousand hands caressing my body, making me quiver. I close my eyes, snuggling into his neck. "And very horny!" he growls.

I pull back from him, making a choking sound.

I didn't see that coming.

In the six months since the accident, Nick has done everything in his power to assure me he's happy to wait until I'm ready to accept him as my husband, if at all, but tonight, as I look into the depths of his stormy steel-blue eyes, I can see that time is running out.

"Six months is a long, *long* time, Mrs. Pierce."

I purse my lips, lost for words.

"I don't know how much longer I can wait." His voice is

so deep and gritty it almost rumbles. He glides his hand down my thigh, raising the side of my dress, gauging my reaction when he lightly brushes the back of his hand against my inner thigh. I gasp, the sexual tension between us shifting into overdrive. He moves his gaze to my mouth, slowly inching his face toward mine.

He sweeps his lips, soft and tender, against mine and I close my eyes, overcome by an unfamiliar emotion, a permeating giddiness of nervous excitement that lightens my heavy heart. As we part, he glances briefly to my left.

"Later," he whispers and he's gone, leaving me curious and longing for more.

I spin around to see what caught Nick's eye, to find Mitch, Tash and Tayla behind me.

The girls try desperately to monopolize Mitch's attention, but he has his gaze fixed firmly on me. I start to smile, but he shifts on his feet and looks away. I step inside from the terrace, heading toward them, only to be ambushed by my Uncle Ben and his new wife Joan, making small talk, but the only things I hear are Nick's words, playing over and over in my head. He's right. Six months is a long time.

He's a loving, caring, incredibly amazing man who I just happen to be married to, not to mention extremely attracted to, so what's stopping me?

Nothing.

The girls let out a loud, cackling laugh and I glance over to find them draped all over Mitch, who now looks as though *he's* in desperate need of rescuing. I excuse myself and make my way over to him. Just as I arrive, Mitch pulls his car keys from his pocket.

"You're not leaving?" Tash shrieks.

"I'm afraid so. I've got an early start in the morning."

I step forward. "I'll walk you out."

He gives me a gratified nod then turns to the girls. "Ladies, it was a pleasure to meet you both."

Tash fumbles around in her purse, emerging with a business card in her hand.

"Here, take my card," she says a little too eagerly. "Maybe we could catch up sometime?"

Mitch takes the card politely and slips it into his pocket, though I get the distinct impression that's one call he won't be making. I shrug out of Nick's jacket and place it on the chair beside me as we head toward the front door, the girls' giggles following us indecently all the way down the hall.

I glance across at Mitch, arching an eyebrow. "I'm so sorry about that. They're—"

"Tanked!" he interrupts, unable to hide his amusement.

"For want of a better word."

"It's no problem. They both seem like lovely girls."

"They are, even more so when they're sober. They've really been there for me through all of this."

"Oh, I'm sure," he replies sincerely.

As we reach the foyer, I pause, turning toward him. "Thank you for coming tonight and for doing the rounds with my mother. She can be quite the handful when she gets excited about something."

"She's fine. I met her at the hospital the night of the accident and she calls every couple of months to thank me again."

"Oh, God, you gave her your number? Are you crazy?"

He presses his lips together, fighting a grin. "Yeah, I did. She's been trying to get us all together for a while now, as a surprise, but it just didn't pan out until now."

"Well, it certainly was a surprise."

"A good one, I hope."

"A very good one. Everyone loved you."

"Well, not everyone."

I frown as though I have no idea what he's talking about, though I know very well.

"Well, everyone I talked to did," I insist.

"I just got their attention. It was you who won their hearts."

His lips steal up into a warm, generous smile that somehow makes me feel more whole.

I open the front door and Mitch walks through the entrance, stopping to face me. "I've been meaning to ask you. Do you like boats?"

"Boats?"

"Yeah, you know, those watertight contraptions that people float around in on the ocean?"

I roll my eyes. "I know what boats are!"

"I'm glad." He chuckles. "Do you like them?"

"Well, I haven't been in one. At least not that I can remember."

He reaches into his pocket. "Well. This is my card. If you decide you want to come out for the day, just to get away from it all or something, give me a call. You'd love it out there, the wind in your hair, the sun on your face," he continues, watching me as though waiting for a reaction.

"Uh, okay. Sure. Thanks. Nick would probably like that."

His expression is impossible to read. I reach out to hug him. "Thank you again, for everything."

He wraps his arms around me, pressing his body against mine, nuzzling his nose into my hair. I feel his chest rise, drawing in a deep breath, and I twist out of his embrace, suddenly acutely aware of him.

"It was really good to see you again, Scarlet."

"Yeah, it was nice to finally meet you."

He dips his head as though defeated, then turns to leave. I stand at the door, rubbing my arms as I watch him walk away, instantly feeling colder. He doesn't look back.

How strange. Mitch is a complete stranger to me, not family, not a friend, yet it feels as if a part of me is leaving with him. Nick's voice startles me.

"Seeing your boyfriend off?" he asks, folding his arms across his chest as he leans against the wall behind me.

"Oh. My. God. You *scared* me!" I shout, clutching at my chest.

"I'm sorry. Are you okay?" he asks, his eyes filled with amusement.

"*No.*"

He laughs louder, pulling me to his side, looking down at the business card in my hand. "What did he give you there?"

I hold up the simple white rectangle that reads *Mitchell Morgan, Handscraftsman*. A cell number and business address occupy the bottom of the plain white rectangle. He takes the card, tossing it onto the end table then directing me back toward our guests.

"So, you and Captain America seemed to get along pretty well."

"Yeah. He seems nice enough."

He nods in Tash's and Tayla's direction. "Think one of the Bobbsey Twins is in?"

I shake my head vehemently.

He chuckles. "Me, neither. It seemed to me someone else was snaking him."

"Who?" I ask innocently.

"Please! He didn't take his eyes off you the whole night."

"Yeah? Well, he's gay."

Nick raises an eyebrow. "Hmmm…maybe he was looking at me, then?"

I laugh wholeheartedly. "Very funny!" I slip out of his grasp and turn to walk away.

"What? I'm an attractive man!" he shouts matter-of-factly down the hallway behind me.

"Yes. You. Are!" a female voice replies.

I spin around to see my much older, very tipsy Aunt Carol pinch Nick on the backside and wink.

"You see! I knew it!" he shouts to me, holding his arms out triumphantly. "Now, if only I was five years older, Carol, you'd be in trouble."

My Uncle Bill lets out a riotous laugh. "Don't you mean thirty-five years older?"

Nick shakes his head, giving my Uncle Bill a stern, serious look. "Nope. Five, Bill. Just five."

The corridor fills with laughter as Nick turns and struts off like a true god. *I have to give it to the man – he's certainly charming when he wants to be.*

Chapter Two

The Morning After

I awake the next morning to the sound of voices downstairs, the aroma of fresh coffee beans filling the air. The voices are familiar — our groundsman-chauffeur, Gabriel, and our housekeeper, Malaylie, both of Spanish decent, who frequently speak to each other around the house in their own tongue. Gabe is a kind and obliging older man, Malaylie an attractive, dark-haired, animated woman for her fifty-five years. Both are single and around the same age. I can't help but wonder why they aren't dating. Perhaps secretly they are?

I glance anxiously across at Nick's side of the bed. It hasn't been slept in. After his comments last night, I half-expect to find him lying in bed beside me this morning. During the past few months, desperate to be close, he'd sneak in during the night and I'd wake to find him curled up in his PJs on top of the covers beside me, the perfect gentleman. Previously, I've felt a little uncomfortable waking with him next to me, but this morning, I actually feel a little disappointed.

I rise slowly and wander over to the balcony doors. The sunlight shines through the glass panes and onto the carpet, stretching its arms out to me in long, defined lines. I open the doors and step out into the warm, fresh air, gazing out over the grounds. The view from our balcony never fails to inspire. The lush green acres and rolling hills, screaming with vitality beneath the sprawling arms of the apple, oak and twisted cotton trees that stretch across the landscape and line the white rail fences along the long, winding driveway. I hear a splash below and glance down to see Nick doing laps in the pool, as he does most mornings, powering his strong biceps through the water in swift, smooth strokes.

"Good morning, beautiful!" he calls out from below, mid-lap.

"Uh, morning," I reply, startled.

"Breakfast is ready if you want to come down."

"I'll be right there."

I turn and wander into the bathroom. As I approach the mirror, my reflection comes into view and I catch myself scowling, exasperated by the monotony of it all. Every morning the same, starting with me staring into the mirror, a complete stranger looking back at me. Never diverging, never changing. I shake my head, confounded. How can someone just forget the way they look? Forget who they are, forget their name. A lifetime of feelings, triumphs, losses, childhood, schooling, jobs, dating, marriage, I've missed it all. I try hard to find a positive in all this, but if there is one, I haven't found it yet.

Day after day, I study every line of my face. The shape of my lips, the dark brown in my eyes, the soft waves in my long brown hair, the tiny scars on my forehead, the healed gashes that lurk just below my hairline, and every day I ask myself the same question. *Who are you?* And wait for an answer that never comes. I splash water up onto the mirror, distorting my reflection, and push away from the vanity, tired of the whole routine.

I dress slowly and dawdle downstairs, forcing myself out of my melancholy mood. As I enter the expansive sunlit kitchen, Gabe and Malaylie both look up, greeting me more like a daughter than an employer, which I love. Malaylie slides a plate of breakfast in front of Gabe, his pleasure unmistakable as he tucks a napkin into his shirt and snatches at his fork. I put my hand on his shoulder as I pass, then wander out to the sundrenched terrace to find Nick sitting at the table, drinking juice and reading the newspaper. No shirt.

The sun shines on his broad, muscular shoulders and gleams across his perfectly tan, toned chest and biceps.

My whole body reacts, a jittery, tingling sensation spreading through me like wildfire.

He glances up at me, flicking his dark, damp hair back from his forehead.

"Good morning, sleepyhead," he singsongs, rising to kiss my cheek. Just at that moment, I turn my head, touching his lips to mine. His eyes light up. "Well! It *is* a good morning."

I purse my lips, settling into the cushioned wicker chair opposite him and glance down at my plate. Waffles and bacon. It smells amazing.

"Sleep well?" Nick asks, sawing at his bacon.

"Mmmh, really well, must have been the wine. What about you? How did you sleep?"

"Like the dead. I think your Aunt Carol slipped me a roofie."

I let out a sharp, short burst of laughter. I love his sense of humor.

"I've missed your laugh," he says, a jubilant smile spreading across his lips. "In fact, I considered crashing your bed last night but—"

"You should have," I interrupt.

He stares at me, parting his lips.

I shrug. "I feel terrible that you don't get to sleep in your own bed anymore."

He puts down his knife and fork then leans back in his chair, his eyes inscrutable.

"Are you saying what I think you're saying?"

I bite my bottom lip. "I think I am."

"Wow, Scarlet, that's made my day!" He rises from his chair, leans across the table and seizes my face in his hands. He brushes his lips across mine, softly yet fervently, and I reach up, grasping his powerful forearms, soaking in his spirited strength. As we part, he rests his forehead against mine.

"You've made me a very happy man." Nick glances down at my mouth, gliding his thumb over my lips, pressing my bottom lip down so they part, then slides his finger inside. I close my lips around it he trails it down my tongue. He exhales loudly, a deep indentation in his brow as he slowly withdraws his finger. Right at that moment, Malaylie approaches with toast and coffee. Nick recedes into his chair, staring across at me, his eyes ablaze as she places the tray down on the table in front of us.

"Can I get you anything else, Mrs. Pierce?" she asks.

"No, thank you, Malaylie," I reply, picking up my fork and starting on my breakfast in an attempt to stow my giggles. Nick clears his throat, shifting in his seat as Malaylie flitters around the table, pouring out coffee and taking away plates. I peek up at him, pressing my lips together, knowing exactly what's making him so uncomfortable.

"You're home late this morning. Are you staying home today?"

"Uh, no," he replies, absentmindedly. "I've got a meeting at ten-thirty and new clients after that, but I won't be home too late."

I look down at my plate, trying to hide my disappointment.

"I'm sorry," Nick says. "I know I've been working a lot lately but taking over as partner is a whole new level of responsibility. It's really bad timing, I know. There's nothing I'd like more than to spend time with you, but this company is a part of us now. The other partners are away for two weeks. This is my chance to shine, to show them I can run this company on my own."

I don't respond.

He leans back, regarding me thoughtfully. "Why don't you get out of the house for the day? Gabe can take you anywhere you want to go, shopping, maybe?"

I force a halfhearted smile. I know Nick has just become a partner at his firm, one of the largest international finance and trading companies in the world. It's apparently the dream partnership he's worked tirelessly to secure. I should be happy for him. How can I be anything *but* happy for him?

Yet, I'm not.

This new partnership means he spends a lot less time at home lately than I'd like, but then again, maybe that's something I've been doing too much of. I look up at him as he takes a sip of his orange juice.

"I've been thinking about going back to work."

He swallows his juice hastily then slams his glass down, his breath hissing from his lips. He's been completely against the idea of my returning to work and I don't understand it. It's my own business. I can't see how going back to work for a couple of hours here and there can possibly hurt.

I shrug. "I need to go back sometime. I feel as if I'm ready to at least pop my head in and see what goes on there."

"Baby, I really think you need more time. It's a very hectic place and the clients are demanding. One hint that you're back and they'll start leaning on you hard again. You were run off your feet before the accident."

I frown.

"I've put Marcy in charge. She's doing a great job and I've got the rest covered. There's plenty of time, so why rush?"

"I still don't see how dropping in for an hour or two would matter."

"It's not that, Scarlet. It's a very busy office. I'm just worried it might be too much on you too soon. You need time to rest, time to get your head together."

"My head *is* together," I snap, throwing my napkin down onto the table. "I may have lost my memory, but I haven't lost my mind. I *am* capable of relearning things."

"Okay, poor choice of words, but you know what I mean."

"Is that how things go around here?"

"What?" Nick snaps.

I wave my hand at him dismissively. I'm not in the mood for an argument. He glances down at his watch then pushes back from the table, rising to his feet. "I've got to go or I'm

27

going to be late. We'll talk about this tonight, okay?"

I don't answer. He walks around the table, helping me up then wrapping those darn biceps around me, gently touching his lips to mine.

"Why don't we have a romantic dinner tonight? Just you and me. Out here under the stars?"

His blue eyes stare down at me, instantly dissolving my anger, the infectious smile on his lips spreading to mine.

"I'll take that as a yes. I'll arrange everything. In the meantime, no more worrying about business. Go shopping, buy yourself something, have some fun. That's an order."

"Yes, sir!" I salute him like a bratty teenager.

He raises an eyebrow.

"What?"

"You used to do that." He touches his finger to my nose. "Gotta go."

"I did?" I yell.

"Uh-uh," he calls behind him.

I fall back into the chair behind me to finish my breakfast. "I'll take that!" I murmur to myself, happy with my progress, no matter how minute. It was no breakthrough but it was something. Shortly after, the front door shuts and he is gone.

After breakfast, I wander aimlessly through our ridiculously oversized house. It's far too large for just the two of us, the Italian marble tiles and floor-to-ceiling glass panels in the lounge and dining rooms making it look even bigger than it is. The dark beige and stone walls render a warm, relaxing feeling, but the vast open spaces and voids of silence haunt me, the thought of being completely alone here sometimes overpowering.

Most of the time, there's no sign of Malaylie or Gabe. Malaylie seems to steal in and out of rooms like a ninja and Gabe spends most of his time outside in the garden, so when Nick's not home, the house has an eerie emptiness to it. The kind of emptiness that could probably gobble someone right up if they let it.

I wander up to our bedroom, finally settling on the dressing room floor. Another thing that's far too big for just the two of us — the entire population of a small town could fit in here. I look up at all the drawers and hangers.

Too many clothes. Too many shoes.

Did he really just tell me to go shopping? By the look of this dressing room, that was all I ever did. I yearn for something of importance to do.

I need a hobby.

Apparently, I had *no* hobbies before the accident — didn't have time for them.

Sounds like all work and no play. Maybe Nick is right, not wanting me to go back to work so soon. I wander back out into the bedroom and stretch out on the bed, when the phone rings.

"*Hola!*" Tayla answers.

"*Bula,*" I reply.

Greeting each other in foreign tongues is something Tayla and I have been doing since the accident. She's traveled all over the world, to so many countries she's probably lost count, yet only managed to master the one word that matters, in her mind. The word that allows her to start conversations with men all over the world. *Hello.* Some might frown upon that but, according to her, "little fish are sweet". She's proud of herself and that's all that matters.

"We're going to your brother's restaurant for lunch, coming with?"

I hesitate.

"Come on! Tash's sister, Nikki, is here for a few days. Girls' day out, it'll be fun!"

I don't doubt it will be. I finally agree, before heading back into the dressing room to change. Picking an outfit will be difficult today. Most of my clothes are far too flamboyant for my melancholy mood. I choose a dress hanging at the back, the plainest one I can find, beige, but it comes in at the waist with a black band and flares out at the bottom, giving me just a little something. I put on my makeup, pull my hair back in a ponytail and wander downstairs to ask Gabe to drive me to town.

As we pull up outside my brother's restaurant, anxiety sets in. I sink my fingernails firmly into the armrest and have no desire to let go. I sit there, waiting for Gabe to open my door. Normally, I jump out of the car before he even gets close, but today I feel so apprehensive that I wait.

Gabe holds out his hand to me and I step out onto the sidewalk, looking up at the impressive wall of glass in front of me. A big sign over the door reads *Arias*. I swallow hard, suddenly feeling infinitely small. The vibrancy of the city makes me even more nervous. The honking horns, petrol fumes and towering buildings make me want to find a corner and cower in it. People in suits hurry past me, trailing along the sidewalk in formation like ants. *Is this what I did every day? Was I one of these faceless people, staring down at the sidewalk day after day, forsaking the beauty above them?*

"Scarlet!" Tayla yells.

I look up at her and wave, then run the gantlet, ducking and weaving through all the Mr. and Mrs. Smiths hustling and bustling toward me. She snatches me up in a quick hug, then pushes the door open and we tumble inside. The moment I enter the foyer, my nostrils fill with delicious aromas of food that I can't wait to taste. That has to be the best thing about my condition, tasting food for the first time. The restaurant is incredible. So warm and inviting, its exposed shiplap timber walls and Japanese-inspired theme giving off a relaxed, enticing atmosphere.

Tash and her tiny sister, Nikki, wave to us from the bar and we hurry toward them, bypassing the line of guests waiting for a table. I glance in the direction of the kitchen and catch a glimpse of my brother, Ari, striding toward us, his short dark hair slicked back at the front, his most accomplished smile on his face.

"Scarlet!" He scoops me up in his long, lean arms, swinging me around, and I giggle like a schoolgirl when he sets me down, planting a big, sloppy kiss on my cheek.

"It's so good to see you. I'm sorry I couldn't make it to your homecoming party last night. We had a function and our head chef's wife just had a baby. I just couldn't get away."

"It's fine. Really. You didn't miss a thing."

Ari nods graciously, then turns to the girls, greeting them like family. He's such a joy to be around, instantly making everyone feel better about themselves, exuding a lovable, comforting charm that draws people in and holds them there. There's only a year between us, but no one would know it, and when people guess how old he is, they usually think he's in his mid-thirties, but I won't tell him that. My mother constantly reminds me how tirelessly he works and how having this business has aged him.

"Well, come on over," he says. "There's a great table in the far corner. Rosa will show you and I'll join you when I can." His hostess, Rosa, shows us to our table, with in-floor seating and scattered cushions, overlooking a small Japanese-style garden. Raked sand and stones lead the way to a delicate handcrafted timber bridge that descends to a cascading water feature, the trickling water adding to the atmosphere and soothing my weary soul. As soon as Rosa leaves, Tash turns to me, hot as Haiti.

"Mama Mia, your brother! Why, oh, why does he have to like boys?"

Nikki clucks her tongue. "It makes me wanna be one."

They giggle, looking toward the kitchen in hopes of catching sight of him. I think back to a couple of months ago when my mother had told me my brother 'likes boys'. I asked her what she meant by that and she whispered, "He's gay," as though it was something she shouldn't say out loud. I don't understand it. It's just a word, like any other, and frankly the connotation of the way people use or don't use it annoys me. He's my brother. I don't care what he 'likes' or doesn't 'like'. I just know I'm lucky to have him.

As we eat and sip wine all afternoon, the girls remind me of all the crazy things we used to do, before I got married. The skydiving, jet skiing, the weekend getaways and the hilarious drunken antics of our nightclubbing days. Finally, it gets to me.

"Why do you keep referring to things we did *before* I got married?"

Tayla pauses before answering, as though choosing her words carefully.

"Well, it's just that we so rarely got to see you *after* you got married."

I take a sip of my wine, swallowing hard. "Why's that?"

They steal glances at one another.

"Let's just say that Nick liked to keep a close eye on you," Tash replies.

"A close eye?" I can't understand how Nick could possibly keep a close eye on me when he works so often.

Tayla nods. "He was *way* possessive."

"Possessive? I don't get that vibe from him at all," I reply.

Tash shrugs. "Well, maybe the accident gave him a new perspective."

"Or maybe he's changed. People change, right?" Tayla adds.

I swallow hard, resting my glass on the table. "What are you two not telling me?"

"Nothing, nothing. Nick is great and you both seem very happy together, just enjoy it," Tayla replies.

And though I get the impression there is so much more to be said, I'm certain I'm not going to hear it today.

Chapter Three

Old Fires Burn Deep

After a long afternoon with Ari and the girls, I head home to get ready for dinner with Nick. I hear the front door open and feel him before I see him. "Honey, I'm home," he calls, walking toward me, an impressive bunch of long-stemmed red roses in his hand. As beautiful as they are, they pale in comparison to him. His glistening blue eyes, his sensuous, curled smile and ruby-red lips. I zero in on the material of his well-tailored jacket, tugging gently on his biceps. The top three buttons of his crisp white-collared shirt are undone, revealing just enough of his chest to make my bottom lip quiver. Every muscle in my body tightens and a thousand butterflies that I didn't order arrive at my doorstep, free of charge.

I must be grinning like an idiot.

He gives me a knowing look.

Yep, I'm definitely grinning like an idiot.

"They're beautiful." I take the flowers, breathing in their delicate scent.

"*You* are beautiful," he says, touching his lips to mine. It's quick but very sweet. "Mmmh. I missed you today," he murmurs, his voice deep and raspy.

My breath hitches in my throat. "Me too."

He takes my face in his hands, bringing his mouth back to mine, his kiss warm and tender. Nick opens his mouth wider, closing his lips entirely over mine, and trails his hands down my shoulders to my arms, holding me to him. The air shallows in my lungs and I press my hand firmly against his chest, disoriented and breathless, but he holds me tighter. I push again and he releases me, his eyes burning into mine, impassioned, hurt, confused.

"Nick, I need to take this slow. This is new to me."

He swallows his ragged breath. "Of course. Of course," he replies, glancing down at the flowers in my hand. "Why don't you finish getting ready? I'll put these in some water and get dinner organized."

He takes the flowers and I nod, turning toward the stairs, my knees like jelly, my body like snow melting in the sun. I clutch at the balustrade, looking up at the top of the stairs, wondering how I'm going to get there, but somehow, I do. I take my time getting ready, while my mind tries to process the kiss. I wanted him to kiss me, but when he did, it was too much.

"Ugh!" I shout in frustration. *Great. First, I'm confused, now he's confused. Beam me up, Scotty!*

I pause.

What does that mean? And who's Scotty?

My thoughts are interrupted by the doorbell, followed by the amazing smell that begins to waft through the house. Downstairs, the kitchen smells like Italian. I love Italian. I wander outside to find Nick out on the terrace, setting the roses down in the middle of the table. Softly lit lanterns hang overhead, swaying gently in the breeze, their reflection dancing on the surface of the pool while Dean Martin, someone I've learned I love, sings just for me from afar.

"Wow. This is amazing."

"I'm glad you like it. I had a little bit of help." He winks, dishing our food onto our plates.

"*Italiano?*" I ask in my best Italian accent.

"Uh-huh. We have the best little Italian restaurant not far from here, makes the best *puttanesca* ever, just a-lika-mama-makes-it," he jokes.

"Well, it smells great!"

"Wait until you taste it." He pulls out the chair in front of me, gesturing for me to sit. I take my seat, studying him as he walks around the table to take his own, amazed by how good his body can make a shirt look. The smell of the food interrupts my thoughts and I look down at my plate, barely able to contain myself.

"Try it," he insists.

He pours me a glass of wine while I take a mouthful of pasta. "Oh, my God!"

"It's good, right?"

I roll my eyes, taking another mouthful and hastily swallowing it down. He chuckles, taking a sip of his beer.

"Your mom cooks this?"

"Even better than this."

"I can't wait to meet your family."

"Well, they're coming over in the spring. They can't wait to see you. They're only sorry they couldn't get here sooner."

"It's fine, really. Do you think they'll move here eventually, or stay in Sicily?"

He leans back in his chair, wiping his mouth with his napkin. "Well, they come over on holidays from time and time, and we usually go over there every two years or so, but I don't think they'll ever move here. I think my mother would move here, but my father is too set in his ways."

"And you've got a brother, right?"

"Uh-huh. Yeah, Antonio. Tony for short. He's a *lot* of fun. He's a couple years younger than me, twenty-nine this year. He's a force to be reckoned with." He chuckles. "The ladies *love* him. I don't think he'll ever settle down. He's off traveling the world. He calls from time to time, but he's a free spirit."

"Does he look like you?"

"Uh, yeah, a little, I guess. I'll have to dig out some photos. He's a little shorter than me and we're a similar build, but personality-wise, we couldn't be more different. Like you and Ari, huh? Chalk and cheese," he says, his smile lighting his face then mine.

As we eat, he tells me of all the places we've been, things we've done, things we planned to do. Traveling the world, racing each other down the autobahn, Pagani versus Bugatti at the top of the list. Nick loves his cars. Especially fast Italian ones. A love of cars was apparently something we shared. Surprisingly, that doesn't shock me. There's something about a sleek, shiny supercar that makes me want to grit my teeth and growl.

I sip my fine Italian *vino*, listening to him reminisce about how we met, how we fell in love and our wedding. His fond memories warm my heart as the wine glows in my cheeks and warms my toes. It sounds as though we've led a very happy life and have a very happy marriage.

"Did we want to have children?" I ask guardedly.

His face grows serious. "We were trying to have children before the accident."

"So, you *want* children then?"

"Oh, very much."

"Did I?"

"More than anything."

His sincerity shocks me. I swallow hard, taking another sip of wine, not knowing how I feel about that right now. He takes smaller mouthfuls of pasta, growing quiet and thoughtful.

"Will you tell me about the accident?"

He rests his fork on his plate. "I'd prefer that you remember that on your own, Scarlet. It's very hard for me to talk about. I thought I lost you." His eyes grow deep, like dark pools of sorrow.

"What if I don't remember? What if I never get my memory back?"

He reaches across the table, taking my hand in his. "It will come back. I know it. It has to."

My heart hurts. His hand tightens around mine and I stand then clamber onto his lap. He holds me so tightly against his chest that it hurts, but he needs this. I need this. After a moment, I pull back to look at him. "Do you think fate is inevitable?"

"Inevitable?" He frowns, tilting his head to the side. "I think we're destined to do certain things in our lives. That certain choices we make lead us to a certain destination, but *inevitable*?"

He shrugs, regarding me thoughtfully, the moonlight illuminating his brilliant white shirt and reflecting in his dark, metallic-colored eyes. I let my gaze drift down his shirt to where the fold of the fabric meets his rippling chest, lingering there.

"That's a really big question. That's what's weighing on your mind right now?"

I shrug. "People throw around these sayings, that everything happens for a reason, that you can't fight fate, that whatever is meant to be will be, and I just wonder if there's any substance to them."

He rests his beer on the table, drawing my absolute attention. "Well. In my honest opinion, and in my capacity as a highly respected philosopher—"

I swipe at his shoulder, amused.

"I think that ultimately, we're all architects of our own design, and as long as there is free will and coincidence, there can be no inevitability. Now, pass me the wine, God damn it."

I laugh, but his answer actually makes a lot of sense. The first part, and the last. He glances up at me, all humor gone.

"I'm just grateful we've been given a second chance."

I touch my hand to his face, charmed by the quiet power of him. "Me, too." A new song starts playing in the background, filling the silence in the air.

"Dance with me, Scarlet."

We rise and he takes my hand in his, slipping his other hand around my waist as we sway to the music. I lean my head against his chest, listening to the words of the song, something about being nobody till somebody loves you. The soulful depths of Dean Martin's voice softly stroke my soul like soft ribbons of silk sweeping over my skin.

At the song's bridge, he steps away, twirling me around, then pulling me back into his arms. It's messy. I tilt my head back, consumed with laughter, caught completely off-guard. He looks down at me, sharing my spirit, his dark eyes flickering with silver and steel.

Oh, God, he's intoxicating.

I'd been warned about the effects of drugs, but not about the blue-eyed ones with two left feet and a heartbeat. I snuggle into his chest as Nick tightens his arms around me, comforting me, protecting me, and I know that deep in the dark, forgotten void which imprisons my soul, I know this man, and I know there's nowhere else I want to be.

His eyes bind me as he brushes his tender lips across mine. I feel the strength of his body, feel his breath on my face and I tremble in his arms. He pulls his head back, gauging my reaction, then brings his mouth back to mine, deepening his kiss. He licks at my lips and I part them willingly, our tongues meeting, twirling, circling, invoked in a sacred dance. A deep burning desire ignites inside me and I can't fight it, I don't want to fight it. I respond, putting all that I am into the kiss. Our breathing spirals out of control. Nick tightens his arms around me. I can't breathe. I push against his chest and we spring apart, his eyes open wide with concern.

"I'm sorry," he murmurs. "I know, it's too much."

"No, it's—" I shake my head, not really knowing what it is. "It's fine."

He watches me as though he's willing me to look at him, but I can't. I turn back to the table, collect the dishes and head for the kitchen. He follows closely behind me, our empty glasses in his hands. As I place the dishes in the sink, 'Scotty' springs to mind again.

"Nick, what does 'Beam me up, Scotty' mean?"

He blinks in surprise, then chuckles, the thick cloud of fog surrounding us, receding. "What? Where did that come from?"

"I don't know, it just popped into my head earlier."

"It's a catchphrase, from a movie. *Star Trek*."

I frown, even more confused.

"It's a line from a movie. Well, TV series, too, I guess, set in space on board a spaceship. Scotty transports people from the ship to planets and when they want to return to the ship, they say 'Beam me up, Scotty'."

"Sounds crazy."

"It is, it was made in the sixties. Too many drugs." He grins. "That's really interesting, though, that things like *that* are coming back to you, not your husband, or anything of any importance. Just a catchphrase from a movie." He shakes his head, still grinning as he takes the dishes from my hand. "Leave it. Malaylie can do this in the morning. It's such a lovely night out there. Why don't we go for a swim?"

I beam up at him like an excitable child, nodding emphatically, then turn on my heel toward the bedroom. He grabs my hand and I spin back around.

"Where are you going?"

"To put my swimsuit on." I twist my hand out of his grasp and rush off.

"Hey!" he shouts, behind me. "I don't know what goes on in other people's pools, but there's a strictly no-swimsuit rule in this one, lady." I laugh, then hear him splash into the water.

Without swimmers, I suspect.

I rush upstairs and slip into my most revealing bikini, which just happens to be red, then hurry back down to the pool. He ravishes my body with his eyes as I approach.

"*Very* nice, Mrs. Pierce."

I bat my eyelids at him. "Can I see yours?"

"You could if I was wearing any."

Just as I suspected. "How did I know you were going to say that?" I step down onto the top stair. The water's surprisingly quite warm. He steals toward me like a crocodile stalking a deer on a riverbank, swiftly pulling me into his arms, and I gasp as we sink below the water.

He really isn't wearing swimmers.

He drags his gaze slowly down my body to my breasts, caught firmly against his chest. The air expels forcefully from his lungs as he slides his hand down to the small of my back, pressing me against him, making sure that I feel all of him, and I do. My breathing shallows and my body trembles, so scared and unsure.

"Nick—"

"I'm sorry." His eyes are soft and rueful, his voice sincere and low. "It's just that I've missed you so much, and you're here with me tonight, looking the way you do…"

He moves his lips down my neck, whispering his breath against my ear, darting his tongue on my skin. I don't stop him. I close my eyes and tilt my head to the side, allowing him better access.

Apparently, I like playing with fire.

Insistent, he brings his lips to mine, weaving his hand into my hair as the warm, moonlit water ripples and swirls around us, the heat from our bodies increasing its temperature. He slides his tongue inside my mouth, circling mine, gathering speed, begging me to give in to the multitude of feelings welling up inside me, and I surrender willingly.

He seizes his victory, sliding his hand down my hip, pulling my leg up to wrap it around him. Nick brushes his fingers lightly against my inner thigh and I moan into his mouth, my body suddenly a vessel of pure desire.

A deep, animalistic growl vibrates in his throat and every thought leaves my body, every last shred of reason gone. There's nothing now, only him and me. Our tongues circling. Our eyes closed. Our bodies trembling. Breathless, we spring apart. His eyes, filled with fire, flicker euphorically. He knows he's breaking me down.

He sweeps the hair from the side of my neck, lowering his mouth to my ear.

"Say yes," he whispers against my skin.

"To what?" I breathe.

"To being my wife."

He pulls back to look at me, his eyes drenched in desire and devotion. I can't resist him. I won't resist him.

"Yes," I whisper.

His eyes ignite. He stands swiftly, scooping me up in his powerful arms, carrying me to the bedroom, his mouth never leaving mine.

We fall onto the bed, a tangled mess of arms and legs, our bodies dripping wet. He anchors himself above me, his heart pounding, his arms tensed, rippling with strength. He looks down at me, his disheveled dark hair falling onto his forehead, his eyes laced with concern.

"Are you sure you're ready for this?"

I nod.

He draws in a deep, ragged breath and slowly, painstakingly, lowers his body to mine. I feel his erection, almost lithic, pressing against my body, and I gasp, quivering with anticipation. He slips his hand behind my neck, untying my bikini top, his gaze glorying in my nakedness. A double dose of anxiety surges through me. I'm so unsure of my body, unsure of myself, unsure of what comes next.

"You are *so* beautiful," he murmurs, his words squashing my fears. His strong hand glides down my body, and he's trailing his mouth slowly, strategically, down the line of my neck, his tongue stroking, his teeth scraping, threatening to bite and I want him to bite. He caresses my breasts, circling his fingertips, tracing the outline of my perfectly round, erect nipples.

He squeezes gently and I cry out in awe at the way my body responds, gasping and burying my head back in the pillows, every nerve ending awakened, raw and evoked.

"I've wanted for this for so long," he growls.

Nick slides his hand beneath me, forcing my hips up to his as his heady, hungry eyes bore into mine. Suddenly, knowing exactly how I feel about him doesn't matter anymore. He is my husband and I am his wife. I want him.

I want *this*. I'm more sure of that than I am of anything. I seize his face in my hands and raise my head to his, brazen and demanding. His mouth meets mine, his lips sweeping, his tongue lashing, building up a relentless, rhapsodic rhythm. Nick trails his fingers down the curve of my hips to my bikini bottoms, forcing them down with the slide of his hand between my legs, his fingers, circling, teasing.

Oh, my God!

He moves his mouth slowly down my body, his lips on my breasts, my stomach, my hips, then sliding between my thighs. I watch him, unsure of his intentions as he spreads my legs, his adventurous tongue licking me, tasting me, then sliding deep inside me. I gasp, running my hands through my hair, down my throat and over my breasts as I whimper mindlessly at his mercy. He watches me, sweeping my legs open wider, forcing his tongue deeper, a menacing rumble in his chest vibrating all the way to his tongue. My body trembles with greed. I want more, I need more.

I look down at him, begging, pleading, and he obliges, sliding his finger deep inside my body, first one finger, then two. I cry out, arching my back and clutching at the bed sheets beneath me. He increases the pressure slightly, circling his thumb, establishing a slow, steady pattern, so unconditionally invested in my pleasure.

"Oh, Nick," I breathe.

I tighten around his fingers, flexing my hips against his hand, imploring him to explore my deepest depths, to fill me with his touch. I weave my fingers into his hair, tugging gently as he glides his fingers faster and faster between my thighs, the heat inside me rising to a deep burn. He brings his face back up to mine, watching me and forcing his fingers deeper inside me. I smell his scent, hear his breath in my ear. I take his hand in mine, clutching it tightly, willing it to move faster, matching the pulsating rhythm percussing through my body.

He whispers words of encouragement in my ear, conjuring an all-consuming wave of pleasure, and I cry out, thrusting against his hand, as it washes over me. My whole body shudders, tightening involuntarily around his fingers.

"Oh, Scarlet," he groans, his eyes enraptured, his breathing harsh and heavy, my pleasure his own. I never imagined I could feel like this, that his touch could do such things to my body, that I could lose myself so completely.

I run my fingers down my face, to my mouth, closing my lips around my fingertips as my body floats subconsciously, weightlessly like a whisper in the wind before slowly free-falling back down to Earth. I open my eyes, meeting his. He's pleased. So pleased. "Good girl," he breathes. "I almost came just watching you." I look up at him, taking breathless gasps.

"Did you like that?"

I nod, lost for words.

"More?"

"More," I whisper.

Nick moves his hand slowly between my legs as he takes my hand, gliding it over his rock-hard shaft. He groans as I wrap my fingers around his girth, feeling him throbbing against my palm. My breath catches in my throat at the thought of him inside me, wondering if it's going to hurt, though the thought of it hurting is intriguing.

I close my eyes and feel his mouth on my neck, moving slowly down to my breasts, engulfing my nipple, tantalizing me with his tongue. He sucks hard with deliberate pleasure, then bites, and my whole body reacts. My eyes flash open and I cry out, arching my back, my body craving him inside me. Sensing my need, he moves his body over mine and I clutch at his biceps, exuberant yet apprehensive about what comes next. I let my gaze drift slowly down his body, admiring the strength in his chest, the power in his arms. Nick slides his hand down between us, urging my legs apart, and I feel him between my thighs, circling then pressing the tip of his hard, thick cock firmly against me.

"Look at me," he whispers, and I do, to watch him slowly force himself inside me, just a little, though it feels like a lot.

I gasp, the pressure of him inside me stripping me of the ability to breathe. He eases back then pushes deeper and I cry out, sinking my fingernails into his arms. He winces, bowing his head to mine.

"Are you okay?" he breathes.

I nod solemnly. He tightens his jaw, pulling back swiftly then plunging in more strongly. I throw my head back against the pillows, a soft cry escaping my lips. He lowers his mouth to mine, biting gently on my bottom lip then pulling his head back so that my head rises off the pillow until he lets go, and I fall back, whimpering.

He waits until my gaze meets his again, then draws back, groaning, thrusting harder, filling me over and over, each stroke deeper than the last.

"Oh, my God. Oh, Nick!" I cry out.

I arch my back, rolling my hips against his.

"That's it, baby — move with me."

I do what he says, flexing my hips up to his then down against the bed, tightening around him as he builds to a steady rhythm. He pushes my knees up, spreading my legs wide, so that I can take the rest of him. His insatiable dark-blue eyes stay locked with mine, willing me to trust him unequivocally, and I do. He pulls back, slamming his hips against mine, and I clench tightly around him.

"Oh, Scarlet," he groans.

I close my eyes, sucking in breathless urgent gasps through my mouth, drawing the heat from his body, feeling the friction of our skin. A raw, throbbing sensation manifests deep inside me, blood coursing through my veins like liquid energy, and I buck my hips against his, clamping down around him again and again, clutching at his sides, raking my nails over his skin. His breathing turns rapid and erratic as he thrusts faster and harder.

"Give yourself to me," he whispers. His breath in my ear rattles my spine. I throw my arms around his neck, pulling him closer, crushing his body against me.

"*Nick*," I cry out, shaking, trembling, unraveling beneath

him, my body taut, my soul suspended, somewhere, nowhere. I don't ever want to come back from here, from this feeling, this heaven, this primal meaning of life.

He moves slowly inside me, drenched in my pleasure, watching, waiting. "*Baby*," he breathes.

I look up at him, weary and exhausted, my body limp.

"Ready to come again?"

I nod, wetting my lips. He tenses his body and anchors his feet, driving himself into me hard and fast, grunting with vigor as I whimper and writhe beneath him.

Fueled by his enthusiasm, I raise my hips, tightening around him rapidly, successively, my body greedy, craving the euphoric pleasure he has to give. His thrusts grow wild and uncoordinated, his breathing completely out of control.

I close my eyes, feeling the pull of my desire, so close to the edge I can't stand it. He groans, bringing my leg up to his shoulder, diving deep and hard. The shaking and throbbing inside me turns fierce and overpowering and I scream out, exploding around him.

He tilts his head back, a feverish, satisfied growl resonating in his chest, his heat filling my body, spurting deep inside me.

He lets go of my leg, lowering his body down to mine.

"Oh, baby," he pants, burying his head in my hair, tensing and twitching inside me. "God, I've missed you."

I run my hands across his back into his hair, so completely fulfilled. He lifts his head, kissing my cheeks, my nose and eyes, and withdraws slowly, collapsing onto the bed beside me.

"You're an amazing woman."

I lie there, exhausted. I can't speak—I can barely think.

"Are you okay?"

"Yes. That was unbelievable."

"That's nothing," he replies. "There are so many more places I can touch you."

I arch an eyebrow and roll onto my side to look at him, his bare chest heaving, glistening with sweat. "Really? When do we start?"

A mischievous look forms in his eyes and quickly spreads to his lips. "Slow down. We have the rest of our lives together, remember?"

"That's right. I forgot."

Chapter Four

Awakenings

I wake the next morning, feeling alive, refreshed and renewed, lying in Nick's arms. Big strong arms that hold me to him as we lie on our bed in a loosely woven web of limbs. He realizes I'm awake and tightens his embrace. I clutch his arm tightly, so blissfully happy.

"Good morning," he says, brushing the hair away from my neck and kissing softly down the nape.

"Mmmh. Good morning."

"I had a great time last night, Mrs. Pierce." He thrusts his hips against mine just once, a not-so-subtle reminder of the night before.

"It was the best night of my life," I reply.

His chest vibrates with laughter. I love his laugh. So deep and manly. I hadn't realized just how much, until now. I turn around to face him. He brushes the back of his hand lightly against my face, a tenderness developing in his eyes as he touches his lips to mine. Nick's mouth closes over mine, his masterful tongue courting, caressing, seducing mine. His deep, sensuous strokes building up to a crescendo, like a symphony to my soul. His kisses like whipped cream and candy, entirely their own kind of sex.

His cell phone rings on the bedside table beside him, startling us both. He looks down at his watch.

"No!" he growls. "No, no, no!" He snatches at his phone, every muscle in his face tightening.

"Mara," he snaps. I hear a woman's voice in the background. "I'll be right there." He throws the phone down onto the bed and I roll my eyes, knowing exactly what he's about to say. "I have to go into the office. I need to authorize the codes to unlock the safe."

"I know," I grumble, unable to mask my disappointment.

"I'll only be an hour or two, then we can pick up where we left off."

He presses against me suggestively and I roll over and groan into the pillows. He then jumps out of bed, heading for the bathroom. I watch him walking away, naked, raising my head for a better view, my eyebrow arching all by itself, obviously as aroused as I am. I throw my head back down, wallowing in frustration.

"Call in sick," I shout.

He steps back into the doorway so I can see him. "I'd love to, but I can't," he mumbles with his toothbrush in his mouth.

I huff.

He rushes back into the bedroom, running his hands through his dampened hair, and I watch him dash around the room, getting ready. His perfection never ceases to make me feel so horribly inadequate. I let out a long-suffering sigh as visions of our night of passion consume me. I can't believe how happy I am. How happy we both are. What on Earth was I so afraid of? *Nick is wonderful.* He's attractive, funny, sexy, successful and he definitely lights my fire. There can only be good things to come.

He hurries into the dressing room, appearing moments later dressed in my favorite dark-gray suit with a black collared shirt, the first three buttons undone, revealing just a glimpse of his tan, toned pecs.

I whistle. "You must have every woman in your office worshipping you."

"I do. It gets the job done, but you're the only one I want." He kneels over me, touching his lips to mine, when his cell rings again. He reaches for the phone, looking down at the screen. "It's Pete," he murmurs. "I have to go. I hate to leave you like this, baby. You'll be okay?"

"I'll be fine, go."

He swipes his finger across the screen to answer the call.

"Pete! I'm on my way," he barks, turning toward the door.

"I miss you already," I shout.

"I miss you more," he yells, chuckling as he closes the front door. I inhale sharply, catching a hint of his scent, and roll onto his side of the bed, burying my head in his pillows like a dog rolling on a bone, inhaling every last breath of him.

This is all happening so quickly. How is it possible to feel this way about him so suddenly? Is this the new me feeling, or the old me awakening? There's no way of knowing and honestly, right now, I don't care.

* * * *

The next few days are a blur of meeting up with family and friends, morning teas, afternoon teas and cups of tea, but the long, sensual nights with Nick have changed everything. Altering me in every way. No matter where I am or what I'm doing, he's with me, in my mind, touching me, kissing me, his arms around me.

The mere idea of him steals the air from my lungs, the sight of him electrifies the blood in my veins, the ghost of him still lingers inside my body. I wander out onto the balcony, breathing in the crisp morning air, looking out over the grounds. The sun is softer today, the light crisscross-patterned clouds stretching out across the pale-blue sky, lightening its glare, shadowing the prospering hills and valleys below. I exhale loudly.

Today is mine.

There's nowhere I need to be, but there is something I want to do. I decide on finding a bookstore, grabbing some lunch, choosing a good bottle of wine, then heading home for a nice hot soak in the tub. I do just that, having Gabe drop me off at the mall, then set about finding a bookstore.

The mall is buzzing today. I've come here to unwind, but

I can see that's not the case for others. People rush past me in a hurry to get somewhere, only to stop at the first thing that catches their eye, lingering there as though debating whether or not to buy it. It makes no sense to be in such a hurry in the first place. I stroll right to the other end of the mall before finding a bookstore, but it's well worth the walk.

As I open the door, warm air and the aroma of fresh, hot coffee waft toward me like an old friend inviting me in. The store is vast and wondrous. People everywhere, talking and reading. Innocent giggles cascade down a spiral staircase that leads to the children's section, accompanied by the soft buzz of conversation from the oval-shaped coffee shop in the center of the store. Its timber floors and old-fashioned furniture with high-backed armchairs transport me to another time. I never imagined a bookstore to be such an experience. I drift toward a sign that reads *Latest Arrivals*, admiring the rows of new books promising me an escape, or at least temporary relief from my new world of self-discovery.

I flip through the first book I come to, bringing it closer to my face, inhaling deeply. I love the way new books smell, the whole soft, shiny, innocent feeling in my hands. To consider the possibility of no one having opened it before, that it could be mine and mine completely, to read at my own will, to live vicariously in someone else's world, to see life through their eyes and feel their emotions without fear or favor is a truly intriguing prospect. Funny, considering my own life feels like someone else's right now.

Reading is something I've learned to love since the accident. Books of all kinds, inspiring me, not just in knowledge, but in truth. To know that hope is not a foolish concept, that love can save us, that faith can transform us, that our friends can also be our enemies, that heroes can be small and monsters can be vanquished.

I place the book back on the shelf, scanning the covers for a standout, when a hand reaches for a book in front of me.

A man, I guess by his cologne, which smells oddly familiar. He passes the book to me.

"This is a good one."

I look up, instantly recognizing his voice.

"Mitch!"

His eyes light up as I say his name. "Hi, Scarlet."

"Wow, what are you doing here?" He holds up his book, twitching his lips. "You're buying a book," I reply, answering my own ridiculous question. "So, you read then?"

His grin broadens into a hearty laugh. "Yes, I *read*. I can also write."

This time, *I* laugh. "I just meant that I hadn't pegged you as a reader."

"I know what you meant. I'm sorry, I couldn't resist."

I shake my head and look down at the book in my hands in an attempt to hide my flushed cheeks.

"So, this is the one to read, huh?"

"It's my pick."

I turn the book over to its back. It looks interesting enough.

"This one it is, then."

I glance up at him. He looks completely different in the light of day. He's taller than I remember, his broad shoulders filling his white long-sleeved knit shirt that hangs loosely over the waist of his jeans.

"It's really good to see you again."

"Yeah, you, too," I reply ingenuously.

He flicks his fingertips against the side of his neck. "Uh, I don't have to be back at work for a while. Do you wanna grab a coffee or something?"

"Um, yeah, I'd love a coffee."

"Great. After you," he replies, relief flooding into his eyes as he motions for me to lead the way.

As we approach the cashier, Mitch slides the book from my hand and places it on the counter with his.

"Just these two," he says, taking his wallet from his pocket.

The cashier scans the books, flashing him her widest white-fanged smile and flipping her long red locks as she hands him the book bag, making sure her dainty pale-white fingers touch his hand in the exchange. Mitch doesn't seem to notice her at all. If he did, he hid it well. He reaches into the bag, handing me my book.

"There you are, all yours."

"Thank you. That's very kind."

"No, it's smart. At least this way, if you don't like it, I won't wear it," he says, returning my smile.

We head over to the coffee shop and order, then seek out a quiet spot to sit. The furniture is like nothing I've ever seen before, the high-backed armchairs like those of a knights' castle. I lean back against my red king-size chair, gliding my fingers over the soft, woven fabric, adoring the aged timber and old-fashioned tacking holding the fabric firmly in place. I scan the store for exits, wondering how I could possibly get one of these out of here, when Mitch's voice interrupts me.

"You want one too, huh?"

I look up at him, amused. "Am I that transparent?"

He chuckles. "No, but I think everyone who's ever sat in them has thought it."

I grin, resting my head against the back of the chair, its comfort like a giant hug.

To my surprise, the conversation comes easily. We laugh and talk like two old friends and, for a nice change, there's no mention of the past. I sit listening to him, captivated by the way he speaks, so earthy and honest, so different from anyone I know. I watch the way he moves his hands when he talks, the way two soft dimples punctuate his cheeks when he smiles, the way his short dark hair with just a hint of gray kicks up at the front just above the soft lines of his forehead and the way his brown eyes, with just a hint of green, seem to soothe my soul.

I wonder how old he is. Thirty-two, thirty-three, perhaps? It's not his looks that make me feel he's older, or the things he says or does — it's the way he projects himself. He's lived. He knows who he is, unlike me. Most of all, he makes me laugh. I love how good it feels to laugh. A real laugh, the kind that make me tilt my head back, my stomach tighten and after a while, my cheeks hurt. Every now and then, when he shifts in his seat, I catch a faint hint of his cologne, sending my senses into overdrive. Nick smells incredible, but Mitch's scent stops me. My pulse quickens. I take a sip of my coffee and swallow hard, fighting the dreaded red-cheek syndrome away. If he notices, he doesn't falter.

We talk briefly about the accident, how he saw my car go into the water and jumped in to save me. He tones down his heroics and oversimplifies it all, but I feel strangely better hearing his account of things. I put my napkin onto the table and look up at him.

"Well, this has been really good."

He nods, drinking down the last mouthful of his coffee. "Yeah, it's been great. We should definitely do this again sometime."

He places his cup down on the table and runs his hand through his hair haphazardly, and it hits me like a ton of bricks, as if someone had kicked the chair out from underneath me. I sit bolt upright, embedding my fingernails deep into the armrests of my chair.

"Are you okay?"

I clutch at my chest, suddenly out of breath.

"What just happened?" he asks.

"I don't know. It was like a rerun, in my head."

"A rerun?"

He comes around to sit beside me.

"What do you mean?"

"It was so strange. You put your cup down and ran your fingers through your hair, then I saw you do the exact same thing, but it was different."

"Different?"

"*You* looked different. You were wearing different clothes and there was a different background."

He draws his eyebrows together to form a hard line, a distinctly distant look forming in his eyes.

"It was as though I've seen you do that before. Like a memory."

He doesn't answer. Not a single word.

"Only it couldn't be a memory. Because I didn't know you before the accident."

His silence is deafening. I look up at him, searching his face until finally, he speaks.

"No. It couldn't be a memory," he replies, but his eyes betray him. He stands abruptly. "We should probably get you home—you should rest." He scoops the books up from the table and takes my arm, helping me to my feet.

As we step out into the mall, people rush past us, busy going about their day, but not me. Everything moves frame by frame. I float through the plaza in a daze, the fact that Mitch has his arm linked with mine my only lifeline to the outside world. As we near the exit, two uniformed police officers approach us.

"Mitch!" one of them calls out.

He groans, tightening his grip on me as we come to a stop in front of them. The officers greet us with smiles and extend their hands to shake his. The tallest one glances from Mitch to me. I look down at his name badge but it's just a number—1059812.

"Long time, no see, boss," 1059812 says cheerfully.

Mitch grunts. "Ah, yeah. Hi, fellas."

"Ma'am," the other officer says, dipping his hat, his sprightly blue eyes making him look much younger than he is.

I feign a smile as my gaze settles on his name badge. Thankfully, he has a name—Constable Matthews. Mitch glances across at me but doesn't introduce us.

"So, what are you up to these days?" 1059812 asks. "It's sure not the same without you around."

Mitch shifts on his feet, clearly uncomfortable.

"Hey, Jade's here if you want to say hello," Matthews

interrupts. "She's right over there." He points toward a tall, athletic-looking brunette police officer talking to a man in an electrical goods store just across from us. She's staring right at us and she doesn't look happy. Mitch turns swiftly back to face them, his body tense.

"Look, guys, I don't mean to be rude, but Scarlet here isn't feeling too well. I'm just taking her home."

They both glance at me, concerned.

"Uh, okay, yeah, sure. Anything we can help with?" 1059812 asks.

Mitch shakes his head. "No. Thanks though."

They both nod. "Well, it was good to see you, Sarge. Catch up soon for a cold one, hey?"

I turn to Mitch.

Sarge?

He tightens his fingers around my arm but doesn't look at me. "Yep, see ya round," He replies, whisking me away and through the exit to the underground carpark.

"Do you have a car here?" he asks.

My head is spinning. *Mitch is a police officer?*

"*Scarlet.*"

I flash back to the here and now, glimpsing up at him.

"Do you have a car here?" he snaps.

"Uh, no."

"I'll drive you home. My car's right down there." He points toward a black SUV parked at the end of the row. He presses a button on his remote and the doors open, presses another and the Chevy roars to life. He helps me into the front seat, then hurries around to the driver's side and slides behind the wheel.

A sharp, stabbing pain shoots down behind the back of my eyes and I hang my head, cupping my face in my hands.

He bows his head to mine. "Are you okay, Scar?"

My eyelids flutter involuntarily, an unfamiliar feeling rippling through my body. "Why did you call me that?"

"Call you what?"

"Scar," I snap.

He pauses. "I don't know, it just came out. People must shorten your name to Scar?" he asks, more a statement than a question.

"No. No one ever calls me that."

The cabin is so deadly quiet I can hear him chasing his breath. He reaches across for my seat belt and I snatch it from his hand. "I can do it."

He straightens in his seat, putting his own belt on before shifting to drive and pulling out onto the street, neither of us saying a word. He drives out of the city, toward the motorway, when my cell phone rings.

It's Nick. I can't talk to him right now. I send the call to voicemail and rest the phone in my lap, deep in thought. Mitch changes lanes then glances across at me.

"Nick?" he asks.

I look up at him, his voice tugging me from my thoughts. "Yes," I whisper, my gaze slowly returning to the phone. I feel him looking at me. I glance up at him and he looks away, turning his attention back to the road.

My cell rings again and this time I turn it off, tossing it into my purse, the sudden movement making my head throb against my temples. I take two of my painkillers from their bottle and try to swallow them without water. They taste terrible. Mitch looks down at the pill bottle in my hands, then reaches into the center console, passing me a bottle of water. I take the lid off and gulp it down. "Thank you."

"What are the pills for?" he asks softly.

I frown, looking out of my window. "My head hurts."

"Does that happen often?"

"Yes."

He exhales loudly, flicking on his indicator and merging between two cars before taking my exit. I'm suddenly filled with emotion. Anxiety, curiosity? I'm not sure. I stare across at him, waiting for his dark, brooding eyes to meet mine, but they don't, or won't. I decide not to wait.

"So. *Sarge*, is it?" I ask, studying him closely. He tightens his fingers on the wheel but keeps his attention on the road.

"I thought you were a boat builder?"

Mitch clenches his jaw, but he still doesn't look at me. "I *am* a boat builder."

"But you're also a police officer."

"I *was* a police officer. Well, *technically* I still am. I'm just not at the moment."

"Why didn't you tell me?"

He shrugs, his poker face well-hinged. "It didn't come up."

I raise an eyebrow. *Well played.*

He doesn't offer anything more and, frankly, I'm not in the mood for an interrogation.

A loud ringing sound echoes through the stereo, shattering the deafening silence. A name appearing on the small screen in front of me.

Jade.

A green Answer button and red Decline button glow beneath it. He looks down at the screen and presses Decline. It rings again straight away. Again, he declines the call, leaving me wondering who Jade is to him. A girlfriend, perhaps, though he never mentioned one. He reaches for his cell phone, to turn it off before putting it down on the console between us. I stare across at him, realizing he's not the boat-building, accidental hero that I thought he was. He's much more than that. He's a mystery, evidently a cop, and I really don't know him at all. I sink down in my seat and close my eyes, going over fragments of the vision until, finally, we turn in to my street. He drives slowly up the driveway and shuts off the engine, resting his hands on his knees.

"Well. Here we are," he murmurs. He sits completely still, looking straight ahead, his brow furrowed.

"I saw water."

He looks across at me, bewildered. "What?"

"Behind you, in the vision. I saw water, like the ocean. All around you. You were on a boat."

He turns his head slowly, resuming his stare straight

ahead, not saying a word.

"You build boats. Can you explain that?"

He doesn't answer.

I throw myself back in the seat. "Ugh, I don't understand any of this. You know something, I can *feel* it. What are you hiding?"

Right at that second, he snatches at his seat belt and seizes my face in his hands, bringing his mouth down on mine, without warning. His lips engulf mine, kissing me urgently, ardently. I can't breathe. I clutch at his fingers, desperately trying to pry them from my face, but he only tightens his grip. I whimper, tears welling in my eyes. He stops suddenly, releasing me, and I pull away from him, cupping my mouth in my hand.

"Oh, God. I'm sorry," he starts.

The frenzied rhythm of my heart resonates through my body. I desperately press my seat belt release, then snatch at my purse and jump out of the vehicle.

"Scar." I hear his car door open. "Scarlet, please, stop!" he shouts, but I don't stop. I can't stop. I run. I reach the front door, fumbling for my house keys, and I hear him behind me. My hands are trembling, shaking so vigorously that I can barely push the key into the lock. I can almost feel his breath on the back of my neck. I turn the key in the lock, the door opens and I tumble inside.

"Scar, please! Just let me explain." He jams his foot inside the door so I can't close it.

"Mitch, please, just go."

"I didn't mean to frighten you, please, just listen to me," he pleads.

"Go away!" I sob.

"It's not what you think, Scar." He presses his head against the door.

"Please, Mitch. Go!" I look up at him, tears streaming down my face.

His face twists up as though he's in pain. "I'm sorry."

I push on the door again and he steps back. The door

slams shut and I lock it, sliding slowly down to the floor. Malaylie rushes into the room in a panic, crouching in front of me.

"Oh, my Lord, Mrs. Pierce, are you okay?"

I nod, fighting back the tsunami of tears threatening to crush me.

I hear Mitch's car start up and drive away, and hug my knees to my chest, my tears paralyzing me.

"Come, come." Malaylie tugs gently on my arm, helping me to the couch. "I'll make you a hot cup of tea, antioxidants, they are good for you, you'll be fine, you'll see. Just breathe." She pats my arm, sets my purse down in my lap then rushes out of the room.

I lean back against the couch, trying to make sense of what just happened, but the more I try, the more I sob and so I stop. I sit there listening to the kettle boiling, then hear the front door open and shut with a thud. It's Nick.

"Hey you," he says cheerfully, tossing his keys onto the end table. "I've been ringing your cell but it's switched off, I thought I'd —" He looks into my eyes and stops talking.

"Hey!" He rushes to me. "What's wrong?"

I look up at him through my messy fringe like a scared child, tears re-forming in my eyes. He kneels in front of me, wrapping his arms around me, which only makes the tears fall faster.

"Hey, hey, what happened? Are you okay?" he asks, his voice shrouded in concern.

I have no idea where to start or what exactly I should tell him. "Scarlet, tell me what happened."

I wipe the tears from my face, summoning courage. "I saw something today."

His whole body stiffens. "You saw something?"

"I had a vision."

"A vision? Like a memory?"

"I don't know if it's a memory. If it is, it doesn't make any sense."

He rests his hands on mine. "Why's that?"

"I don't understand how it could possibly be a memory, when I didn't meet him until after the accident, and I haven't had a cup of coffee with him since I met him."

"Hold up," he interrupts. "Who's *he*?"

"Mitch."

"Mitch? The guy who rescued you from the crash?"

I nod. "I ran into him at the bookstore. We had a coffee, then he put his cup down on the table and ran his fingers through his hair. Then it replayed in my head, but it was completely different."

His eyes grow darker. "Different how?"

"He was wearing different clothes and we were in another place, not that one at all."

He stares at me, as though trying to make an ounce of sense from what I'm saying. "So. You're telling me, you were with Mitch today and it triggered some kind of memory. Of him?"

"Yes."

He holds my gaze. I have no idea what he's thinking or feeling and his eyes give nothing away. Malaylie rushes into the room, holding my cup of tea.

"Oh, Mr. Pierce, I'm so glad you're home. That man, he scared Mrs. Pierce, I didn't think he would leave."

He pulls his hands from mine, rising swiftly to his feet. "*He was here?*"

Now, there's no mistaking how he's feeling – he's furious. His eyes reduce me to ash. I inhale sharply as Malaylie puts my cup of tea in front of me, looking up at me nervously, then leaves the room as quickly as she entered. I take the tea and look up at him, tears forming in my eyes.

"In the black Chevy I just saw in the street outside?"

I nod.

"Why was he here? What did he do?" he snaps.

"Nothing."

"Then why are you crying? Did he hurt you?" he growls, searching my face and arms for injuries.

Should I tell him about the kiss? *No. He's angry enough.*

"No. He just scared me, that's all."

"Scared you how?" he asks, his eyes as dark as the docks at midnight and his voice just as threatening.

I look up at him, alarmed. I've never seen him like this.

"Tell me," he snarls.

The truth is the only thing in my head and it's on my lips before I realize it. "He kissed me," I murmur.

"*What?*"

I bow my head. Nothing in the world is going to make me repeat that. Nick grits his teeth as he paces across the room. "Who the hell is this guy? Thinks he can kiss my wife—" He balls his hands into fists, twitching them at his sides. "I'll fucking kill him," he roars.

I flinch. "He saved my life, Nick."

"He kissed you! You were scared, crying, now you're *defending him?*" he shouts.

My bottom lip quivers involuntarily, my hands shaking. "I'm not defending him," I mumble.

He runs his hand through his hair, glaring down at me. "Christ, Scarlet, I just got you back!"

"Why are you so angry with me?"

He pauses, then light seems to flow back into his eyes. "I'm not angry with *you*. I'm just angry! Some miserable excuse for a man has just manhandled my wife and I wasn't here to protect you."

He relaxes his fists, stretching out his fingers as he sits down beside me. "I'm sorry for shouting. I'm just trying to understand," he concedes, his expression suddenly rueful.

"Well, that makes two of us."

He exhales loudly, pulling me into his arms. "I don't want you to have anything more to do with him," he insists. "Promise me." He tilts my head up to look at him. "I'll handle this. Okay?"

I have no idea what he means by that and I have no energy to ask.

He brushes the back of his hand against my face and my eyes grow heavy. "You should rest. It's been a big day.

Come on, I'll run you a nice warm bath and organize some dinner."

He takes my hand, leading me up to the bathroom. There, I walk over to the mirror, taking off my clothes as I do so, and he starts the bath, swirling his hand in the water, checking the temperature.

"Are you okay?" he asks.

"Yes," I reply, walking toward him.

He slides his arms underneath mine to undo my bra, then slides down my panties. He trails his fingers lightly over the curves of my hips before he takes me in his arms, touching his lips to mine.

"Did he hold you like this when he kissed you?" he asks.

My brow creases. "No," I whisper. "We were in his truck."

He swallows hard. "I'll be downstairs. Leave the door open. Just yell out if you need anything."

I nod hesitantly and watch him exit, hoping that I did the right thing not telling him everything, though it fills me with an uneasy feeling. I step into the bath, sliding slowly beneath the warm water as it dips and swirls around me, sinking into my skin, soothing my body.

I turn off the tap and lie back in the tub, closing my eyes, doing all that I can to avoid thinking about the day's events, but they are inescapable. I slink beneath the water until my head is completely submerged, holding my breath until I can't hold it anymore, trying to drown out my thoughts, but there's no escaping them. I come up for air, gasping, the feverish rhythm of my heart temporarily suppressing my fears. The bathwater rears up, slopping out onto the floor, lapping at my body and whirling around me in the tub. The room grows quiet again as the water settles. Too quiet.

Suddenly, being alone with my thoughts doesn't seem so appealing.

I wash quickly and slip into my robe, then head downstairs to find Nick sitting on the couch, an informal dinner for two set out on the coffee table in front of him. The lights are dim, the TV on, the fire kindling in the fireplace. He looks up, flashing me a sympathetic smile that has the effect of a tranquilizer dart. I return the only smile I can find and flop down onto the couch beside him.

"This is really nice. Thank you."

"Don't get too excited. It's just leftovers."

"Leftovers sounds great."

We eat dinner in front of the warm, numbing glow of the fire and though there is much to say, neither of us dares to go there.

Chapter Five

Enter the Sandman

Black rain falls all around, without a sound. Light shines in my eyes. Too bright. I shield my face with my forearm. A car horn blares. I can hear the rain now, angry, smashing its tiny fists against the windshield in a wild, relentless rampage. I glance down, tightening my fingers around the steering wheel.

Another car horn blasts. I look up and lights blind me. I panic, yanking on the wheel, the tires bearing down on the gravel beneath them, the car spinning. I scream but there's no sound. Fear ripples and echoes through my body, searing my spine. I close my eyes, gasping, breathless, spinning, spinning, then falling, silently into the darkness.

I open my eyes. I can hear my scream now. I sit up, clutching my chest. Still, there's only darkness, then light, everywhere. My eyelids are fluttering wildly like newborn butterflies when I hear Nick's voice.

"Scarlet?" I feel his hand on my back. "Are you okay?"

I have no idea. It's hard to think with my pulse thudding so loudly in my ears. I clutch at my nightgown until the material clings to my body, constricting my chest, as though it's the only thing holding me together.

His brow creases. "A nightmare?"

I nod.

"I'll get you a glass of water." He jumps out of bed and rushes into the bathroom.

I take a deep breath, shocked by the magnitude of fear I'd brought out of my dream. The first I've had of the accident. Nick rushes back in, passing me the water the instant he reaches me. My mouth is so dry that I gulp it down quickly, letting it run over my chin onto my nightgown.

"What was it about?"

"The accident."

He frowns. "What did you see? Do you remember what happened?"

I clutch my forehead, squeezing my eyes shut. "Just snippets of the car spinning and falling."

"Is your head hurting? Do you want some painkillers?"

"Yes, please."

He takes the glass from my hand and walks into the bathroom, to return with a full cup of water and my pain medication. He sits as I swallow them, then takes the tumbler from my hand and puts it on the nightstand.

"How long have the headaches been back for?" I look up at him, startled. "Your bottle's nearly empty."

"They never stopped," I murmur.

"You told me they were better."

"I didn't want you to worry."

He pulls me into his arms, cradling my head against his chest.

"You're going back to the neurologist."

"No, I'm fine."

"You're *not* fine."

Tears come out of nowhere, pooling in my eyes.

"It's okay. I'm here," he whispers, tightening his arms around me. "It's progress, I guess."

However painful.

We fall asleep like that, wrapped in each other's arms. In the morning, when I wake, he's gone, instilling a feeling in me I've never known. Like a fledgling, peering over the edge of its nest, not yet sure it can fly. I sit up to find a note on the pillow beside me.

Good morning, beautiful girl,

Attending to urgent business. You were sleeping so soundly that I couldn't wake you. I'm only a phone call away if you need me.

Love, Nick. xx

P.S. You have an appointment with your neurologist next Thursday at 10:30.

I lie back down and close my eyes. *Damn.*

I hope his 'urgent business' isn't tracking Mitch down and beating him with a stick. *Or maybe I do?*

No. I wouldn't wish that on anyone. I roll over onto Nick's pillows. I miss him. I can't believe how much. How empty I feel without him. The way my feelings for him have changed so profoundly in such a short time amazes me. Just weeks ago I felt so alone, my own entity. Now *I* has turned to *we,* and I honestly don't know what I'd do without him. He's my rock, and I do mean rock, clinging to him so often lately for his love and support, though I saw a completely different side to him last night. I've never seen him angry like that, not even close. He sure doesn't like Mitch very much. Not that I blame him. I'm not sure *I* like Mitch very much right now.

I close my eyes and see a flash of his face coming toward me, his ashen, brimstone eyes, his hands on my face, his mouth on mine. I still have no idea why he kissed me.

Nick's last words spring to mind, that he would *'handle this'.* The thought makes me nothing short of nervous.

I rise slowly, get dressed and wander down to the kitchen. The house is eerily quiet this morning, with the only sound to be heard the coffee machine, percolating in the corner. I take a cup out of the cupboard and hear Malaylie and Gabe talking outside.

I spot them in the vegetable garden, picking fruit and pottering around. I can't help but smile. Malaylie sits on the corner of the garden bed, picking cherry tomatoes and placing them in her aproned lap. Gabe swipes a tomato from her collection, quickly popping it into his mouth, grinning, tilting his head back as though her smile is the warmth of the sun on his face. He says something and she giggles, then lightly touches his arm. It lightens my heart and fills me with hope, that feelings like those don't fade with age, that life can still hold so much intrigue and emotion, irrespective of where your foot is in time.

The phone rings beside me and I jump out of my skin, answering it quickly, expecting it to be my mother or Nick checking in, completely unprepared for who it is.

"Scarlet, it's Mitch." I stop breathing. "Please don't hang up, I *need* to talk to you," he pleads.

"How did you get this number?"

"Please, Scarlet, just let me explain what happened yesterday. You need to know the truth."

I take a deep breath, debating whether or not I want to. "Just tell me one thing," I snap.

"Anything."

"Was it a memory?"

For a moment, there's only silence, then just one word.

"*Yes.*"

I stand there trembling, trying to comprehend what that means.

"It's complicated, but if you just give me a chance, there are things to say."

I put down the phone, my brain unable to handle any more information. I clutch at the kitchen bench, steadying myself as the room spins around me, a thousand questions fighting to reach the forefront of my mind. Seconds later, the phone rings again. I ignore it. I stumble into the lounge and sit, trying to gather my thoughts.

What does that mean? I knew Mitch *before* the accident?

The phone rings again.

I jump up and snatch at the receiver. "Leave me alone!" I shout into the mouthpiece.

To my surprise, it's Nick's voice that answers. "Whoa, hey, it's me." And that's that, all my worries, fears and tears find me at once. "I'm on my way home."

He hangs up in my ear and I drop the phone, six months of turmoil finally engulfing me. I drop to my knees, curling up in a ball on the floor and, for the first time, I cry myself a river.

When the tears finally subside, I hear a rapping at the front door. I look around, searching for Malaylie, but there's no sign of her. I rise slowly, wiping the salty remnants from my face as I walk over and open the front door.

"*Mitch.*"

He stands before me, his tortured, bloodshot eyes pleading with me to let him in.

There are no words.

I stand there staring at him, when I should be shouting at him. I should be angry, furious that he's here, furious that he kissed me, furious that he called. Instead, I bow my head and drift back from the door, allowing him entry. I gesture toward the lounge and he walks in ahead of me, setting himself down on the couch. I take a seat opposite him, afraid to look into his eyes, afraid of what I might find there.

"Scar, please, look at me."

"It's *Scarlet*," I snap, unintentionally obliging his request.

"I'm sorry that I kissed you yesterday. I shouldn't have done that."

"Why did you?"

"You were remembering things. I needed to see, if you remembered…"

"Remembered what?"

He stands and takes a step toward me, and I shift nervously in my seat.

"Please. Just think, Scarlet. I need you to think."

I shake my head, unsure what I'm supposed to be '*thinking*' about.

"You *have* to remember!" he demands, taking another step toward me.

He's too close. I jump to my feet in fear and anger and he seizes my upper arms. I glance down at his hands, outraged.

"Stop it! Just stop it! You don't know what you're asking! I don't remember. What am I supposed to remember?"

"Me. *Us*," he whispers.

I had feared it, but hearing it is entirely another thing. I stand there frozen, searching my mind, searching his face, but there's nothing.

No *us*.

I can't help him. I just don't remember. He drops his head in defeat, releasing me, and I step back, instantly reaching up to where his hands were. He paces the room, running his hands through his hair in frustration.

"I promised myself I wouldn't do this," he says bitterly. "For six months, I promised myself I wouldn't do this."

"Do what?"

"Tell you. Confront you. I wanted you to remember for yourself, but when you had the memory at the bookstore yesterday I thought maybe if I just pushed a little harder…"

"What are you saying?"

"I'm saying that we knew each other before the accident. *Really* knew each other."

He reaches into his pocket and pulls out his cell phone, swiping his finger across the screen before holding it up in front of me.

It's a picture.

I float forward, staring at the two people in front of me.

Mitch and I. Together.

He's looking straight at the camera, smiling, so innocent, so happy, and there I am, right beside him, kissing his cheek. I can see there are other photos, but I can't bear to look.

"What. How can this…?" I have no words.

"We were in love, Scarlet."

I see that. I see it in his face. I see it in mine. I swallow hard, studying the picture as I fall onto the couch behind me, my hand over my mouth. I see it with my own eyes, but I still can't believe it. I don't want to believe it.

I betrayed Nick? Is this the kind of person I am? A liar? A cheat?

The screen grows dark and I pass the phone back to Mitch,

shaking my head. "That's not who I am now."

"You don't know *who* you are now, Scarlet, and you certainly don't know the man you've been living with for the past six months."

My brow creases. "I do know him. Nick and I are happy. Really happy."

"Oh, come on! He's not who you think he is, Scar. You were scared of him."

"*What?*"

"It's only a matter of time before you see the real Nick."

I shake my head in horrified denial.

"You called me. Before the accident. I was rushing here, to you, when I saw your car go off the road."

Tears stream down my cheeks. I've heard enough. "Stop!"

He walks toward me and I thrust out my palm to stop him coming any closer. He takes another step, pressing his body firmly against my hand. I look down at his chest, watching as it rises and falls beneath my fingers. I can feel his heart racing, feel the warmth of his skin, feel his eyes searching for mine.

"You were leaving him, Scarlet. You told him that night. I was worried about what he'd do so I stayed close, in case you needed me. You called me. You were crying hysterically. I drove toward you and that's when I saw your car go off the road."

"*That's not true!*"

"It *is* true."

"If I left him before the accident, why on Earth would he pretend otherwise?"

"Who knows how his mind works? There was a second car that night, Scarlet. Someone was right behind you. I saw it. Saw it force you off the road."

"Stop it! Just stop it!" I shout.

Suddenly the front door bursts open, swinging back against the wall with a loud *thud*. Nick's tall, powerful frame fills the doorway and he's in the lounge in an instant.

"What the fuck are you doing here?" Nick shouts, his

anger filling the parts of the room I hadn't filled with mine. He strides toward Mitch, his eyes filled with rage, his hands balled up into fists. Overcome by a sudden urge to protect Mitch, I step in front of Nick, blocking his path. I clutch at his shirt, begging him to look at me, but his gaze is fixed on Mitch.

"He came to talk to me," I splutter.

"*Really?*" he snaps. "What is it *exactly* that you have to say to my wife that you feel the need to sneak around behind my back to do so?"

Mitch squares his shoulders. "I came to explain about the memory Scar had. Of me."

Nick's eyes ignite with pure hate.

"*Scar?* Her name is Scarlet. Mrs. Pierce to you!"

"Really? I think you and I both know that card's been played," Mitch slams back.

Nick tilts his head. "What?"

"It's worked out pretty well for you, hasn't it? Scarlet losing her memory…" Their eyes stay locked, filled with fury.

"It was you, wasn't it?" Nick growls. "You're the reason."

I have no idea what Nick's referring to, but I get the feeling that Mitch does, and his response, or lack of it, seems to answer Nick's question. Without warning, Nick reaches across to my shoulder, sweeping me out of his path as they both launch at each other.

"Stop! Stop!" I yell, though I know neither will. Nick swings his big, powerful arm at Mitch's face then locks it around his throat, holding him in a viselike grip. Mitch fights back, elbowing Nick in the stomach, then in the face. Nick stumbles backward then turns, driving his body into Mitch's stomach, lifting him off the ground and slamming him down, the two of them landing together with a loud *thud* on the floor in front of me.

I scream. I have to stop this. I rush forward, taking a firm grip of Nick's arm, trying to pull him away, but his focus is on Mitch. Nick rips his arm from my grasp and I hurtle backward, hitting my head on the coffee table, my eyelids fluttering. I close my eyes momentarily, then try to sit up, but my head hurts. I drop back down onto my elbow, running my fingers through my hair until I find the spot where the pain is. It feels wet.

I bring my hand down to look at it and wince, shocked to see blood on my fingers. I glance across at them, still wrestling on the floor. Nick is on top of Mitch, about to punch him again.

"Nick, stop! He's a cop!" I shout. Nick turns to look at me, his eyes zeroing in on the blood on my hand.

"Scarlet?" He lets go of Mitch's collar and scrambles over to me. "Are you okay?"

"I think so."

"Oh, my God, what happened? Did I do that?"

"It's not your fault."

I glance up at him, his eyes filled with remorse, his face an absolute mess. Blood trickles from a cut above his eye and oozes from a split in his lip. Mitch comes into view behind him, his chest heaving, his shirt ripped open, blood spilling from the corner of his mouth.

"Scar," he gasps.

I can see there's nothing he wants more than to rush to my side. Suddenly any anger I felt toward him is gone. Nick puts pressure on the wound, holding my head against his chest possessively, then glares up at Mitch.

"You're a cop?"

He gives Nick a fierce, hateful glare then returns his gaze to me, twitching his hands at his sides. Nick's body grows tense. He stands swiftly, grabs Mitch by the shirt and swings him around toward the front door.

"Get the fuck out of my house!" Nick snarls, emphasizing every word.

Mitch steadies himself, clenching his jaw, visibly fighting every desire in his body to stay, then turns abruptly, marching toward the door.

"And stay the fuck away from my wife!" Nick shouts, as

Mitch slams the door behind him.

I flinch. I wasn't sure of Mitch's motives, but I have to consider that what he said was the truth and, judging by the look in his eyes, he has a lot more to say. I hear his car start, his tires screeching out of the driveway. I sit up just as Nick reaches me, scooping me into his arms and setting me down on the couch.

"Let me see," he says, sitting beside me, searching through my hair for the wound. "He's really a cop?"

"Yes."

"Why tell us he's a boat builder?"

"He is a boat builder, but he's also a cop."

"What?"

I wince as he finds the spot, leaning in to take a closer look.

"It's not bad, but you might have a concussion. We should take you to the emergency room just in case."

"No." A drop of blood drips down from the cut above his eye onto his white shirt. "Look at *you*. Maybe we should take *you* to the emergency room."

"I'm fine." He reaches down to take my hand and I pull away, Mitch's words resonating in my mind.

Nick looks up at me, his eyes clouded and intense. "What's wrong?"

I frown, not sure I should ask but knowing that I have to. "Is what Mitch said true? That I was leaving you?"

He stares at me, every muscle in his face tense, then leans back against the couch, folding his arms behind his head as if acknowledging something he long feared. Finally, he answers.

"Yes."

And there it is. One little word that changes everything.

The air from my lungs wisps from my lips, deflating my entire body. I stand, glowering at him, my anger suddenly returning. "And you didn't think I should know something like that?"

He drops his hands from behind his head, his eyes hazy

shadows of their former selves.

"I battled with it, but things were so good between us after the accident, I just couldn't tell you."

I can hear the heartbreak in his voice, see his apology in his eyes, but there's just no making sense of it. I shake my head and turn, walking out of the room.

"Scarlet!"

I ignore him and keep walking, returning a few minutes later with a first-aid kit. He looks up at me, surprised as I kneel down in front of him. I take out a piece of gauze and apply it to the cut above his eye. He winces, closing his eyes briefly then opening them again, looking straight into mine. I ignore him, focusing my attention on his injuries, but the silence closes in, screaming at me.

"Why was I leaving you?"

He hangs his head, taking a deep breath as he draws his conclusions. I sense I'm not going to get the whole truth, but I need to hear some kind of explanation.

"You told me you weren't happy anymore."

I take the antiseptic from the box, dabbing it on his cuts, somehow finding solace in his suffering. "Why wasn't I happy?"

"You didn't really say why. I tried to talk to you about it, but you wanted to leave. I asked you if there was someone else. You said there wasn't. I held you by the arms, trying to get you to talk to me, but you were hysterical, adamant that it was over between us. You rushed out of the house and…you know the rest." I shake my head, expecting more, wanting more.

"So, I wasn't happy in our marriage and you have *no* idea why?"

His expression darkens. He stands abruptly and walks over to the patio door, staring out at the pool, his back to me.

"I didn't say I had no idea why," he mutters.

"Then tell me."

He turns back to face me slowly, his eyes red, altered. "I

think you just stopped loving me."

My brow creases. That's hard to believe, given the way I've come to feel about him. I'm not sure that it's love, exactly. I'm not even sure what love is, but it has to be close. My heart aches. His eyes, layered with hurt, remorse and loss, stay on mine. I walk toward him, straight into his big strong arms, and he closes them around me.

Very few people in this world get a second chance to start over, but here I am, standing at the precipice of mine. I have no idea how I felt about Nick before the accident. I only know how I feel about him right now. Things aren't the same anymore. *I'm* not the same anymore and the past is exactly that. We're happy now — how can I possibly let a decision I don't remember making ruin that?

There's only one answer to that question. *I won't.*

"Make love to me," I whisper.

He doesn't falter. He brings his lips down on mine and forces his powerful tongue inside my mouth. I clutch at his collar, drawing him closer as he slides his hands down to my hips, lifting me up. I throw my arms around his neck, returning his kiss. I feel his pulse on my tongue, taste the sweet coppery tang of the blood from his lip. If it's hurting, he doesn't complain. He tilts his head, grazing my lips with his teeth.

I knot my hands in his hair, tugging gently, and he growls into my mouth, hungry and needy. He lowers me onto the rug in the middle of the floor, pinning me against the soft wool. He thrusts his hips against me and uses his eager mouth to engulf mine. I slide my hands down his body, slipping them under his shirt, wanting it gone.

In one swift movement, he breaks the kiss, reaches behind his shoulder and pulls his shirt over his head, revealing his tan, muscular chest, screaming with strength.

Nick snatches at my top, raising my arms and sliding the fabric up over my head with my bra. His eyes glisten, him seeming to revel in the sight of my breasts, and I arch my back so they rise, begging for his mouth. He obliges, wrapping his lips around my nipple, sucking hard as he slides his hand down my thigh, hitching up my skirt and clutching at my panties, tugging hard. I hear the fabric tear and I whimper – he rips them from my body.

Nick moves his mouth slowly, strategically, down the line of my stomach, his tongue licking, his teeth nipping. He spreads my legs, lowering his mouth to the inside of my thigh, circling his swift, skilled tongue, caressing my soft skin, then sliding it deep inside my body.

"Oh, Nick," I moan. His breathing accelerates. He pulls me closer, spreading my legs wider, his tongue licking, plunging, probing so fiercely inside me. I reach down to touch him, but he snatches my wrists, holding them firmly back against the floor. I whimper, twisting them in his hands, and he tightens his grip, digging his fingers into my skin. He drives his ambitious, determined tongue deep, insisting on making me scream. I close my eyes, thrusting my hips against his mouth. He growls with predilection and pleasure, the vibration rippling through me as I climax hard and loud in his mouth.

"Oh, baby," he groans, releasing my wrists, moving his body on top of mine. I trail my hand down his chest, over his rock-hard erection, rubbing him, teasing him, feeling him bursting against his pants. He draws in a raw, savage breath, tugging at his zipper, tearing his pants down with his underwear, unable to bear another second without my touch. I take him in my hand, sliding my fingers down the length of his smooth, velvety shaft. He throws back his head and gasps, closing his eyes as I wrap my fingers around him, gently pulling up and down. I wish I knew what I was doing, but he doesn't correct me and he sure isn't complaining.

His eyes grow deep like the jungle and I tremble with desire. I want him. I need him, more than my next breath.

"Please, Nick," I beg.

He digs his fingers into my thighs and I open my legs to him, feeling him pressing the tip of his thick, threatening shaft firmly against me.

"Is this what you want?" he whispers.

"Yes," I breathe.

"You want me to fuck you?" he rasps, increasing the pressure. "Huh?"

"Yes," I cry, bucking my hips against him.

He groans, forcing himself inside me, then pulls back, driving into me fast and hard, over and over, but it's not enough. I know he has more and I want it. I arch my back, wriggling and writhing beneath him.

He knows what I want and ignores my request, slowing his strokes, thrusting deliberately, methodically, never deviating from his slow, steady torture. He watches me, controlling his breathing, exerting his power over me, enjoying every last moment of my denial. I wrap my legs tightly around him, my body greedy and demanding. Nick weaves his hand into my hair, tilting my head back so he can watch my torment.

"Oh, Scarlet," he breathes, bringing his mouth down on mine, savage and besieging. I close my eyes, losing myself in his sudden wild, animalistic presence, meeting him thrust for thrust, tightening around him as he slides his hand down my thigh, pulling my knee up to his hip. Nick clenches his jaw and plants his feet, plunging deep, deeper than ever before, touching a place inside me he's never been. I cry out, clutching him to me. There's nothing but him and me, lost, deep in the depths of our souls — nothing can touch us here.

In one swift movement, he withdraws and sinks back to his knees, turning me over then pulling me back toward him so that my back is against his chest. He positions himself beneath me, forcing me down onto his hard, waiting cock to thrust up inside me. I gasp, closing my eyes and tilting my head back against him. Nick glides his hands across my skin, cupping my breasts, pinching my nipples with his fingertips as my hips rise and fall with his. The throbbing inside me grows deep and distinct. I tighten around him as he increases his stroke, my body burning from the inside out. I push back against him, my fingers clinging to the ledge, my toes curling, my spine tingling.

As if sensing my impending climax, he thrusts his whole body against me, and I jolt forward without resistance onto my hands and knees, gasping, kneeling in front of him, trembling, my thighs wet, clutching the rug beneath me. I feel him right behind me and I bite down on my bottom lip, knowing there's more, so much more. He sinks his fingers into my hips and dives deep inside me, then pulls me back firmly against him.

"Oh, Nick. Oh God!" I scream, as he rams himself into me over and over. I close my eyes, balancing perilously on the edge of destruction, taking everything he has to offer. My excitement consumes me, my body transcending my mind to places I've never been as I scream his name. Flying, floating freely, then slowly falling, drifting, descending back to Earth.

He groans, slowing his thrusts, giving us a chance to slow our breathing.

"We're not done yet, baby," he threatens. A soft moan escapes my lips, my body weak and tired. I've got nothing left to give, but his stamina is enough for two. He stays inside me, leaning back on his ankles, pulling me up with him, taking my hands in his and raising my arms above my head.

Nick glides his hands down my arms, trailing his fingers over my breasts, slipping between my thighs, rubbing me, teasing me with his thrusts. He sweeps the hair from my neck, replacing it with his mouth, licking and sucking hard. I bend my arms at the elbows behind his head, knotting my fingers in his hair. He reaches up for my hand, bringing it down, placing it where his had been, guiding my fingers, circling and stroking, urging me to explore myself.

He keeps his hand on mine, controlling and insistent. I throw my head back against him, whimpering as he clutches my hand tighter, moving my fingers faster. I can't think, only feel. He pounds into me hard and fast, then lets go of my hand, slamming his hips against mine. I keep my fingers where they are. I'm close, so close.

"Come for me, baby," he whispers, his voice deep and gritty in my ear. I arch my back, rising quickly and falling hard on his shaft, crying out as we come, our bodies bucking against each other in a wild, uncivilized, uncoordinated rhythm.

"Oh, fuck," he moans, his hot, wet cum filling me, warming my body.

He clasps my chin, turning my face to meet his, kissing me urgently, ardently from behind as his body jerks and twitches against mine.

"Oh, that was incredible," I gasp as he withdraws slowly, our bodies falling forward, collapsing onto the floor.

I look across at him, his sweat beading on the rises of his chest, then cascading down into tiny valleys, pooling in the hollows where his skin clings tightly to his muscles.

He turns to me, his eyes ablaze, his hair slicked back with sweat. He curves his lips into a devilish grin and I grin back at him, wicked with desire.

He's mine. All mine, and I am the luckiest girl in the world.

Chapter Six

In Dreams

Finally, it's the weekend and I have Nick all to myself. We don't speak again about what happened with Mitch, but we do promise one another a fresh start. Like newlyweds, we can't keep our hands off each other, occupying every waking and even some sleeping moments getting to know the other inside and out. Gabe and Malaylie couldn't be happier to have the entire weekend off and, without their presence, we manage to conquer almost every room in the house, and it's a very, very big house.

I'm actually thankful when Nick ducks into the office on Sunday afternoon to switch off an alarm. I'm weak and sore and I desperately want more, so I'm glad for the hour off. It *is* a day of rest, after all, no matter how small. I fall asleep on his chest that night and, in the early hours of the morning, he slides between my thighs where he stays even when we're done. We lie there, drifting back to sleep, body to body, heart to heart, soul to soul and though we couldn't be any closer, it's still not close enough.

It's raining, hard. Water pelts against the windscreen in front of me so fiercely I fear it might break. It's dark. So dark, I can't see. I swipe my forearm against the glass in a feeble attempt to clear the fog from the window, but it returns just as quickly. I turn the wipers on faster, but it doesn't help. Tears stream down my face, stinging my skin, rivaling the wrath of the rain. In an instant, the deluge slows almost to a stop, then smacks down harder, lashing at the windscreen, unleashing a relentless, angry onslaught.

Headlights flash in my eyes, shining brightly. I panic, my heart drumming in my ears. I can't breathe. I can't breathe.

I sit up, clutching at my chest, gasping for air. It's daylight. The sun pours in from all directions, blinding me. I squint and throw up my arm to shield my eyes from the sun. I'm in my bedroom, in my bed.

I was dreaming. I look across at Nick, lying beside me, sound asleep on his stomach. His toned, sculptured arm drapes over his pillow, a light growth of bristles shadowing his face, his innocent beauty stealing what air I have left.

I recline against the pillows and pull the covers up under my chin, listening to my breaths whisper shallowly from my lips, my terror still imminent. Nick stirs beside me and I watch his eyelids flicker then open.

"Hey, you." He slides across the bed and puts his arm around me.

"Hi," I reply, snuggling into him.

"Hmmm. This is starting to become a habit. Me in your bed."

"It's your bed, too."

He tightens his arm around me. "I like the sound of that."

"Me, too."

"Come here," he whispers with the devil in his eyes as he pulls me closer. He brushes his lips tenderly across mine, his soft, wispy growth lightly tickling my skin. I feel him pressing against me. He's hard and I'm sore and, honestly, I'm just not in the mood. Thoughts of my dream catch me off-guard and I break away just a little, ending his kiss prematurely. He pulls his head back to look at me but doesn't say anything.

I touch my finger to his cheek. "I like this stubble on your face."

His eyes soften. "Yeah?"

"It tickles a little, but you look so different. It suits you."

He twitches his lips, as though he's pleased. "I'll grow it a little then."

Nick tightens his arm around me and I know he wants to

kiss me, but my head is still embedded firmly in my dream. "I've been meaning to ask you something."

"Sex," he declares.

I sit up, looking down at him. "What?"

"Sex. Sex is the answer to everything." The spirit in his eyes spreading to his lips.

I shake my head. "Not to this."

"You sure?"

"Quite sure, and I think you've had your fill of that, anyway."

"Never!" he replies, pulling me down the bed, tickling me while I scream and laugh, thrashing around beneath him.

"Stop! Stop! I'm gonna pee myself," I shout. I wasn't really, but I had to do something. It doesn't stop him, anyway – he only laughs louder.

I cover my face with my hands, wiping away my tears of laughter. "Oh, my God!" He looks down at me, propping his head on his hand.

"So! What did you want to ask me?"

I roll onto my side to face him, catching my breath. "I'm afraid to ask."

He shakes his head, a serious look taking over his face. "Ask me."

"I was wondering what happened to my car?"

"Well! Funny you should ask. See, one cold wet night, you decided to take it swimming, and cars can't swim."

He squeezes one eye shut as I swing my hand in the air, swatting his shoulder.

"That's a terrible joke."

"It was, wasn't it?" he says, his grin returning.

"Yes!"

He drapes his arm back over me, the sparkle in his eyes slowly losing its luster. "Your car was a total wreck. The insurance company kept it, cut me a check."

"Can I get another one?"

He reaches up, touching his fingers to my forehead, sweeping the hair out of my eyes. "You don't like Gabe driving you around in the estate car?"

"No, it's fine. I'd just like a little independence from time to time."

"Didn't the doctor say you shouldn't drive for twelve months?"

I shrug. "I think that was more of a rough estimate than a rule. It's been six months now without issue, no blackouts or anything."

"Still, you should check with the doctor before you do."

"Well, thanks to you, I have an appointment on Thursday. I'll check with him then, but I'm sure it'll be fine."

He nods, his gaze fixed firmly on me but his mind elsewhere. "Okay. I'll get you one. When the doctor says it's okay. An early Christmas present."

"Really?"

"Of course," he says pointedly. "Any requests?"

I pause. I haven't got that far yet. "You know, I think I'd really like to choose my own if that's okay."

"Are you sure? I have a couple of high-end clients with dealerships. I can have them bring some cars here to you, if you like? Something fast and sexy," he says, his eyes lighting up.

"No, I think I'll ask Tayla to take me. We'll make a day of it. It'll be fun."

"Okay. Sure," he says casually, but his eyes don't match his face. He rolls over, hops out of bed and pulls up his underwear. "I'm gonna grab a drink. Would you like one?"

"No, thanks."

"What about some breakfast? You must be hungry?"

"Yeah, I am a little."

He walks around to my side of the bed and kneels over me, kissing my forehead.

"I'm on it. I'll see you in a bit."

I watch him leave. I can tell he's not pleased by my request, but being driven everywhere is starting to feel as if someone's keeping tabs on me. Besides, if I'm going to find myself again, I need to get lost from time to time.

I settle back into the pillows, glancing around the room, my mind sifting through the remnants of my dream. Everything is so shrouded in darkness. I wish I knew how to bring everything out into the light, to lay it all out straight and begin to sort through it, but it's not like that. Everything is fragmented, splintered and shattered. A puzzle without purpose.

The images in my mind lead to Mitch. The picture from his phone, of him and me together, are permanently imprinted in my brain. I've been in denial as far as he and I are concerned, and that's fine, I guess, on the surface. I don't remember it, I can deny it all I want, but that isn't going to stop the nagging questions in my head, building up to the point that I almost feel suffocated by them.

A sudden pang of fear hits hard. Fear of the unknown, fear of what I'm thinking of doing. I have to see Mitch. I need to talk to him. To know what he knows. He said there was a second car behind me that night. He said I was afraid of Nick, that I'd left him. I know now that I did leave him, and though I've heard his explanation as to why, I have to know for sure. I swallow hard and sit up, suddenly acutely aware of my immediate future.

* * * *

The traffic is heavy this morning, backed up in two stagnant lanes that snake for miles in front of us. Its increasing numbers of mergers and acquisitions make it appear more like a parking lot than a motorway. Gabe looks back at me in the rear-vision mirror, equally as unimpressed.

"Is there some way around this, Gabe?" I ask. I'm anxious enough about my first visit to the office without the added stress.

"I wish there was, Mrs. Pierce. We're stuck here, I'm afraid. We're just going to have to grin and bear it."

After a few minutes, the traffic starts to move ahead.

"Finally," Gabe mutters, clapping his hands.

I glance up at him, straightening in my seat, suddenly more nervous than I was before. For a while, it's smooth sailing, but once we exit the motorway and head into the city, things only get worse. After a seemingly never-ending series of stop-starts we snail-pace into the city center, arriving at the office much later than I had anticipated. Gabe pulls up at the entrance and I glance up at the strikingly modern, yet somehow futuristic-looking façade, at least ten stories high. The words *Modus Vivendi* seem to float weightlessly above the entry. I love it. I love the building, I love the name, Latin for 'a way of life'. My concoction, evidently. The place where elite clients' lifestyles are transformed into easy street, letting us organize everything and anything from laundering their clothes to arranging their red-carpet events.

Nick drove me past here a couple of times and pointed it out, but I don't remember the building ever being this intimidating. Maybe it's just my small mood.

Gabe rushes to my door and I step out—trembling like a child on her first day at grade school, I suspect. I feel nauseated. I got up early this morning to watch Nick do laps and joined him for an early breakfast. Now, I'm suddenly wishing I hadn't.

"This entire building is mine?" I ask doubtfully.

"Well, it's your father's building," Gabe replies, closing the car door behind me. "But to all intents and purposes, it's yours. When he retired from practicing law, he passed the building on to you. His staff are now your legal team—they're on the first two floors and your office is way up there. Top floor."

I follow his pointing finger to the top of the building, my eyes widening. "Huh, I must remember to thank him."

His eyes wrinkle at the corners. "Should I come back later, Mrs. Pierce, or would you like me to wait?"

"Well, I'm just going up to say hello, really. Maybe just give me an hour or so?" I reply, clutching my purse tightly.

He glances down at my hands briefly. "Are you sure

you're okay to do this on your own, Mrs. Pierce? Maybe Mr. Pierce could come with you—"

"No," I interrupt. "I'd like to do this on my own."

He bows his head. "Of course."

"I'll see you in an hour, then?"

"Yes, ma'am."

I turn, stepping up onto the sidewalk and through the big glass entry doors. People line the foyer, busily going about their business. *My business.* It's hard to believe.

I stand there, astounded, casting my gaze upward to the extravagant chandelier hanging over the ridiculously loud water fountain beneath. It's not my taste at all. Perhaps this is how my father left it? I certainly hope I didn't do this. I find myself frowning, disappointed by the outlandish outpour of money spent in here. It's surely enough to save all those starving children I see on TV.

"Wow. Someone had their head fair up their own ass," I mutter to myself.

"Mrs. Pierce."

I hear a female's voice behind me and turn to find a young, vivacious dark-haired woman.

Oh, God, I hope she didn't hear me.

She stares at me, wide-eyed, her big dark eyes accentuated by her lashings of black mascara and pouty, crimson-red lips.

"Oh, my God! You're really here. How lovely to see you."

I force a tight-lipped smile, though I have no idea who she is, which she quickly realizes. She holds out a pale white hand with long black manicured nails to shake mine.

"I'm Larissa. I'm head of HR. I take care of all your hiring and firing here, and, boy, let me tell you, there's been plenty of that since you've been gone, but I don't want you to worry about that."

She takes my hand and leads me through the foyer to the elevator, swaying her mesmerizing hips to and fro in her high-waisted 1950s-style dress and platform shoes.

"I wish I'd known you were coming. I'd have had

something organized. You'll have to forgive me. You know there's this peachy new little bakery that's opened up just down the street, everyone goes there, well, they have these tiny little—"

"Welcome back, Mrs. Pierce," a man's voice interrupts from behind me.

I manage to turn and give a slight wave before Larissa takes my arm, dragging me forward.

"Oh, listen to me, rambling on," she continues. The elevator doors open and she ushers me inside, squeezing into the already overcrowded space before pressing the tenth-floor button. I'm grateful for the distraction, for anything that stops her mouth moving for just a second. If I wasn't stressed before, I am now.

"So how are you feeling?" she asks, studying my face.

Freaked out.

I feign a smile. "I'm fine. Thank you for asking."

"That's so good to hear. I keep asking after you and I wanted to call you after the accident, but Mr. Pierce felt it would be best for you to come to terms with the office in your own time."

"He means well," I reply, staring at the elevator doors, wishing they'd open.

Larissa nods hesitantly. "Okay. So. I'll take you up to see Marcy. Marcy is the new you. She's been absolutely wonderful at it, too." She pauses then rolls her eyes. "Well, not as wonderful as you, of course, but she's doing a great job all the same. Everyone likes her. The clients love her. She's added twenty-three new clients to our dossier in the past six months alone, far exceeding our target figures."

I watch her, her hands flapping faster than a falcon in flight, her lips motoring more rapidly than the speedway. The elevator doors open and she rushes out, practically pulling me along behind her like a toddler.

She leads me through a vast, open office space filled with ridiculously overdressed people talking to one another and on telephones while tapping away on computers with that sharp, useless kind of look about them. Curious, unfamiliar faces stop what they're doing as we pass, their jaws dropping, bowing their heads to me as though I'm royalty. Finally, we reach the farthest corner of the office, stopping in front of a tremendously cumbersome but exquisite hand-carved timber door. The plaque on the door reads *Scarlet Pierce – Director.*

Larissa opens the door, leading me into an impressive brilliant-white office with a burnt-orange feature wall. Everything looks so clean and shiny. I'm immediately drawn to the desk and to the fifty-something blonde-haired woman sitting behind it, her glasses tipped to the end of her nose. She looks up at us and blinks, her hardened, expressionless face suddenly bright and exhilarated.

"Sorry for barging in like this," Larissa gushes. "But I have someone here who needs no introduction."

The woman jumps to her feet. "Holy shit! Scarlet!" She throws her glasses down on the desk and runs to me, hugging me tightly and I hug her back.

"You must be Marcy."

"Yes, I'm Marcy!" She pulls her head back to look at me, clutching my upper arms. She's stronger than she looks. "It's so good to see you. Why didn't you call and tell us you were coming? I'd have had a big welcome party planned."

"That's what I was afraid of."

She squints, wriggling her nose.

"Come, sit down." She ushers me over to a lounge area in the corner of the office, overlooking the city. I glance up at the big glass panels behind her, spanning the entire length of the wall from floor to ceiling. The view is nothing less than impressive, if one's not afraid of heights like I am. I draw in a deep breath to settle my nerves, the overpowering smell of Marcy's perfume filling my nostrils.

I can see it's going to take some time to de-Marcy in here before I come back. I peer around the office, dazed, unable to comprehend that any of this is mine. Nothing in the room looks like anything I'd choose willingly, let alone surround myself with. It's really quite clinical, not at all like our home, with its warm stony-beige and dark gray. I sit down, both Larissa and Marcy sitting opposite me, staring, and I have no idea what to say.

"It's hard to believe this is my office," is the best I can do.

Marcy frowns. "So. Nothing's familiar here then?"

I shake my head, absentmindedly. "No."

They both glance around the room but not directly at each other. They're worried.

"What about in general? Has anything at all come back?" Marcy asks.

I pause. "Uh, there has been some progress, but it's early days yet. The doctors are optimistic. So, how are things here?" I ask, changing the subject.

Marcy nods, deep in thought. "Really good. Yeah. We've had about a couple dozen new clients come on board, so, needless to say, it's been quite hectic. Larissa has had to hire a couple new people. We ran all that past Nick, though, and he helped sort out salaries and such. We've had a couple of bumps in the road. We had some clients leave, insistent on dealing with only you, but that can't be helped. And when you return, I'm sure they will, too."

I wince.

She waves her hand at me. "No, no. Truly. It's fine. They understand you can't be here."

Larissa nudges Marcy. "The security portfolio," she murmurs.

Marcy's eyes spring to life. "Oh, yes, the security portfolio."

My brow creases. I have no idea what she's talking about.

"We have a group of fat cats, politicians, high-profile celebrities and the like who require personal bodyguards and security when they attend functions, speeches, events, stuff like that. We call it our security portfolio. Anyhow, our security liaison, you won't remember him, Mitchell Morgan…"

She pauses, seeing if I recognize the name. I do my best

not to react, though my heart starts banging away like a bass drum. Marcy continues to ramble, not missing a beat. I keep my eyes on her, trying to control my breathing.

"Well," she continues. "He resigned as security liaison right after your accident and we still haven't found a suitable replacement. Rostering security has been a bit of a nightmare, and then there's those particular clients who won't divulge their calendars to just anyone and, seeing as you and Mitch were the only ones who knew anything about it, there's not a lot I can do there. I haven't had a chance to discuss it with Nick yet. He's always so busy. He really only signs the paychecks these days and leaves the business side of things to me."

I part my lips. "Uh, no need to discuss it with Nick. I think I may be able to help you with that. Just give me a few days."

"Oh, well, that'd be great," she replies cheerfully, though I'm sure she's wondering how.

"It's a big market, Mrs. Pierce. We really do need to sort it out as soon as possible," Larissa adds.

I nod, pretending I'm listening, but truth is, everything that's been said since Marcy uttered Mitch's name is vague at best.

"It would be great if we could get Mitchell back on board. He knows the clients and they trust him."

I dip my head, still getting over the first time she spoke his name, let alone dealing with a second. I just can't escape him. The walls begin to close in on me. I look down at my watch, then pick up my purse. Gabe will be here soon.

Marcy rises swiftly from her seat. "Oh, look at us, bombarding you with our problems on your first visit. I hope it wasn't too much for you."

"No, it's fine," I reply, fighting the sudden urge to mess my hair and run screaming all the way down the hall. "My driver is coming to pick me up shortly. I'd better go. It was just a short visit."

Marcy pulls me into a hug. "It's so good to see you, honey.

Thank you so much for coming to see us."

"I'm glad I came, and thank you for telling me about the security issue. I'll see what I can do."

She nods. "I would have called, you know, to check on you, see how you are, but I don't have your number."

I stop dead in my tracks, confused and somehow alarmed.

"I tried to call your cell phone a couple times after the accident, but your number's disconnected and your home number's not on file. I asked Nick about it and he said your phone was destroyed in the crash, but when I asked him for a number to call you on, he completely evaded the question. I figured he didn't want us to bother you. I knew you'd come in when you're ready and look, here you are."

"Well. I can fix that!" I reply defiantly, striding across to the desk. I scribble out my cell number on a scrap of paper, squaring my shoulders before handing it to Marcy. "There! Now you can call me whenever you want to."

She glances down at the number briefly. "Okay, great, and don't worry too much about things here. We're anxious to have you back, Scarlet, but on *your* terms. There's no rush. I can handle things here until you're ready."

"I know you can, and I'm eternally grateful. I'll stop by when I can."

"We'll look forward to it," Marcy replies.

I look over her shoulder at Larissa, smiling warmly at me. Everything is in good hands here. One less worry on my mind.

I leave the office as quickly as I can, rushing downstairs in a panic to find Gabe waiting for me at the door. He straightens his back as I approach him, scanning the foyer behind me as though looking for whoever's chasing me. I slow down, reminding myself to breathe. I hate to say it, but Nick was right. I'm nowhere near ready to take on the office yet. I told Marcy I'd come in when I can, but I'm honestly in no hurry to subject myself to these uptight, anxious feelings anytime soon. Gabe opens the door for me, then slides behind the wheel, looking back at me in the rear-vision mirror.

"Where to, Mrs. Pierce?"

I stare out of the window at the street, deep in thought. "Uh, do you know the boatyard, down by the Coomera River?" I ask timidly.

Gabe looks back me, his expression guarded. "You mean the old Morgan shipyard?"

I nod.

"Uh, yes, ma'am. I know the place," he replies, his voice altered.

"Can you take me there, please?"

He gives me a look that worries me. "As you wish," he answers, his tone concerning me even more. He's accelerating out of the car park toward the motorway when my cell phone rings. It's my mother. I tuck the phone back in my purse. *There's no way that's happening.*

My mother is a wonderful person, but somehow, and without trying, seems to have an uncanny way of sending my blood pressure through the roof. She worries about me, I know, but I have to be in the right mindset to speak to her and now is not one of those times.

The drive is long, around fifteen minutes or more, to the outer city limits. We turn off the motorway onto a long, straight road. I can almost see the river at the end. My nerves ignite. My hands trembling, my palms sweating, I grip the door handle so tightly my fingertips are turning purple.

Gabe glances back at me in the mirror, looking as nervous as I feel. Dread stirs the cauldron in the pit of my stomach.

What if he tells Nick, what am I going to say?

I look up at the end of the road just ahead. *Too late now.*

As we reach the river, Gabe slows, creeping along the waterfront until coming to a stop outside a large fenced lot. An old timber-and-red brick building sits proud at the front. It's a big parcel of land, maybe a couple of acres, that stretches along the entire length of the river access. A big sign outside reads *River Precinct*. I scan up and down the street. It's quite deserted for a weekday. Monstrous steel sheds line the surrounding blocks and though there are cars all around, it really doesn't seem as if there's a lot going on.

"Here we are," Gabe says quietly.

He drives inside the gates. Mitch's big black Chevy is parked out front. *He's here.* I swallow hard. I feel wretched, guilty even, just being here. Gabe parks next to Mitch's truck and shuts off the engine. I glance around the yard. It looks more like a boat cemetery than a boatyard. Crustacean-covered boats sitting upright on blocks, others overturned on their bellies or on trailers. I stare up at the entrance of the building, my hands shaking.

"Are you okay, Mrs. Pierce?" Gabe asks.

"Uh, yeah. I'm fine. I'll be just a minute." I snatch at the door handle and walk slowly across the lot, looking up at the monstrous time-worn building, the big sign above its door reading *Morgans' Shipyard*. As I grow closer, I see the building is even older than I thought. The façade has clearly been upgraded, but it doesn't detract from the building's heritage. I walk up to the front entrance. The door's locked. I scan the yard, unsure what to do, when I notice the side gate's wide open.

I peer across at Gabe, wondering if I should leave, but the gate gets the better of me.

I gravitate toward it, walking slowly down the side of the building and around to the backyard. There's not a soul in sight. It feels deserted, like one of those places viewers beg the poor, clueless girl in a horror film not to go. I weave my way through the stacks of aged timber piled neatly on shelves at the rear of the building and hear the faint hint of music in the air. I stop, listening, my eyes searching.

"Can I help you, miss?" a man's voice asks from behind me. I trot on the spot, startled, then spin around to find a man standing there. Without a knife, thank God. He's about my age, tall and gangly with long light-brown hair and dark-brown eyes. He reminds me of Mitch. I clutch at my chest.

"Scarlet?" His welcoming smile is blinding. "I'm sorry, I didn't mean to scare you." He rushes toward me as though coming in for a hug, then stops.

"I... I'm sorry. I don't—"

"Oh!" he interrupts. "Wow, you really don't remember. I'm Matt. Mitch's little brother."

"Oh. Well, I can see the resemblance."

"That's what they say," he replies, straightening his stance.

I nod, glancing around nervously. "So you build boats, too?"

"Uh, no, not really. Mitch teaches me stuff from time to time, but boats are his thing. I play lead guitar in the house band down at the Gatzby in the city. You know it?"

"Um, no, I don't think I do."

"Yeah, well, it's only open at night. It's a pretty high-end club. It's not really my scene, but it pays well. Mitch got me the gig, actually. A friend of his owns the place."

"Oh, well, that's great. Gotta do what you love."

"Yeah, you should swing by sometime. It's on Third and Main. Mitch plays with me there sometimes, just for fun and just for a song or two. I don't let him play more than that. He shows me up too much." His fondness for his brother sparkles in his eyes.

I tilt my head to the side, fascinated by him. He really is just a younger version of Mitch without Mitch's characteristics. He's shy and nervous, not what I'd expect from a lead guitarist in a band.

"I didn't know Mitch played the guitar."

He lets out a sharp rattle of laughter.

"What?" I ask.

He presses his closed fist to his mouth to quash his outburst. "I'm sorry, it's just strange hearing you say that. Music is Mitch's life. Apart from you, of course. He used to play to you all the time. We had a bonfire here one night and you sang with him. You've got a great voice."

I shake my head, incredulous.

"You do. You sang this awesome rendition of *Day After Day* by Badfinger together. Mitch plays it every day, ten times a day, since you've been gone."

He drops his gaze briefly, shifting on his feet, as though he's said too much.

"He's over there in the workshop, if you wanna go in. He'll be real glad to see you." He points toward an open roller door at the back of the building.

"Uh, okay. Thank you."

He slides his hands into his pockets like a nervous ten-year-old boy, flashing me a warm, honest smile. "It's good to see you again, Scarlet."

I dip my head graciously and turn toward the building.

"Oh, and Scarlet—"

I spin back around to face him.

"Go easy on him. He's not the big, tough cop he makes out."

I flash him a tight-lipped smile, then turn and head toward the roller door, with concrete boots on.

As soon as I set foot inside the workshop, I see him leaning over an upturned boat, sanding the hull, his hair tinted lighter with sawdust. His strong, toned chest is bare, glistening with sweat. My gaze lingers there, watching the sweat bead down the hollow between his defined pecs, following the light trail of hair down the line of his stomach to the top of his worn-out jeans that hang loosely around his hips.

I swallow hard, staying completely still, studying him, searching for something familiar. His eyes are narrowed, focusing on his work. He doesn't see me. His hands are on sandpaper, sliding back and forth in long, smooth strokes along the surface of the sculptured timber hull. He bends down, aligning his eyes with the lines of the timber, gliding his fingertips back and forth over his work, feeling for imperfections.

I glance around the workshop. Old, battered red bricks line the walls, meeting with the rusty tin of the once-strong roof and aged timber rafters hanging overhead as sawdust blows freely on the floor, dancing in the breeze, like an old Western movie set. Old-fashioned music emits from the far corner of the workshop, the sound quality poor and crackly, and though the song is very old, it sounds vaguely familiar. A lady's voice, as exquisite as a songbird, singing about living in a daydream. It's beautiful, almost hauntingly so, and absolutely not what I expected him to be listening to.

I take a step toward him and he stops sanding, looking up at me. I don't move, unsure how he'll react to my being there.

"Scarlet?"

I wince. "I didn't know if I should come."

He tosses the sandpaper down on the hull, dusting his hands as he walks toward me. "This is a surprise. I thought you were angry with me."

I nod, his sublime bare chest temporarily stealing my ability to form words.

He stops right in front of me. "Is everything okay?"

"Uh, yeah. I just—"

"I'm glad you came," he interrupts, twitching his lips at the corners.

"Uh, I just met your brother out back," I stammer, rather inarticulately.

"Oh, yeah?"

"He seems nice."

"Yeah, Matty's great. He comes here a couple days a week to hang out and helps out a bit. He's the only family I have now. He means the world to me."

"He's your younger brother?"

"Yeah, he's, uh, your age, twenty-nine in September."

I hear a yelp and look behind Mitch. A blue-gray and tan-colored dog limps toward us.

"And who is this?" I ask, bending down and holding out my arms.

"His name is Blue. He's a Blue Heeler," he says, crouching and rubbing him roughly. "He's my protector, aren't ya, boy?" Blue falls down on the concrete and I kneel, rubbing his belly. "Not that he does much protecting these days. He's almost fourteen now. He's settling into retirement, aren't ya, fella?"

I watch them, their bond radiating far beyond them. "He's beautiful."

Mitch looks up at me. "*You're* beautiful."

I stand abruptly, brushing my hands together. He rises to his feet and I turn, motioning toward the boat he was working on.

"I was watching you. You really love this, don't you?"

"It's in my blood."

"It looks like a lot of work. It must take a long time to make one of these."

"Yeah, well, I try not to keep track of time when I'm building these. Time can be a bit of a wrecking ball."

"I bet."

He walks across to his workbench, reaching for his shirt. I watch him, allowing my gaze to stray down his strong, defined back. He throws his shirt on over his head and wanders slowly toward me, stopping just inches in front of me, reaching his hand out to mine. I pull away, looking up at him, alarmed.

"Humor me," he says, without an ounce of it. He reaches for my hand again, taking it loosely in his.

"What are you doing?" I ask.

"Teaching you to feel." He closes his fingers around my hand and I don't pull away. I feel the heat of his skin warming mine, his thumb lightly stroking the back of my hand, as though soothing me. I swallow hard, looking down at our hands, conscience-stricken.

"Close your eyes," he murmurs. "Trust me."

I draw in a deep breath, slowly narrowing my eyes when he guides my hand across to the hull of the boat beside us, gliding it across the smooth, soft timber. It feels nothing like I expected. It's almost like velvet. I bite my bottom lip, savoring the sensation when I feel his chest brush against my back. My whole body tenses. I stop breathing, attuning to his proximity. His hand moves on mine, sliding across my skin, diverting my focus. I can smell his scent, feel his breath in my hair. He's so close.

"It doesn't feel like timber, does it?" he says, innocently enough, but it sends a shiver rocketing down my spine. My eyes spring open, my breathing quick and shallow. I step forward, not daring to look at him.

"No, it doesn't. It's so soft." The music stops playing in the background and I turn back to look at him. He's right behind me, his face just inches from mine. I look stare up into his penetrating brown eyes, losing ground when his cell phone rings in his pocket, startling us both. He takes out his phone, staring down at the screen as though debating whether or not to answer it, then looks up at me.

"Could you excuse me for a sec? I've just gotta take this quick."

"Uh-huh."

He turns, marching away.

"Morgan," he says sternly. "What's with the private number?" he asks, glancing across at me briefly. "No, it's not a good time. I can't talk right now." He exhales loudly. "Because I can't. I have to go," he snaps. He shakes his head then hangs up, turning back to me. "Uh, could you give me a second? I just have to duck out front for a minute."

"Um, yeah. Sure."

He hurries through the workshop to a side door and strides hastily outside. I drift slowly toward the window at the front of the workshop, my curiosity getting the better of me, watching him sprint across the carpark toward a tall brunette woman in a police uniform.

She's around my age, her long hair pulled back in a ponytail, her uniform clinging to her body, accentuating her athletic build. They speak briefly before the woman throws her arms up in the air, shouting and pointing in my direction. My breath hitches in my throat. She dodges him, heading toward the office, but he grabs her forearm, turning her back to face him. She shouts at him, ripping her arm from his clutches before shoving him backward. He shouts back at her and she pushes him again. He holds his hands up in surrender, as though talking her down, then finally takes her by the arm, ushering her back to a big blue Statesman parked beside his Chevy, folding his arms across his chest to watch her drive away.

I draw in a ragged breath, relieved that she's gone. Mitch turns around suddenly, looking straight up at the window where I'm standing. I turn swiftly and hurry back over to the boat, spinning around to face the doorway as he charges through it.

"Sorry about that," he murmurs, running his hand through his hair.

"That's okay. Is everything all right?"

"Uh, yeah. Just a friend going through a rough time." He stops in front of me, his demeanor completely different from before his visitor arrived. "So, was there something you wanted to ask me?"

"Yes. I came to talk to you about business, actually."

"Business?"

"I just came from my office—"

He leans against a timber crate behind him, folding his arms across his chest.

"Why didn't you tell me you used to work for me?"

He considers me carefully. "Would it have made a difference?"

I shrug. "Probably not. It's just another thing in a string of things you didn't tell me."

He screws up his face. "What *string*? You didn't want to hear anything I had to say, Scarlet. None of it matters anymore, anyway."

I pause. "I need you to come back to work. *Marcy* needs you to come back to work. To get the security portfolio up and running, or at least hand it over to someone who can. The clients won't disclose their schedules to just anyone. They need a head of security. Someone they can trust."

Mitch looks up at me, his eyes suddenly darker. "So that's why you're here? Your security portfolio?"

I swallow hard, standing my ground. "Yes."

"Does Nick know you're here?"

I don't answer.

"I thought not."

He unfolds his arms, turning away, and I notice two skin-colored stitches between his hairline and the side of his eye. I gasp.

"What happened to your face?"

"Let me guess—he didn't tell you," he replies with weary resignation.

"Tell me what?"

"Nick. He came here yesterday, warning me to stay away from you."

"*What?*"

"He wanted to know about us. Before the accident. So, I told him."

I shake my head. "Nick was with me all day yesterday."

"Not at three o'clock he wasn't. He was here."

My brow furrows as I remember the alarm at Nick's office. I steady myself against the sawhorse behind me.

"What did you tell him?"

"He already knew. He just wanted to hear me say it out loud. He was suspicious that you were leaving him for someone else. He just didn't know who it was. I reminded him that you chose me. That you left him for me once, and I'm not going away. He didn't like that very much."

"I'm so sorry. Are you okay?" I reach out to touch his face and he jerks his head back.

"I can take care of myself," he snaps.

I step back from him, my hand recoiling to my chest.

His dog, Blue, wanders over to us, throwing himself at Mitch's feet, and he crouches down to pat him.

"He never said anything," I murmur. "I had no idea he was here. There were no marks on him."

"Because I didn't hit him back."

"Why?"

His eyes ignite. "I should have! I should have arrested him there and then, locked him in a fucking jail cell like he deserves."

My whole body tenses at his harsh, abrasive tone and for the first time I can see the cop in him. "Why didn't you?"

He stands up, brushing his hands against his jeans. "Because you wouldn't want me to." He walks toward me. "Why are you really here?"

"I told you."

"You forget, I know you, Scarlet. I know why you're here. I can see it in your eyes."

He inches toward me and I step back, trapped between him and the boat behind me. He rests his hands on the hull on either side of me, locking me in place.

"I have to go." I push on his arm but he reaches up, taking my face in his hands. He looks down at me, making sure that I'm looking back at him.

"Do you know how beautiful you are?" he breathes. "You're so beautiful that I wish I'd never seen you, so that I'd never feel this pain or know the love I've lost."

His eyes harden with a fierce, uncompromising sorrow, tearing at my heart, gnawing at my soul. My eyes fill with tears. I shove him, breaking free, rushing out toward the yard.

"You can't run away from this, Scarlet," he yells.

But I *do* run, not stopping until I reach the car, snatching at the door handle and tumbling inside. Gabe looks back at me, alarmed.

"Is everything okay, Mrs. Pierce?"

Tears stream down my face and I can't stop them. "Yes, Gabe. Take me home."

He starts the engine immediately and accelerates out of the lot. I rest my head against the seat, curling toward the window, letting myself cry. I can't believe the way Mitch affects me, the way my body reacts to his touch, the way his eyes search mine, not to find a trace of himself, but because he knows he's already a part of me. I swipe at my tears, useless, relentless tears that solve nothing. One thing is for certain now. Nick knows everything. That I was cheating on him, that I was leaving him for Mitch and that Mitch won't give up. He knew yesterday. He knew last night. He knew this morning, but he hasn't uttered a word. I can't imagine what he must be feeling, or what would drive me to do such a thing. I close my eyes, images of Nick and Mitch fighting flashing though my mind. I can't believe Nick didn't tell me.

He has to be crazy, beating up a cop. This has gotten completely out of hand.

I spend the entire trip home debating whether I should tell Nick that I know he's been to see Mitch, or even that *I've* been to see Mitch, though I'm almost certain he'll find out either way. My head is spinning, a relentless, throbbing pain manifesting in my temples. I reach into my purse for my painkillers, eagerly swallowing them down as we pull into the driveway. I glance down at my watch. It's almost two-thirty. Nick won't be home for a couple of hours. Plenty of time to work out what I'm going to do.

I wander through the house and up to the bedroom. It's darker than usual today. I open the balcony doors and step out onto the terrace, the cool westerly breeze chilling my skin. I wrap my arms around myself, breathing in the crisp afternoon air, watching the soft-winged butterflies and vibrantly colored finches flittering across the green meadows like skimming stones across a lake. The sky is ghostly today, a vastness of gloom, the sinking sun hidden behind a dense canopy of countless, forbidding clouds, darkening my already bleak mood.

I close my eyes and see Mitch's face, so close to mine, his dark eyes fierce and consuming. My heart flutters, and that, I don't understand. I open my eyes, listening to my breath echoing in my ear, cupping my mouth in my hand. It's Nick I want to see when I close my eyes. I love Nick. I have to put Mitch out of my mind, no matter what happened in the past, or what choices I made. I need to, but more than that, I want to focus all my attention on the man who I married, the same man who's lied to me, numerous times now. I shake my head, disheartened, then turn and walk inside, lying down on the bed, tired and weary.

Everything is black. I can't see anything. I hear Nick's voice in my ear. "No peeking." I giggle, catching a glimpse of light through his fingers, his hands over my eyes. He's leading me somewhere.

"Are you ready?" he queries.

"Yes!"

He takes his hands from my eyes. "Ta-da!"

I stand there, looking up at the spectacular white two-story mansion in front of me, its lush green landscape with aggregate paths leading to double wooden doors with glass panes that reflect and shine like crystals in the bright, incandescent sunlight. The rolling hills beyond reach up to the heavens like patchworks of green, with grazing horses and prospering trees of farmers' dreams.

I turn to Nick. "Is this…"

"It's all ours, baby!"

"What?"

"Ten a.m. this morning, it's officially ours."

"Oh, my God, Nick!" I jump into his arms, never happier.

I hear my cell phone ringing, the ringtone growing louder and louder. I sit up and look around. I'm in my room, on my bed. I must have fallen asleep. I throw myself across to the nightstand and pick it up. It's Nick.

"Hello."

"Hi, baby."

"Hi," I reply, yawning.

"I called the house earlier. Malaylie said you were asleep."

I rub my eyes, sleepily. "Yeah, I must've drifted off. I dreamed of you."

"What?"

"I dreamed of the first time I saw this house and you told me it was officially ours. I saw you."

"Really? I can't believe it. That's great!"

"It is, isn't it?" I reply, still trying to wake up.

"That's your first memory of me?"

"Mmm. I've heard your voice before, but never seen your face."

"Oh, my God! I'm so happy. That's made my day."

"Mine, too," I reply.

"I'm on my way home. We have dinner with your parents tonight, remember, so get dressed."

"That's right. I'm on it."

"See you soon, baby."

"Okay, bye."

He hangs up and I rush into the dressing room to change, suddenly wide awake and excited. Dinner with my family never fails to entertain. My pressing worries about confronting Nick are the furthest thing from my mind.

Chapter Seven

A Long Story

As we reach the front door of my parents' house, I'm instantly filled with nerves. I glance up at the grand two-story brick façade with its white timber, for-show shutters and oversize Roman-style columns. There's nothing familiar about the outside, nor the people who live inside it. To know that I grew up here in this house that holds so many fond memories for my family, but not me, fills me with a complicated mixture of salvation and grief. Nick presses the doorbell, squeezing my hand, grinning away my nerves.

"You look beautiful."

It's *him* who looks amazing in his tailored blue jeans and long-sleeved black knitted shirt I bought for him. It's a size too small and clings to his body in all the right places, making his shoulders look big and his arms even bigger. The top three buttons are undone, the sleeves pulled up to his elbows, revealing the veins on his tan, taut forearms. It's completely unintentional on his part, but the whole ensemble, coupled with his genetically engineered perfection, could only be defined as a symphony of greatness. I flash him a tepid smile, then run my eyes over my low-cut silver-blue silk dress, making sure everything is where it should be. My mother answers the door almost immediately, her shoulder-length gray hair styled faultlessly as usual, her lips, plump and red, matching the color of her dress and complementing her long flyaway scarf that slowly cascades down around her bodice. She's completely overdressed for a night with the family, but that's my mother.

"Honey, it's the lovebirds," she shouts, beaming at us as we step inside.

"Hi, Mom."

"Hi, Mom," Nick choruses.

I glance across at him. I haven't heard him call my mother Mom before, but there's something oddly familiar about it. My father rushes out to the foyer to greet us, snatching me up in a loving embrace that satisfies me like no other.

"Hi, Daddy."

"Hello, darling," he replies, the wrinkled lines on his forehead receding into his gray hair as his face comes to life. My father was a highly respected barrister in his time, apparently the big man on campus around here, but since his retirement and ongoing health problems, he's much quieter and far less scary than he used to be, according to Nick. Strange, as all I've witnessed is my mother running the circus and my father tending to the sideshow. They're adorable, all the same.

I hear my brother's voice in the background and my mother spins around to us.

"Oh, yes, your brother and his new partner, Nigel, are here, joining us for dinner and I have another surprise for you." She winks at Nick.

"Great," he says, rubbing his hands together. "I just *love* surprises."

"Nick," my brother shouts, rushing toward him before shaking his hand. "Beautiful sister, you look darling," Ari shrieks, scooping me up in a mammoth bear hug. The joy in my heart spreads to my lips as he lowers me down to the ground, turning quickly toward a tall man with glasses standing behind him. Ari waves him madly toward us. He's slightly older and taller than Ari, his light-colored hair a direct contrast to Ari's.

"This is Nigel, my partner," he gushes. "This is my sister, Scarlet, and her husband, Nick."

Nigel draws his lips back to let out a high-pitched squeal

and charges toward us. Nick jumps back, startled, Nigel's reaction obviously surpassing his expectations. Nigel bundles me up in his arms like a long-lost friend, then deliberately steps back to shake Nick's hand.

Ari snatches my forearm, tugging me toward the lounge, raving about Nigel and pouring us glasses of champagne while Nick follows closely behind, talking to my father and Nigel about football.

"State of Origin Wednesday, huh? Any tips, Nick?" my father asks.

Nick shrugs. "I'd like to say New South Wales, but I think Queensland's got a pretty good lineup this year."

"Every year!" Nigel interrupts.

My father turns to Nigel. "You follow NRL, Nigel?"

"Oh, yes, sir! I'm an avid Broncos fan."

My father raises an eyebrow, patting Nick's shoulder.

"Nick here was a professional football player in his day."

"In his day?" Nigel squawks. "He still looks as if he's in his *day* to me! Well, I should have known. Look at you, so strong and magnificent."

Nick hangs his head briefly before flashing me a mischievous grin.

"Ari, darling," Nigel calls, "you didn't tell me you had a celebrity in the family."

"Yes, well, you keep your hands to yourself now, my love, won't you?" Ari replies.

Nigel swipes at Nick's shoulder, letting out a ridiculously loud laugh. "Oh, isn't he gorgeous? He gets so jealous."

Nick looks at me, screaming silently for help, before quickly turning his attention back to Nigel.

"Now, where were we?" Nigel asks, stroking his chin. "Oh yes! Football. Whoever did you play for?"

"Uh, the South Sydney Rabbitohs for a bit."

"Ah, a New South Welshman!" Nigel says with a refined inflection. "Oooh. Isn't that that actor's team, what's his name now, that big strapping sexy hunk of a man with the deep manly voice. Russell…"

"Russell Crowe," Nick replies.

"That's it, yes! Russell Crowe, oh, don't tell me you know him, that's just too much!" Nigel exclaims, waving his hand in the air.

"Yes. I know him."

"Oh! Strike a light, what's he like? Is he as rugged and manly as he seems on the screen?"

Nick screws up his face. "I can't really say. Rugged men aren't really my thing."

"Oh, they're *my* thing, let me tell you," Nigel gasps.

Nick glances down at me, completely out of his depth, not knowing what to say, while my father chokes on his champagne and my mother's eyes bulge. *Poor souls, I can see Nigel's flamboyant personality is going to take them some getting used to.*

"Did you make it to Origin?" Nigel asks.

"Uh, no, I was in contention, but I suffered a knee injury that year. I had surgery and a lot of physio, played one game afterward, but it was way too damaged to run on. I never really played after that," he says, his brilliant blue eyes slowly fading.

His whole energy seems to change, like a battery running low, and I want to comfort him, but I know he wouldn't want me to right now. I'm surprised to hear him talk about it, really—he can hardly bear to watch it on television these days. It's been ten years now since he played and though he says he doesn't miss it, he loses the sparkle in his eye at the mere mention of the word football.

"Okay! Everyone, over here, over here," Ari gushes, handing us all glasses of champagne. "We're celebrating tonight!" Everyone crowds around him, accepting their glasses, except Nick, who comes around behind me, taking me in his arms. Nigel settles in next to Ari, nodding at him to begin.

"My Nigel and I have decided to move in together," Ari announces, his joy unmistakable.

"Yay!" Nigel cheers, golf clapping beside him.

Ari looks directly at me. "I know that we haven't known each other for very long, but, what can I say—when you know, you know. *You know?*"

He lets out a riotous burst of laughter and I smile my widest smile—being around Ari tends to make me do that. We all congratulate them, when the doorbell rings. My mother's eyes light up as we all look at one another curiously, wondering who on Earth she's invited to dinner.

"Oh," my mother says, setting her glass down on the table. "I've got a surprise for you." She rushes to the front door, bringing back with her a surprise I could do without.

Mitch.

His presence fills the room, thick and heavy. I feel faint.

"Look who's here," she shrieks. "Finally! Oh, I had so much trouble getting him here."

"Hello," he says hesitantly, setting his sights on me.

"Oh! Mitchell, dear, it's so good to see you again." She takes his arm, walking him toward us.

"Ari, Nigel, this is Mitchell. He's the man who saved Scarlet's life." She turns to Mitch. "Ari has been dying to meet you."

Mitch smiles nervously as Ari and Nigel stampede toward him, shaking his hand.

"A real-life hero!" Nigel squeals. "Color me happy. What a wonderful night!"

My father steps forward, offering Mitch a glass of champagne, and I take the opportunity to check in with Nick. He's not taking it well. At all. He turns his head slowly to look at me, a brand-new wrinkle forming in his forehead.

Holy Hell. She's really done it this time.

"Honey, say hello," my mother says loudly.

Everyone stops. Mitch squares his shoulders, his brow furrowed. I notice Nick's hands twitching and I panic, though I'm certain he won't start something here. They all watch me, waiting for a big, tearful reunion.

I've never been more afraid to move in my life.

"Hi, Scarlet," Mitch says softly.

"Hi," I reply, feigning cheerfulness as I walk toward him. He drifts toward me and I put my arms around him, careful not to touch my body to his, but he pulls me closer, holding me tighter, rubbing his hand across my back. My body grows tense. My heart beats slower and faster at the same time, though it never beats quite right when I'm around him. I step away quickly, striding back to Nick, who reaches out and pulls me tightly to his side. I look up at him and he lowers his lips to mine, kissing me fiercely, feverishly, as though no one else is in the room.

I hear Ari and Nigel coo in the background and I pull back from him, sparing everyone the details.

"We're celebrating something ourselves tonight!" Nick says proudly. "Scarlet had a dream, a memory of me, the day we bought the house."

Everyone cheers and congratulates us, but Nick stands fast, smirking at Mitch, Mitch who glares back.

"Isn't that wonderful?" my mother says to Mitch, who's taking a sip of his champagne, seemingly swallowing his unease.

Nick sits on the couch behind him and pulls me onto his lap, no doubt smiling audaciously at Mitch.

"Oh, before I forget." Ari dashes over to the coffee table, returning with a gorgeously wrapped gift, passing it to me.

It's presented so perfectly I don't want to open it.

"What is it?"

"Open it," Ari insists.

I don't delay. I love presents. I tear at the beautiful paper and delicate bow as Ari watches on, wild with anticipation.

It's a book. *Wuthering Heights*. I turn it over front to back then look up at him curiously.

"Thank you."

Ari's whole body sags. "Nothing?"

I frown, unsure what he means.

"Really? Nothing at all?"

I glance back down at the book. "Am I missing something?"

He takes the book from my hand, holding it up in front of me. *"Wuthering Heights*? Emily Brontë? Cathy and Heathcliff? You loved this book when we were younger. It was practically glued to your hand. Took it everywhere you went. Cathy this and Heathcliff that, you drove me so crazy that eventually I had to read it, and *I* don't do books! It's absolutely not my bag, couldn't stand all the pompous nonsense they went on with back then."

I can't help but laugh, ever amused by the way Ari sensationalizes things.

"I didn't really understand it at the time, I guess. I was a bit younger than you, but you did."

"Well, thank you, I'll be sure to read it," I reply to him.

"Ha! Why not? It would only be the ninety-ninth time." He flops down on the couch next to Nigel. "I was sure she'd remember that," he blubbers into Nigel's arm.

Nigel winks at me, patting Ari's knee in comfort. I feel terrible. Nick snickers into a couch cushion behind me, like a schoolboy. As much as Nick loves my brother, his overdramatized antics never fail to amuse him.

Thankfully, dinner is served quickly, but Mitch is seated directly opposite Nick and the tension between them is suffocating. My father slams beers down in front of the boys, insisting they abandon the girlie champagne they've been drinking, except for Nigel, who refuses to conform. My father clutches Nick's shoulder as he takes his seat at the head of the table.

"I've got a superb coffee liqueur for after dinner," he says with a wink.

Nick's eyes light up with a gleam of deviltry, and I know what that means — Dad's famous double Black Russians with a Bundaberg Rum liqueur chaser. They'll be off their trolleys in no time and, given the current climate, I'm not sure that's such a good thing.

Surprisingly, the conversation flows freely, but the air between Nick and Mitch grows thicker by the minute, so thick I could cut it with a knife. "So, how's business,

Mitchell? Are they keeping you busy?" my father asks.

Mitch looks up at my father, swallowing his mouthful of food hastily. "Yes, sir, I'm actually building a couple of racing skiffs for the regatta at the moment."

"Oh, yes, yes. That's the big surf lifesaving regatta down at Kirra in a couple of months?"

"That's the one."

There are three other conversations going on around the table, but I can't tear myself from theirs.

Nick drops his fork on his plate, glaring at Mitch. "I thought you were a cop!"

Everyone stops, turning their heads to Mitch and Nick like a stadium wave.

"Uh, I was a cop, yeah."

My father frowns. "You're a policeman, Mitchell?"

Mitch wipes his mouth with his napkin. "Uh, yes, sir. I'm on a long-term leave of absence, though, just concentrating on the boats at the moment."

My mother gasps. "I had no idea, Mitchell. That's wonderful."

"Yes, yes, it is," my father adds. "What rank are you?"

"I'm a sergeant," he replies.

My father's eyes light up. "Really?"

"My goodness! A policeman. Have you ever shot anyone?" Nigel asks, resting his hand across his collarbone.

Mitch bows his head. "Yes. I have."

"Ooooh," Nigel coos.

"Any particular specialty, Mitchell?" my father asks, beaming at him like a proud father.

Nick shifts in his seat and I glance up at him, catching him mid-eye-roll, his act of sabotage failing dismally.

"I've pretty much done it all. I did a couple of years in generals then about four years undercover in the criminal investigation branch."

I glance around the table. No one is eating, only listening with their mouths open as my father bounces questions off Mitch like a quiz show host.

"I was seconded to prosecutions for three months, which turned into three years," he continues. "I didn't mind that, though I really didn't have the time to study to progress there."

My father tilts his head back. "Ah, prosecutions. That's a fine place to work. I used to be a barrister myself. I tell you, all that courtroom experience certainly won't hurt your career if you ever want to move on to private practice. I have a lot of connections. If you ever want to make the move one day, come and see me."

Mitch smiles warmly. "Thank you. That's very kind."

My father returns his smile, their mutual respect unmistakable.

Nick pushes back in his seat, standing abruptly, then storms out of the room. Everyone whips their heads around to look at me as though I'd kicked them under the table, and I stare right back at them as though I did.

"Excuse me," I murmur, rising swiftly from my seat. I wander through the bottom floor of the house, calling his name, but I can't find him anywhere. I return to the table without him when the back door opens and he steps inside.

"Sorry," is all he says as he strides around the table to resume his seat. I sit down beside him and everyone continues talking and eating as though we'd never left the room.

After a minute, he rests his hand on my leg. "Sorry about that. Are you okay?"

"Uh, yeah, I'm fine," I reply, my shaky voice saying just the opposite. "You?"

He doesn't answer, but his clenched jaw and indignant eyes say it all. I summon a smile and he lowers his lips to mine, sliding his hand between my legs.

"Okay, you two, people are trying to eat here," my brother taunts. Everyone stops and looks at us, the energy in the room shifting instantly.

"Hey, we just met six months ago. Give us a break," Nick jokes.

Everyone laughs but Mitch, his gaze fixed on Nick. If eyes were knives, Nick would be dead. As soon as dinner is finished, Mitch excuses himself, saying he has an early start.

The minute he leaves, my father whisks Nick and the boys into his den to liquor them up while he smokes cigars and tells stories of the good ol' days, when music had meaning and wasn't just noise. When people valued their social standing and respected their neighbors and how going to war didn't determine who was right, only who was left.

I wander into the kitchen, refilling my champagne glass, my mother in hot pursuit. I can't shake her tonight. She's like thunder on the heels of lightning. She props herself up on a stool at the end of the bench, topping her glass up, needlessly so.

"So, how did you enjoy dinner, darling? I bet you got a big surprise seeing Mitch. He's a very nice young man, isn't he, and he's a police officer, no less."

I take a sip of my champagne. "Yes, he's nice. It was just a shock to see him."

"Well, your brother didn't get to meet him at the party that night and I knew how desperately he wanted to. I thought it was the perfect opportunity." I nod, not answering. "There's something going on with you. What's troubling you, my sweet?"

"What do you mean?"

She presses her lips together tightly. "Well, I can't quite put my finger on it, but there's a sadness behind those eyes tonight. I've seen it before and it usually means you're bottling things up. What's going on?"

I shake my head and glance toward the dining room.

She follows my gaze, her brow creasing. "Is everything okay with you and Nick?"

"Yeah, good. Things have become really comfortable with him. I still don't remember him as such, but the dream I had of him actually happened, so that's promising."

"It is, darling, very promising. What happened tonight

114

when he stormed out of dinner?"

"Uh, I haven't really had a chance to talk to him, so I don't know."

Thankfully, Ari and Nigel laugh loudly in the next room, interrupting us.

"It sounds as though there may be a wedding soon, huh?"

She arches an eyebrow, as though she has no idea what I mean.

"Ari. He and Nigel seem pretty serious."

She smirks. "Yes, well, you can marry your cat these days, can't you?" She takes a generous gulp of her champagne, bringing her glass down too hard on the bench in front of her. "Ah, marriage. It doesn't mean what it used to. In the old days, when your father and I got married, marriage was a very different ball game. Pardon the pun." She giggles. "Marriage meant forever back then. People don't respect vows anymore. They're just words without substance or consequence. People seem to get married and divorced as often as they update their cars these days, some much earlier. Times are changing, that's for sure, and not in a good way."

"How long have you and Dad been married now?"

"Ha!" She rolls her eyes. "Forty-two years this September."

"Wow!"

She nods. "I was only eighteen years old when I married your father. Sweet and innocent. He was twenty-one. Oh, those were the days." Her eyes light up and she laughs. "Strutting around in his tight little flared pants with his long, flowing flaxen hair, and flip-flops." She laughs harder.

"I remember he used to pick me up in this loud, hotted-up old Holden—it was his pride and joy. Of course, my father hated it, called it a 'glorified trash can on wheels'. Your father never quite got over that. My father didn't like him very much, practically disowned me when your father asked for my hand in marriage. So we got married anyway." She shrugs, her eyes glistening. "We were wild and young and free and nothing mattered, only that we were together, nothing was going to stop us."

I rest my elbow on the benchtop, my chin in my hand.

"We didn't have much money back then. Your father worked as a delivery driver for Golden Cockerel Chicken, delivering chickens to all the stores in town. I can still see the truck he drove. It had a big sticker on the back that read *Only the good die young*."

She tilts her head back, giggling like a giddy teenager. It's curious to see her like this, so nostalgic.

"Oh, we were crazy in love. We had nothing and we didn't care. We lived on love. We'd go out for a drive on a Friday night when your father got paid and get a hamburger and a milkshake, then park on top of Coolangatta Hill. It was the place to go back then. The view was to die for. The night lights of the city filled the sky with a hazy glow that reflected off the water all around us. Not that we were doing too much sightseeing, if you know what I mean."

She winks.

"Ew, way too much information."

"It was our favorite place in the world. We'd turn the radio on and dance under the stars, surrounded by other young couples in *their* glorified trash cans on wheels." We laugh.

"Life was so simple then." She glances up at me, a tear in her eye. "Then you and your brother came along and life was never the same, or as your father would say, that's when the shit *really* hit the fan."

We both throw ourselves back, hysterical, the champagne well and truly gone to our heads. I'd never heard my mother swear before, but somehow it made me feel closer to her.

"Mm, kids. They're a *lot* of fun. Takes a beautiful thing and turns it into a sleepless, bottle-making, nappy-changing nightmare."

"Mother! I thought you *wanted* grandchildren? Are you trying to turn me off kids?"

"No, no, I'm joking. I'm joking. Raising children was one of the biggest challenges in my life, but it's also the best thing that ever happened in my life. I couldn't survive without you and Ari. You're my world. Whatever choices I've made in my time on this Earth, they led me to you and your brother, so I know I made the right ones. Just as you will."

Her face grows serious. "You're going to face a lot of choices in your life, Scarlet, and then sometimes things just happen, things that are beyond our control and we have to just go with the universe, because fighting it is just a waste of time. You can't see it when it happens, but in the end, you realize that it was meant to be."

I sit there, staring at her in wonder. *Can she read my mind?*

The kitchen door bursts open and my brother and Nigel tumble in, well and truly smashed.

"Well, we have a very early start in the morning, looking for a new shaggers' pad, and therefore we must regretfully bid you adieu. Scarlet, you're coming with us later in the week. When we shortlist our favs, we'll pick you up."

I nod. "I'd be honored."

"Gee, I really hope you find something, honey. It's a sellers' market out there at the moment."

"Ah, we'll find something, Mother. You know me. Failure is not an option."

Nigel raises an eyebrow, amused. "Funny you say that— someone explained the definition of failure to me just the other day. It's when you try to pull your blanket up under your chin and end up punching yourself in the face." He hoots out his ridiculously loud laugh and we all follow his lead, though I'm not quite sure which is funnier.

My brother throws his arms around me and I rise, hugging them both and wishing them well. My mother flashes me a thank-god-they're-leaving look then walks them out, just as Nick comes in, looking a little worse for wear. No doubt my father's doing. He slams his empty glass down on the table, his lips crinkling at the corners.

"Well. *That* was interesting," he jokes, leaning across the corner of the bend, touching his lips to mine. I can smell the alcohol on him.

"Not as interesting as what I just heard. I think *I* was conceived in a trash can."

"What?"

I shake my head. "It's a long story."

"Mmmh. Nearly ready for home?"

I slide my glass across the bench. "Yes. Let's go, and hide the champagne — my mother's had enough."

We make a break for it while Ari and Nigel are leaving, though my mother gushing about Mitch on the way out brings the evening's uneasiness back out into the light.

Gabe is waiting for us when we get outside. He opens the door and I set one foot into the car, but the heel of my other shoe gets caught in the paving stones on the driveway. I tumble inside the vehicle, laughing, the cool night air increasing the effects of the alcohol. Nick reaches down, pulling the shoe from the stones, handing it to me less a heel. I can't stop laughing, though he doesn't seem to find it as funny as I do. I press my lips together, trying to limit my laughter, slipping off my other shoe to match.

"Thank you for waiting for us, Gabe. You were welcome to come in, though, and eat with us."

"Thank you, Mrs. Pierce, but it was a lovely night out. I went for a walk then caught up on my reading," he replies, pulling out onto the street.

I nod and glance across at Nick, my good spirits quickly fading. He stares out of the window, balling his hands up into fists on his knees. I put my hand on his leg and he turns to me, his eyes unreadable.

"Are you okay?" I ask, suddenly sober.

"No," he says sternly. "I can't believe your mother invited your boyfriend to dinner."

"He's not my boyfriend."

He grunts, his dark, venomous eyes like fangs threatening to bite. "Well, he was your something," he growls, his voice darker than his eyes.

I stare up at him, shocked by his demeanor. I knew he

wasn't happy about the night's events but right now, it seems it's me he's not happy with. *Two can play at that game.*

"I don't remember him," I snap.

"Doesn't make it any less painful. It didn't help that you didn't take your eyes off each other the whole night."

"What are we supposed to do? *Not* look at each other?"

He takes my forearm in his hand, gripping it tightly.

"Do you have any idea how hard it was to be in the same room with him tonight and not rip his head off?"

I pull my arm from his clutches, glowering at him. "You already tried that, didn't you?"

"*What?*"

I start to turn away, but he seizes my chin, turning my face back to his. The streetlights grow fewer and the cabin grows darker, but it pales in comparison to the darkness in his eyes.

"Did *he* tell you that?" he growls.

I don't answer.

"So, you've talked to him, then?"

I swallow hard, my heart pulsating like a bass note from a horror movie.

"When?" he shouts, glancing up at Gabe momentarily.

"Today," I murmur.

He scoffs, then lets go of my chin, glaring at the road ahead. "You talked to him *today*."

I nod hesitantly.

"In person?" His eyes flash to mine, watching me like a lion, poised to strike.

"Yes," I reply timidly.

"Huh! And the two of you were in there, pretending you hadn't seen each other since the party. You're both very good actors, I'll give you that."

I don't answer, knowing that anything I say right now is going to be the wrong thing. He shakes his head, studying me with piercing scrutiny.

"You are hell bent on destroying this marriage, aren't you?"

119

"*What?*"

"How can you possibly expect this to work, when you keep going behind my back like this?"

At this point, I should probably be apologizing for not telling him, but instead I embrace the darkness, telling him what I think, letting my words tumble out of my mouth like monkeys in a barrel.

"Oh, and you're not? *You* forgot to mention *your* visit to the boatyard. I do want this marriage to work, Nick, and yes, I should have told you I went to see him, but I knew you'd be mad."

He smashes his hand down on his knee. "Where did you meet him?"

"I went to the boatyard. It was business."

"What the fu — ?"

"It was *business*," I insist. "I went into the office today. Marcy told me that Mitch used to work for me, but he resigned after my accident. I went there to ask him to come back on board, that's all. I noticed his face, he told me what happened and I left. Nothing happened."

"He used to *work for you*? Doing what?"

I swallow hard. "He managed the personal security contracts."

"This just gets better and better. You've been to the office, too! When were you going to mention that?" he shouts, his eyes filled with disdain.

"I didn't have time this afternoon."

"Oh, bull*shit*! You've had plenty of time to tell me. Before we left the house, the drive over to your mother's tonight — you never mentioned a thing. You're so good at keeping secrets, Scarlet. It's what you do best."

"What is *that* supposed to mean?"

"Gee, I don't know. You were apparently sleeping with the guy for three months behind my back. I'd say that makes you pretty accomplished at keeping things from me, and that's putting it nicely. If I call it for what it is, you wouldn't like that very much."

"Don't do that."

"Do what?"

I turn my head, and he clasps my chin, turning my face back to his. "Do what?" he growls.

I swipe at his hand. "Don't punish me for something I don't remember doing."

"Oh, give me a break! I'm not *punishing* you. I only found out you were fucking him yesterday. It's still very raw for me. He's been with you. Inside you. I'm your husband. I wouldn't be human if I said it doesn't hurt me."

I shake my head and look up at Gabe, alarmed, wondering if he can hear us.

"Look at me when I'm talking to you!"

I turn back to face him, shocked at his anger.

"I fucking love you, Scarlet, you're everything to me. If I didn't love you with all that I am, I wouldn't be here."

"I'm sorry, okay! I'm sorry! I can't believe I did that to you. I'm a monster. I feel your pain, Nick. I feel your sadness, but I can't *do* anything about it. I can't even try to work through it, because I don't know what was going on in my head back then. There's nothing. Nothing!"

Tears stream down my face in torrents that would rival Niagara Falls. He closes his eyes briefly then puts his arm around me, pulling me closer. I clutch at his shirt, crying into his chest, and he holds my head against him, stroking my hair.

"I don't want you to see him again, do you hear me? And I don't want him *back on board* at your office."

My whole body tenses at his fierce and uncompromising tone. "Promise me!"

"I promise," I sob.

He takes my hand in his, pressing it against his lips. "We have to be honest with each other from here on in. I should have told you I went there and you should have told me. No more lies," he says sternly.

I shake my head. "No more lies."

The car starts to slow and I look out of the window, to

see the lights of home just up ahead. I collect my things from the floor as we pull up outside the house. Gabe lets us out then leaves quickly, taking the car home with him for the night. I feel bad knowing that he must have heard our conversation, and regretful, knowing it could have been avoided. He's such a wonderful man, and though he feels more a part of the family than an employee, it doesn't seem fair to subject him to our problems.

Nick opens the front door and I walk in ahead of him, throwing my shoes onto the floor. We walk into the lounge and I put my purse down on the lamp table beside the couch, accidently knocking my book onto the floor. He picks it up. "Helen of Troy? What happened to Cathy and what's-his-face?"

He tosses the book down on the coffee table and walks into the kitchen, reappearing seconds later with a beer, though he's already had more than enough. I reach behind my ears, taking off my earrings as he chugs down three-quarters of the beer then throws himself onto the couch. I've never seen him like this, so bitter and broody. I decide to leave him be. I walk past him on my way through the lounge to the bedroom and he grabs my wrist, stopping me.

"You're mad at me."

I exhale loudly. "No. I just feel as if I really don't know you at all, sometimes. Going to Mitch's place and beating him up? The way you've been acting tonight, I don't—"

He stands abruptly, his brow furrowed. "What do you expect from me, Scarlet? He's a homewrecker! He wants you! He's trying to take what's mine. I'm not going to stand back and let him take you away from me. You're my wife. I lost you once—I'm not going to lose you again. As far as I'm concerned, he's lucky he's still breathing."

"He's a cop!" I shout. "Are you crazy?" Though that has nothing to do with my argument.

"Oh!" he shouts. "So, what? He can do whatever he pleases? Steal whoever's wife he chooses? Because he wears a blue uniform and a tin badge? He's not untouchable,

Scarlet. At the end of the day, he's just a common thief trying to pilfer my wife! No! This is war and you are my Helen."

I raise an eyebrow, glancing down at my book on the table.

"Of Troy? Didn't everyone die in that war?"

"*What?*"

I press my lips together, trying not to laugh. "If you start chanting 'Mitch must fall', I'm leaving you. You're too far gone."

He shakes his head, a grin forming on his lips.

"That's funny," he murmurs, his anger dissipating.

I take his hand in mine. "I'm not mad at you. I'm just worried about you. He's a cop. He does have a certain amount of power." That's not my real concern, but it's laced with the truth.

"Point taken." He tugs on my hand, pulling me into his arms. "I love you. I don't want to fight with you anymore."

"Neither do I."

He brings his mouth down on mine, flicking his tongue at my lips. I open my mouth, allowing him in. I taste the alcohol on his tongue, smell it on his breath, mixed with the champagne from my own. An evil concoction that's rendered us both flawed, lesser versions of ourselves.

Out of breath, he pulls his head back from mine, spinning me around so my back is against his chest. "I'm sorry for losing my temper," he utters, brushing the hair away from my neck and replacing it with his lips. I tilt my head to the side, a soft moan escaping my lips as he grazes my skin with his teeth then soothes it with his tongue.

Nick glides his fingers up to my shoulders, slipping the straps of my dress down so that it falls to the ground. He wraps his arms around me, pulling me back firmly against him so that I feel his hard, throbbing cock against my back. "Not mad at me?" he breathes against my ear.

I close my eyes, every nerve in my body standing at attention.

"Not mad at you," I whisper.

He undoes my bra, tearing it from my body, trailing his strong, swift hands down my shoulders to my breasts, squeezing my nipples with his fingers. Hard. So hard that I'm instantly wet. He squeezes them again and I cry out, reaching up to stop him, but it only makes him more determined.

"Nick," I whimper.

"Shut up," he growls, wrapping his fingers around my throat.

He turns my face to reach my mouth with his, kissing me from behind as he grinds against me. His other hand he moves down my thigh, and I whimper when he tears my panties from my body, throwing them to the ground. He steps forward, moving his hand to the back of my neck, clutching it tightly then bending me over the back of the couch.

I breathe deeply, scared but exhilarated. My whole body is trembling, wanting him but so unsure of him right now.

He squeezes my thighs as he spreads my legs, forcing his fingers deep inside me. I cry out, digging my toes into the floor, trying to stand, but he only holds me tighter. He increases the pressure of his strokes, driving his fingers into me over and over without mercy. I hear the tinkling of his belt, the zipper of his pants, the harshness of his breaths. He removes his fingers, forcing himself inside me, and I cry out, shocked by the force of his powerful thrust. I knew what I was in for, but I wasn't expecting it to come so fast and hard. He draws back swiftly, ramming himself into me again and again.

He groans, clutching at my hips, thrusting me forward then pulling me back forcefully against him. "You're not going to see him again, are you?" he growls.

I freeze, caught off-guard. I'd thought this conversation was over. He slams his hips against mine, driving himself into me.

"No," I breathe.

Nick weaves his fingers into my hair, tilting my head back, his other hand forcing my leg up on the back of the couch.

"*Are you?*" he shouts, spreading my legs wider, diving in deeper.

"No! Oh, God, Nick!" I scream.

His chest vibrates with a menacing, possessive rumble as his thrusts grow savage and merciless like a wild animal, and he's squeezing my thighs until they hurt. This is a whole different Nick, alcohol-fueled and simultaneously angry, jealous and horny, but there's something so incredibly erotic about it.

He moves his hands to my breasts, squeezing my nipples so hard they burn. I cry out, relinquishing my body to him, involuntarily tightening and pulsating around him, rising, soaring then falling, sinking, dissolving into my own pleasure. He groans, thrusting faster in deep, vigorous strokes, his breathing unbridled and chaotic as he pumps his hot, wet heat inside me.

"Oh, fuck, Scarlet," he pants, lowering his chest to my back. He wraps his arms around me, our bodies twitching and shuddering. He's never been like that with me before, rough and wild, but I liked it. I lie beneath him, exhausted, panting, intending with all that I am to keep my promise.

* * * *

I wake the next morning, naked, feeling the warmth of the sun on my face, on my body. My eyelids flutter, opening to find the curtains drawn wide open. I must have forgotten to close them last night. I take a deep breath and stretch out when I hear Nick.

"Hey, you," he murmurs, his voice low and doleful.

I look in the direction of his voice to find him sitting on the chair in the corner of the room, his elbows on his knees, his mouth cupped in his hands. He looks terrible, his eyes red, his pillow-bent hair curled up at the ends.

I glimpse up at the clock. It's after nine. He should be at work.

"Hey," I reply, pulling the sheet up around me as I start to rise. Every muscle in my body hurts, but I ignore it, too worried about what's wrong with him.

"What's the matter?" I ask.

He lowers his hand from his mouth. "Look at your body."

I look down, letting go of the sheet around me. He stands slowly, walks over to the bed and sits down beside me. He points to my hips and thighs, and the numerous distinct bruises imprinted into my skin.

"I'm so sorry," he murmurs.

I look up at him, shaking my head. "I didn't feel it."

He closes his eyes and turns away.

I rub my hand across his back, soothing him. "Nick, I didn't feel it!"

"You must have. Look at you."

I take his face in my hands, staring into his eyes. "I didn't. We both had a bit too much to drink. I enjoyed it. I would have said something if it hurt."

"But you're hurting now. That was unacceptable last night. It will *never* happen again." He hangs his head.

"You didn't do it on purpose—"

"Didn't I?" he interrupts. "I was pretty mad at you. Maybe I did." He shakes his head. "I shouldn't drink like that. It's just this *guy*! He makes me so angry. He's like the fucking ghost of Christmas past—he just won't go away. Thinking about the two of you together—" He grits his teeth and clenches his fist. I rest my hand on it and he closes his eyes, momentarily fighting his demons.

"I'm so, so sorry. I had no right to take my anger out on you."

"You didn't. We had incredible, rough, wild sex after a *lot* of drinks. I had a good time. I'm not complaining."

He takes my hands in his, holding them tightly. "I'm sorry for the way I've been acting. I'm just so afraid of losing you again."

I wrap my arms around him, holding on to him as tightly as I can. "You're not going to lose me. I'm not going anywhere." He drapes his arms around my shoulders, as though trying not to hurt me, and I squeeze him tighter.

"Are you staying home today?"

"Yes," he whispers into my hair.

"Good," I reply, rising to my knees and pushing him back down onto the bed. His eyes grow brighter as I slide off his boxer shorts, wrapping my fingers around his stirring shaft that grows rock-hard before my eyes. He stares down at me, biting his bottom lip in anticipation as I lower my mouth to his thighs. I look up at him, wetting my lips just as I'm about to immerse him in my mouth, hungry and bloodthirsty.

"My turn."

Chapter Eight

A New Dawn

I arch my back, burying my head in the pillows, feeling his fingers tighten around my throat. He thrusts deep inside me and I gasp, clutching at the bed beneath me. He thrusts again, so hard that my head hits the headboard, then suddenly he stops. I can't feel him. He groans as though he's in pain. I open my eyes, blinking as they adjust to the light. I see red everywhere. He's kneeling on the bed in front of me, clutching his side. There's blood on his hands. I stop breathing, following the blood trail from his torso to my stomach. I panic, frantically rubbing at the blood on my skin. It's not mine. He cries out, pulling a blood-soaked bandage from his side. Blood oozes out of the wound and runs down his body. I can't breathe. I can't breathe.

I sit up, gasping, crying. The air comes thick and fast into my lungs and I cough—loud, chesty barking coughs that splinter and echo around the room. Suddenly the room lights up, the glare blinding me.

"Scarlet?" Nick splutters.

I glance across at him, terrified.

He pulls back the covers and moves closer. "What happened? Are you okay?"

My heart is thumping so loudly I can't think, my head hammering so hard I can't speak. I nod, sucking in deep successive breaths as he rubs his hand across my back. I look down at my camisole, checking the fabric. There's no blood. I turn to Nick, clutching at his shirt, lifting it up and checking his stomach. No blood, no scars, nothing.

"What are you doing?"

I cry harder. He reaches across, pulling me into his arms. I hear his heart beating and I rest my head against his chest, listening, anything to distract me from the desperate rhythm of my own.

"What did you see?" he murmurs.

My body tenses. I can't tell him. What would I say? That I was having sex with someone? That it wasn't him? That I saw blood? A lot of blood? He'd have me committed. Maybe I *should* be committed. I can't tell him the truth, that's for sure. I lie. "I thought you were hurt."

"Me?"

I look up at him, nodding.

"I'm not hurt, baby. I'm fine." He smooths his hand over my hair then tightens his arms around me as we sit there in silence, waiting for my breathing to settle. A sudden stabbing pain shoots down the center of my skull to the bottom of my spine. I gasp and drop my head to my chest, clutching my forehead. He pulls his head back to look at me.

"What was that? Are you okay?"

I don't want to tell him what's wrong. I've been looking forward to getting a new car, driving and gaining some sort of independence, and this will only cause doubt.

"It's your head again, isn't it?"

"Yes," I whisper.

"Painkillers?"

"Please."

He puts his pillow behind my head, resting me back against it, then rushes into the bathroom, returning seconds later with a glass of water and my pills.

"Your neurologist appointment is tomorrow?" he asks, sitting down on the bed beside me. I nod, swallowing my pills hastily.

"I'm coming with you."

"No. I'll be fine. You had yesterday off work. You can't be away again."

"I don't care. I want to make sure you're okay."

"Nick, it's just a headache. That's all. You're the boss this week. No more time off."

He exhales loudly—his admission that I'm right. He reaches up and tucks my hair behind my ear.

"Tell him everything, these dreams, these headaches, everything."

"I will."

"Okay."

I glance across at the clock. Three o'clock. He follows my gaze.

"Do you want to sit up and watch some TV or something?"

"No. You have to get up soon. I'm sure I'll fall back to sleep."

He nods, watching me as I lie down, then reaches across, turning off the light. I turn onto my side with my back to him.

"Come here." He pulls me back against his chest, wrapping his arms around me.

I close my eyes, feeling his warmth, his strength.

"Sleep, my sweet Scarlet," he breathes against my ear.

I open my eyes.

There'll be none of that.

I spend the remaining hours of the early morning wide awake, listening to the light hum of Nick's breath on my pillow. Strips of daylight begin to peer through thin slits where the curtains bunch together as birds start to chirp and natter outside my window, announcing the dawn of the new day, their song somewhere between light breaths and soft chirps.

I drift off to sleep.

When I wake, Nick's gone. I stretch my arm out across to his side of the bed, sliding my fingers over the soft silk of the sheets, wishing he was there. Nine-fifteen. A sleep-in. I needed that. I roll over, taking my cell phone from the bedside table. There's a text from Nick.

Good morning, baby.

I hope you're feeling better this morning. Ring me when you get up, or after the neurologist appointment and let me know how it went.

Thinking of you.

All my love.

Nick xx

Oh, my God! The neurologist appointment!

I glance across at the clock again—only a little over an hour before I have to be there. I jump out of bed and run to the hallway balcony, panicked.

"Malaylie," I shout.

"Yes, Mrs. Pierce," she hollers back.

"Coffee, please, strong, and can you ask Gabe to bring the car around?"

"Yes, ma'am."

I rush into the dressing room, change quickly, then hurry into the bathroom, applying the bare minimum of makeup and tying my hair back in a bun. I snatch my coat and purse from the bed then bound downstairs to the kitchen at warp speed, throwing my things down on the counter and taking a seat just as Malaylie sets my coffee down in front of me.

"Ah, thank you, so much." The cup is so warm. I wrap my fingers around it and close my eyes as I take my first glorious sip. *Heaven.* I glance down at my watch. I've got a few minutes.

"How are you feeling this morning, Mrs. Pierce? Mr. Pierce said you were up through the night."

"I'm much better, thank you. What about you? How are you?" I ask, taking another sip.

She stares at me as though I'd never asked her that before. I've been so wrapped up in myself lately, maybe I haven't.

Her lips twitch, finally forming a smile. "I'm just fine, Mrs. Pierce. Just fine. Thank you for asking."

"Is there something wrong?"

"No. Not at all, Mrs. Pierce." Her smile widens as she turns, picking up the dish cloth, wiping over the coffee machine and benches. I watch her as I take another sip of coffee.

"Malaylie, can I ask you something?"

"Of course, Mrs. Pierce."

I pause, choosing my words carefully. "Did we seem happy to you? Mr. Pierce and I. Before the accident?"

Her face lights up. "Oh, yes, of course, Mrs. Pierce. You were very happy, you and Mr. Pierce, you were talking about having the little ones." She replies, pretending to cradle something small in her arms.

"I see."

Malaylie motions toward the clock on the wall. "Tick, tock, Mrs. Pierce, tick, tock."

I take a mammoth gulp of coffee, swallowing my discomfort. No clock is going to make me rush into something like that. I snatch my coat and purse from the chair beside me when the home phone rings, startling us both. Malaylie bustles over, picks up the receiver then places it down. She looks up at me, then mutters something in her own language.

"What happened?"

"The phone calls. They are starting again. That's the fourth call this week."

"The phone calls?"

"Yes, before your accident we were getting many, many calls like this. I answer the phone, but when I say hello, there's no reply. Now, last week, they start again. At least ten calls last week, now four this week."

"Maybe we should call the phone company and have them check the line?"

"Ah, yes, we did that last time, but the calls kept coming."

I glance around the room, my thoughts leading to Mitch. I know he has our home number. Maybe he's trying to speak to me but hanging up when Malaylie answers?

"I'll call the phone company. You must go or you will be late. Don't spare a thought of it," she insists, waving her hand at me.

"Yep, I'm going," I reply, rushing toward the door.

Gabe is waiting by the car when I arrive outside, wiping the hood over with a cloth.

"Good morning, Gabe."

"Good morning, Mrs. Pierce," he says cheerfully.

"North and Central, please. I have a specialist appointment at ten-thirty."

"Certainly, Mrs. Pierce."

I hurry around to my door before he has a chance to even think about opening it. The car is already running. He jumps in, then drives us speedily toward the city. My cell phone rings and I rummage through my purse, but I can't find it. I can never find anything in there — what's the use of them? Finally, I locate it. It's my mother. I swipe my finger against the screen.

"Hi, Mom."

"Hello, sweetheart, how are you?"

"I'm fine. How are you, how's Dad?"

"We're okay, we're good. I was just thinking about you. I thought I'd give you a call and see how you are."

"Oh. Well. Thank you, I appreciate that."

"Where are you? You sound as if you're in a tunnel."

"I'm in the car. I'm just on my way to a neurologist appointment, actually."

"Oh, is everything okay? Do you want me to come with you? I can meet you there."

"No, Mom, I'll be fine. It's a good forty-five minutes from your place. You wouldn't make it, anyway."

"Uh." She pauses. "Okay, honey, will you ring me and let me know what the doctor says?"

"Of course, of course."

She sighs, as though she knows that I won't. "All right, I'll wait for your call."

"Yep, talk to you later, Mom."

"Bye, honey. Make sure you ring me, now."

"I will. Bye." I hang up, rolling my eyes and exhaling loudly. Gabe looks back at me in the rearview mirror, grinning.

"Mothers!"

For some reason, after I speak to my mother on the phone, I'm suddenly anxious and uptight to the point where I feel the need to smoke a cigarette and down a schooner of whiskey to calm my nerves. Not that I drink or smoke, but I've seen it in the movies, and it seems to help.

We pull up outside the neurologist's office, my need for a whiskey now a need for a double. I sit there, staring up at its lavish entrance. It looks more like a luxury resort than a specialist building and I grow more anxious by the minute. My mother's phone call hasn't helped the situation. I draw in a deep breath, allowing Gabe to come around and open the door.

"I might be a while, Gabe. You can go home if you like. I'll call you."

"As you wish, Mrs. Pierce."

I straighten my dress and enter the building, abuzz with people, hustling to and fro, taking the elevator to the eleventh floor. The elevator is ridiculously overcrowded. Two men in suits continue to talk loudly as I enter, not caring that their conversation is being overheard by at least twelve complete strangers. The elevator opens on my floor and I couldn't be happier as I rush out into the bustling reception area.

People look up from their books and conversations, watching me as I choose a path through the rows of desperately bored onlookers to the reception desk. The receptionist glances up at me, her perfect blonde hair slicked back from her young, beautiful face, not a single strand out of place. She's one of those girls I just know gets out of bed looking like that in the mornings. I want to like her, but I kind of hate her at the same time. She flashes me a genuinely warm smile.

"Good morning, Mrs. Pierce. It's nice to see you again."

Her face is somewhat familiar, but I can't remember her name. I'm terrible with names. I return her smile, flicking my eyes briefly down to her I.D. badge. *Noelle.* I say it again in my head.

"Hi, Noelle. I've got an appointment with Dr. Bershaq at ten-thirty."

She glances down at her computer briefly then back to me. "Yes, certainly, Mrs. Pierce. You can head straight down to his office if you like. Just take a seat out front. He'll be with you very shortly."

"Okay, thank you," I reply, turning toward his office.

I wander down the hallway and take a seat outside his rooms, thankful to have a moment to myself. I put down my coat on the seat beside me and turn off my cell phone when the door in front of me swings wide open, startling me.

"Mrs. Pierce." Dr. Bershaq's way-too-happy assistant, Carrie, stands before me beaming, a chart tucked tightly under her arm.

Another pretty face. *Are there no average-looking women here?* I flash her the only smile I can muster and toss my cell into my bag.

"How lovely to see you again," she continues. "Dr. Bershaq is available now. Can I take your jacket?"

"Yes, thank you."

She takes the garment from my arm and motions toward Dr. Bershaq's room. "Go right in, he's ready for you."

I walk down the corridor to his office, tapping lightly on his open door. He looks over his glasses at me, rising quickly from his seat to hurry toward me.

"Scarlet," he says cheerfully. "Nice to see you." He reaches out his seasoned hand to take mine, guiding me over to the seat in front of his desk. "How are you? How have you been?" he asks. Carrie closes the door behind us and he sits down, opening my chart.

"I'm okay."

He looks up at me. "Just okay?" I nod.

"What about health-wise, any issues?"

I pause, deciding not to tell him about the headaches.

"No," I reply.

"Great. Very good. Any memories or significant events since we last spoke?"

I frown, setting free a succession of quick nods.

"Great. Tell me everything."

I glance across at the window, wondering where to start, finally settling on Mitch.

"Uh, I met the man who rescued me, the night of the accident. His name is Mitch. Mitchell Morgan."

"Goodness. That's quite a big step for you. And how did that go?" he asks, picking up his pen and scribbling in my chart.

"Uh, it went well, but I ran him into a few days later. At a bookstore—"

He stops writing and glances up at me.

"We had a coffee together and I had some sort of vision of him. He put his cup down and ran his hands through his hair, then I saw him do the exact same thing again, but he was wearing different clothes and there was a different background."

He dips his chin, looking over the top of his glasses at me. "So, this man did something that triggered a different version of the same event to replay in your head?" I nod hesitantly.

"But you met this man after your accident?"

"Well. Yes, but he later admitted that he knew me before the accident."

He takes off his glasses, laying them down gently on the desk in front of him. "So, you knew this man *before* the accident?"

"That's what he says."

"So, it's a memory?"

I shrug. "Is it?"

He leans back in his chair, regarding me thoughtfully. "It does sound like it." He stares at me for the longest time, then puts his glasses back on and picks up his pen. "This is good news, Scarlet. It's progress," he says, moving his pen rapidly across the page. He stops writing and peers up at me. "You don't think so?"

I don't answer, not really sure what I think about it.

"Is that all that's happened?" he asks.

"No. I've had some dreams and a nightmare of the accident, I guess."

"Really. What did you see?"

"In the nightmare?" He nods.

I shift in my seat, uncomfortable about reliving it. "Uh, I was driving in my car. It was raining hard and it was dark outside. I couldn't see. The rain was relentless. Car lights were shining in my eyes. Horns sounding. I was upset, crying, I couldn't breathe. I started gasping for air, then I woke up." I glance up at him, my breathing labored.

"It's okay. Just take a deep breath. Would you like a glass of water?"

"Yes, please."

He strides over to the sink by the window and returns with a glass of water. I take the cup from his hand and he perches on the edge of his desk, deep in thought. "It was raining the night of your accident?" he questions.

I take a gulp of water and nod.

"So, it's quite possible you're dreaming the actual events of the accident." He folds his arms across his chest, knitting his light-gray eyebrows together. "These other dreams, what are they of?"

"Um, I dreamed of Nick, once, and just a couple of other insignificant dreams."

"Nothing is insignificant when it comes to your dreams, Scarlet. Can you remember what they were about?" I shake my head. "I want you to start keeping a dream journal. I want you to write down everything you dream about, anything at all, whether you think it's insignificant or not. Okay?"

I nod. "Do you think my memory's coming back?"

"It's hard to say. You've suffered a fairly significant brain injury. There's been real damage done. To what extent, I can't say. Only time will tell. This is a good thing, though, a good sign."

"Do other patients that start out like this regain their memory?"

"It's not like that, Scarlet. No two brain injuries are the same. They're always different. It may very well be that this is all you ever remember. On the other hand, you may remember much, much more. But in my opinion, going by the results of your last CT scan and the progress you've made, there's definitely hope."

I exhale loudly, conflicted by thoughts of what my memory coming back would mean. What if I don't like the person I was before the accident?

He stands, returning to his side of the desk. "I use the term loosely, though. You have some fairly extensive and irreparable damage and, due to that, what does come back to you will be limited at best."

"Do many of your patients completely regain their memory?"

"I have patients who've regained their early childhood and some remember years or just minutes before their trauma. Some *dream* their lives beforehand, but it goes without saying that that doesn't deem what they dream to be actual and *true*."

"So, what I dream doesn't necessarily mean it happened?"

"No, Scarlet. Sometimes dreams are just dreams, nothing more."

He picks up his pen, writing in my chart again. I wonder exactly what he's scribbling in there.

"How are things between yourself and your husband?"

"Good."

"Anything feeling familiar about him?"

"Not familiar as such, just every now and then I get a feeling that things feel right, comfortable between us."

"Well, that's good news. What about anyone else?" he asks, his pen hard at work.

"Mitch, maybe."

He looks up at me. "Something feels *right* or familiar?"

I part my lips, thinking. "I don't know that it's familiarity, but it's definitely something."

He tips his glasses to the end of his nose, the line between his eyebrows forming a deep crevice. "Scarlet, I know we've been through this before, but I really think you should talk to the resident psychiatrist. We have a very good psychotherapist downstairs."

"I don't—"

"I really think you need to talk to someone, if not about what happened, then about your feelings—"

"I know," I interrupt. "I'll consider it." I'm lying. The last thing I want is to go over and over my every waking and sleeping thought with a complete stranger. The hospital forced a shrink onto me for three months after the accident and it was awful. Talking to a psychiatrist about my thoughts and feelings so they can get a better understanding of who I am when I don't know myself seems pretty redundant to me.

"I understand how you feel. You're a very independent young woman. But if you really want to explore your mind, explore your experiences, harness your progress even, you need to talk things through with someone."

He puts his pen down on the desk, narrowing his eyes. "You do *want* to make progress, don't you, Scarlet?"

"Of course." I reply. I do want to make progress, but that doesn't make me any less afraid of it.

Chapter Nine

Finding Me

I lie there on the bed, my heart sending out erratic electric pulses like Morse code. There's something covering my eyes. I can't see. I can't move. Lips sweep across mine, softly, gently and I return the kiss, hearing the raspy hum in his throat, tasting his mouth, feeling his heartbeat on my tongue. I feel his hands everywhere, caressing my breasts, on the inside of my thighs, spreading my legs. I tremble, trying to move my hands, balling them into fists, but they're restrained. I can't move. His lips are on mine again, licking, tasting, slowly making their way down my neck. I whimper, confounded by the feelings of love and desire that stir inside me.

"Take it off," I breathe.

"No," a whisper replies. His fingers trace the outline of my nipples and down the line of my stomach then glide between my legs, teasing me, tantalizing me, slowly sliding inside me. I whimper, struggling against the restraints, needing to touch him, to watch him as he pleasures my body.

"Take it off," I beg.

Suddenly, I'm blinded by light. I close my eyes while they adjust. He brings his lips down on mine hard and I respond, our tongues twirling, circling, his fingers plunging farther and farther inside me. I gasp, drawing in a deep breath as the scent of his cologne, fierce and raw, fills my nostrils.

I open my eyes and sit up breathless, scanning the room. I'm in my bedroom. I rub my wrists. My hands aren't bound. I'm alone.

I was dreaming.

I throw myself back against the pillows, feeling the dampness between my legs and touch myself there, brushing my fingertips lightly against my underwear as I cling to the images salvaged from my dream.

If Nick were lying beside me right now, I would have him reenact every mouthwatering moment of it, but he's not. I slide off my panties, slipping my fingers between my thighs, circling around and around, forcing them deep inside me, just as Nick showed me. I graze my fingernails against my soft skin and I thrill to the sensation. I keep circling my fingers, searching, exploring until I find a place where it feels just right. I arch my back, whimpering as I flex my hips, moving my fingers faster, thrusting my body against my hand. My temperature rises, the heat inside me spreading through my body like a fever, my head spinning in awe of the way my body responds to its own touch.

I close my eyes, feeling the pull of my excitement deep inside my core. My breathing grows harsh and heavy as I circle faster, thrusting harder against my hand, crying out as the euphoric, exhilarating feeling that I crave courses through my body. Suddenly there I am, in that place that we visit when we leave our bodies for the afterglow.

I reach my other hand up, running it through my hair and down my face to my chest, while I lie there breathless, wanting more. My hand I keep between my legs, stroking slowly, languidly. I long for Nick. I need him, need that feeling again, that high, to come, screaming his name.

My thoughts flash back to my dream, the blindfold, my wrists bound to the bedhead, then suddenly I remember the smell. The cologne so thick that it filled my senses. I sit bolt upright and move to the side of the bed, clutching my chest, knowing the scent, fearing it.

Mitch.

I jump up, wrapping the sheet around me as I pace to the chair by the window. I sit there, clutching the sheet against my chest, looking out as the rain drizzles down, tapping lightly against the glass. I don't understand. It's Nick I want—he's all I want.

I hold my head in my hands, remembering the way I felt in my dream, finding it hard to separate it from reality. I wanted it. I wanted him. *Mitch.* I welcomed his touch. I craved it.

My alarm sounds, startling me. It's nine o'clock. I shake my head, fighting the thought of Mitch, and hurry into the dressing room. Tayla will be here soon.

I get dressed and pull my hair back into a ponytail when I hear a car horn sound downstairs. It's Tayla. She jumps out of the car and waves up to me, her hair windblown and covered in rain.

"Let's go! It's raining cats and dogs down here," she yells.

I look around. I don't see any cats or dogs. Must be another one of those weird sayings. "I'll be right down," I yell back.

I grab my bag and rush downstairs. I can't wait to get to the dealership to pick up my very own new car. I'd planned to go with Tayla to pick out a car myself, but Nick had come across an American import that some big fat cat had ordered through one of his clients and gone broke before delivery, so now it's mine. It feels like Christmas. Of course, I don't know exactly what happens at Christmas yet, but it's approaching fast and getting so very exciting.

People are starting to decorate their houses and the shop owners in town are beginning to hang lights and frost their windows. I can hardly wait. Gabe and Malaylie have taken the boxes of decorations out of the basement and Nick mentioned taking me to buy a tree at the weekend. I dash out to the car, filled with a spirit that cannot be beaten by wind and rain.

"Hi," I giggle as I tumble into the car, wiping the raindrops from my forehead.

"You're very chipper this morning, for such a wet, miserable day."

I flash Tayla my widest smile. "I'm excited. About the car, and about Christmas."

"Oh, yeah, this is like baby's first Christmas for you, isn't it?"

I nod enthusiastically as she pulls out of the driveway onto the street. "Nick's taking me to pick out a tree on the weekend."

"Ooooh, exciting! Things are going well with Nick then, huh?" I blush. "Ah, I knew it. It's written all over your face. Back in the sack, I'd say, by the look of those rosy-red cheeks."

"He's amazing." I grin, biting my bottom lip.

"Good for you. It's good to see you so happy again. You were so miserable there for a while."

"I was?"

"Uh-huh, then right before the accident, you were just plain strange."

"Strange?"

"I probably shouldn't say anything. You seem really happy now and I don't want the past to affect the present. It's of no consequence now, anyway."

"What's of no consequence?"

She shakes her head coyly and I'm suddenly not in the mood for games.

"Tayla, if you know something, please tell me. It may be insignificant to you and I may seem happier than I was, but the truth is, I'm a mess. I don't know who I am or what I'm doing. I'm desperately trying to piece my life back together, but right now it's just a puddle of mud, so please, if you know anything at all, just tell me."

She looks across at me, shaken, as though I've just pulled a pin from a grenade, before reluctantly shifting her gaze back to the road.

"Uh, okay." She pauses before continuing. "Well, I guess it was around two weeks before the accident when I first noticed you were acting strangely. You stopped by the store for a coffee after work, only because I threatened to phone in a bomb scare in your building if you didn't." She smirks. "You seemed really nervous. You kept looking out at the street. I asked you what was going on, but you, being you, wouldn't say. That's the one thing I don't miss about the old you, the borders you put up to keep everyone out." She glances across at me quickly. "No offense."

"None taken."

"So, if that wasn't weird-o-rama enough, about two or three days before your accident, we all went to your cousin Clay's thirty-fifth birthday at the Globe. That was the last time I saw you. Nick was late, he didn't get there till around seven, so Tash and I picked you up. About halfway through the night, you started acting weird. Watching Nick like a hawk, not responding when we talked to you, kind of jumpy and nervous. I asked you what was wrong and you said something really strange."

My brow creases. "What did I say?"

"You said, 'She's going to tell Nick,' then you and Nick just disappeared. Didn't even say goodbye. I rang you the next day to ask you what happened and what you meant by that comment and you said you didn't remember saying it."

I shake my head, deep in thought. Who could *she* possibly be and what could *she* possibly have to tell *Nick*?

"Did I ever tell you anything about my relationship with Nick?"

"Not really. You were pretty tight-lipped when it came to Nick. He barely let you out of his sight, I know that. You were really resentful about that. You'd butt heads about it all the time. I think that's why he's so obsessed with you. You're the one woman he could never control."

"Why would he want to control me?"

The light turns red ahead and she brakes, looking across at me. "I think Nick never really felt he was good enough for you. He's such a strong, confident man, but when it came to you, he was always insecure, always trying to be in charge. And you, with your vibrant personality and rebellious nature, didn't always succumb to his high-handed ways. You loved him deeply, anyone could see that, but sometimes I got the feeling—"

"What?"

She tightens her fingers on the wheel. "I shouldn't say."

"You got the feeling what?"

"I got the feeling you wanted out."

The light turns green and she drives off, neither of us saying a word. I rest my elbow on the armrest, my hand over my mouth. I can barely breathe, shocked that other people could see something so personal.

"I'm sorry, I shouldn't have said anything," she murmurs.

"No. It's fine. I'm glad you told me. I, well, I do see snippets of that kind of behavior from him at times, but I really think he's changed."

"He does seem different." She pauses. "Just remember I'm always here for you if you need to talk."

I look across at her, never having seen her so sincere before. "Thank you."

She indicates and turns the corner, pulling in to the dealership. "Well, here we are," she says, suddenly cheerful. My stomach flutters. Thank goodness, the rain has stopped, the sky lightening to a softer shade of gray, the sun shining sporadically through the gaps between the clouds.

"So how did you convince the doctor to give you an early clearance to drive? I thought you had to wait twelve months."

I wince.

"You didn't ask him, did you?" She puts her hand over her mouth, pretending to be shocked. "Oh. You're such a rebel." She pulls in to a parking space at the end of the lot and shuts off the engine. "I can't believe you're getting a new car — do you even remember how to drive?"

"I've seen it on TV. It can't be that hard."

"Oh, ha-ha," she replies.

I jump out of the car, looking up at the monstrous sign above us. *Dodge.* The manager rushes out to greet us, extending his hand to take mine.

"Good morning. Welcome to Dodge. I'm Rafael. How may I be of assistance to you lovely ladies this morning?"

I shake his hand. "Hi, my name is Scarlet Pierce."

His cool, calm exterior suddenly shifts into first gear. "Oh, Mrs. Pierce, of course! How lovely to finally meet you. We've spoken on the phone."

I nod graciously, but no matter how many times people address me as Mrs. Pierce, I still find myself fighting the urge to spin around, looking for her. I'm just Scarlet. Plain and simple.

"This is my good friend, Tayla Northman."

Rafael holds out his hand to Tayla, taking it in his. "It's an absolute pleasure to make your acquaintance."

I roll my eyes like billiard balls as Tayla bats her eyelashes, engaging him with all her usual seduction techniques. I need to walk her in front of a mirror—the wind is pretty ferocious today and her hair's wild like something out of *Fright Night*. She'd die if she knew. I giggle to myself.

"Is she ready to go?" I interrupt.

He nods, grinning from ear to ear. "She is. She's just been registered, polished, the seats are warm and she's just chomping at the bit for you to take her for a spin." He gestures toward the back. "This way."

He ushers us through the showroom, when I spot a mirror. I push Tayla in front of it. Her jaw drops.

"Jesus Christ, what the— Look at this head."

"I've seen it!" I reply, hardly able to contain my laughter.

She snarls at me, snatching at her hair, pushing it back into place. I rush to catch up to Rafael, who's leading us into the holding bay, and there she is. My big, shiny new candy-apple-red Challenger. She's the most beautiful thing I've ever seen, perhaps more beautiful than Nick, and she too is all mine.

"There she is, the SRT Hellcat. Six-point-two liter V8, seven-oh-seven horsepower, six-hundred-and-fifty pounds of torque. Custom paint, custom exhaust and twenty-inch custom wheels. She's one of a kind."

Tayla stops in her tracks. "Holy shit!"

I stand there beaming like the sun as one of the salesmen

approaches, handing me the remote and opening the door for me. I rush over and jump in. The seat is so comfortable and warm. I tighten my hands around the steering wheel, tracing my fingertips along the intricate stitching on the seams of the fabric. Then I lean forward, sniffing the steering wheel.

"What are you doing?" Tayla asks.

"Smelling the leather."

She raises her eyebrow into the shape of a question mark. "On the steering wheel? How odd."

Tayla doesn't share my enthusiasm when it comes to cars. The mere mention of a new car warrants a tired old speech about how a car is to transport her from Point A to Point B and it doesn't matter what it looks like as long as it gets her there. A speech people who can't afford shiny new cars know by heart.

I run my hands across the dashboard then down over the soft leather seats, intoxicated by the new car smell surrounding me. This memory I was in no danger of forgetting.

Rafael crouches down beside me. "That's Nappa leather and Alcantara suede. The seats are heated front and rear. Everything is digital. An eight-point-four-inch touchscreen display, GPS, wi-fi, a stand-alone mitigation system and press button start." He motions toward the Start button and I eagerly reach out and press it.

The engine roars to life, a deep, soul-rattling vibration rumbling through the chassis to the seat beneath me. I tap the accelerator and she wails out a war cry, gently rocking from side to side. My eyes open wider, flickering with excitement. My heart pumps pure adrenaline through my veins and I am high on the fumes. I can't wipe the ridiculous smile off my face.

"Any questions?"

I shake my head. Rafael stands swiftly, stepping back then closing my door. "Be careful, that's a lot of power."

"I will. Thank you. Do I need to sign anything?"

"Your husband's taken care of everything. Just enjoy."

"All right! This calls for a celebration." Tayla shouts over the pulsing hum of the engine.

"Yes!" I shout back.

"I'll meet you at the Cypress."

"Sounds good—see you there."

I wave as I drive out, the exhaust rumbling and ricocheting off the concrete walls in the holding bay. I idle out of the driveway toward the street, scared but exhilarated. There's a break in the traffic, one of those do-or-die moments, and I stomp on the throttle, opening up all eight American-made cylinders. The back wheels spin, fighting to gain traction as they propel me way too quickly out onto the rain-slicked tar. An elderly lady on the sidewalk grabs her chest and shakes her head at me frantically. A huge smile spreads across my face. I feel terrible but elated at the same time. It's a tough tradeoff.

I lower my window, feeling the wind in my face.

This is living.

I do my best to escape the traffic, turning down side streets and heading out of the city, so I can feel the freedom of being behind the wheel of my very own car. It's better than I imagined. Heads turn everywhere I look, watching my big red warhorse stampeding through town, eating up the bitumen as if she owns it.

Regretfully, I indicate and turn back to the Cypress, our favorite haunt, to meet Tayla for lunch, though all I want to do is head for the hills, screeching the wheels all the way. I tap the accelerator again, my pleasure plastered across my face. There truly is something wonderful about having such power underfoot.

Against my will, I park down a side street near the pub and rush to meet Tayla. We have lunch, but my shiny new remote on the table in front of me wins out. I make up an excuse about running errands to get back to my car quicker, and we leave. As we walk through the bar on our way out, ducking and weaving through people and tables, a glass smashes nearby, diverting my attention. I gaze around the room as people shout words such as *taxi, time to go, last drinks*, and spot him instantly. My heart stops, every muscle in my body tightening.

Mitch.

He's sitting with the female police officer friend of his and four other men, some of them in police uniforms. The woman leans against him, laughing, and he puts his arm around her, whispering in her ear. I swallow hard, a strange feeling sweeping over me. He doesn't see me. I turn quickly back to Tayla, increasing my speed. As we reach the front door, I hug her goodbye and rush toward the car, clutching the remote tightly in my hand.

Almost there.

My heart starts drumming out an intro at a rock concert. I'm almost certain Mitch didn't see me, but not certain enough to glance over my shoulder to check.

"Scarlet," I hear behind me.

Damn! I close my eyes, instantly recognizing his voice, and turn around slowly. "Mitch."

I try to act surprised, though my acting skills failed dismally on all previous attempts.

"What are you doing here?" I ask.

He gestures over his shoulder toward the bar. "I was having a few drinks with some friends from the station and I spotted you leaving."

"Right. Yeah, I just grabbed a bite to eat with Tayla."

"I saw Tayla, yeah."

I dip my head, unsure what to say.

"I'm sorry about the other night, showing up at the dinner. That must have been really uncomfortable for you, but your mother wouldn't take no for an answer."

"Oh, don't I know it."

His eyes soften with humor. "I've got something for you," he says, reaching into his pocket. He pulls out his wallet, takes out a folded piece of paper and holds it out to me.

"What is it?" I ask curiously, stepping forward and taking

149

it.

"It's a copy of the police report from your accident."

"Oh, right. Thank you." I unfold the paper, skimming over the page before tucking it into my purse.

"I thought it might help."

I nod, looking quickly over my shoulder, anxious to leave.

"Well. I should probably get going." I turn to go.

"Scarlet," he says sternly.

I stop, slowly turning back to face him.

"Can't we talk about this?"

"There's nothing to talk *about*, Mitch."

"Come on, Scar! You've seen the pictures—what do I have to do to prove myself to you?"

"You don't have to prove anything to me."

He groans. "Scarlet, please."

My eyes narrow. "Have you been calling the house?"

"What?"

"Have you been calling my house and hanging up?"

He frowns. "Someone's calling your house and hanging up?"

I clutch my remote tightly in my hand, pressing it by accident, and it beeps, the car lights flashing. He looks up at the noise.

"You got a new car?"

"Yeah, Nick bought it for me."

He rolls his eyes. "Compensating for something?"

"Look, I really have to go." I turn toward the car and suddenly he's in front of me, seizing my upper arms.

"Just talk to me, Scarlet."

"I can't! I can't do this, Mitch. I promised Nick I'd have nothing more to do with you." I reach up, clutching at his hands, and he tightens his fingers around my arms.

"Please, Scarlet. Don't do this. You're breaking my heart."

"That's not my intention."

His eyes fill with hurt, anger, pain.

"I'm sorry, Mitch, I just don't remember the things you do."

"So, what? You think I'm making all this up? Why would I do that, Scarlet?" he hisses.

"I don't know. I don't know what to believe. You haven't exactly been honest with me. You didn't tell me you were a police officer. What else are you keeping from me? For all I know, this could all be just one big lie."

His eyes grow darker. He pushes me back against the car, his body pinning me between them. Mitch brings his mouth down on mine, his lips powerful and determined, forcing his tongue inside my mouth, lashing mine, as though punishing me for forgetting him.

I bring my hands up between us, pushing back with all my strength, but he's too powerful. Tears well in my eyes. I whimper, pounding my fists against his chest, but he stands fast, his body unmoving. Out of breath, I stop fighting him. I stop *wanting* to fight him.

He senses my surrender and releases my arms, sliding his hands up to my throat and sweeping his lips softly against mine. My body quivers, my arms hanging limp by my sides. He kisses me, once, twice, three times, then pulls back to look at me, breathless. His eyes pierce my heart, staring straight into my soul.

"Is that a lie?" he snaps.

I stare up at him, not moving, my breathing ragged.

He pushes back from me abruptly and walks away, leaving me standing there in the street, weak, overwhelmed and wanting.

No. It's not a lie.

Chapter Ten

Sweet Surrender

The light is dim. I fall to the floor, looking at the carpet beneath me, and push up with my elbows. I hear Nick shouting my name and I'm frozen with fear. I scan my surroundings – I'm in our bedroom. I swipe at my tears, looking for somewhere to hide. He shouts my name again and a wave of fear surges through my body. He's close. I try to get up, but I hear him behind me. It's too late. He's found me. I cower at the foot of the bed as he towers over me, his hand raised. He's angry, so angry. He shouts down at me. I close my eyes, waiting for the pain, but the shouting stops, replaced by silence.

I feel a cool breeze sweep over my skin and open my eyes, breathless. Nick is gone, but my fear is still imminent. I sit up, looking around the room. The wind howls through the open window, another cool gust of air breezing over me. I shudder, looking down at the bed beside me as my eyes adjust to the darkness. Nick is sound asleep, lying on his stomach, far from angry.

Another dream.

I recline back against my pillow, pulling the blankets up over me, wanting to run but too afraid to move. Moonlight streams in through the glass panes of the terrace doors, the trees in its path swaying gently in the breeze, animating their silhouettes in the shadows on the carpet, like ghosts of the past reaching out for me in the night. I feel Nick move beside me and glance across at him anxiously, filled with dread that he might wake. The desperate rhythm of my heart echoes in my ears. My head hurts. I lie there completely still, reeling, watching his chest rise and fall as he sleeps. I hope it wasn't a memory, though most things I've dreamed so far have been. I desperately want to roll over, but I'm afraid that I might wake him.

Don't be ridiculous. It's just a dream. I'm not going to be afraid of my own husband.

I huff loudly, then roll over, and over, despite myself, until eventually finding sleep.

The next morning, I wake to the sound of the alarm. Nick stirs, then bangs his hand on the top of the alarm clock until it stops. My eyes spring open, the terrifying Nick in my dream still so present. Thankfully, my back is to him. The bed moves, then the shower runs and I find myself thankful there's distance between us. After a minute, the shower stops and I hear him in the dressing room. I lie there, praying he doesn't try to wake me.

What is wrong with me? So much for last words.

I let him get dressed for work and leave, then throw back the covers, reliving the dream. I keep seeing Nick's face, his eyes red, his hand raised. So many questions and doubts fighting at the forefront of my mind. Mitch is adamant there was a second car behind me that night.

What if someone did try to kill me? What if it was Nick?

I shake my head. I don't believe that for a second. Nick loves me. I look across at our picture on the bedside table. *It wasn't him.* I roll over, thinking about yesterday, my encounter with Mitch gnawing at the edge of my consciousness. The darkness in his eyes, the intense power of his kiss, his hands on my throat, his body pressed against mine. So wrong on so many levels, but it felt so right. Even thinking about it feels wrong. *It can't happen again.*

I glance across at the terrace doors. The weather looks beautiful outside, too beautiful to lie in bed. I jump up and walk into the dressing room, flicking through the daunting rows of dresses and skirts, but today I really can't bothered. I spot the string of my bikini hanging out of my drawer. *Perfect.* I put it on and slip on a pair of shorts and head downstairs.

As I walk into the kitchen, I find Gabe and Malaylie flittering around preparing to leave. Malaylie scoops up the dry cleaning while Gabe collects the rubbish to take outside before they head to the shops to pick up some groceries and run errands. I assure them I'll be fine and order them to stop someplace nice and have lunch together today. *Matchmaking?* Meddling, maybe—who can blame me? They're just so darn cute together.

So much has been happening lately I'm just glad to have some time alone. I spend the day around the pool, reading and thinking, thinking and reading. The thinking, not so great, the image of Nick raising his hand to me insisting on rearing its ugly head while Mitch's kiss continues to monopolize my mind. I throw my book down on the table. I'm not taking any of it in, anyway, when I notice a piece of paper sticking out of the pages. I take it out of the book, unfolding it. *The police report from my accident.* I'd completely forgotten about it. I lean back in my chair, skipping through the document to the notes at the bottom.

It reads—

Note: Witness 1. (see appendix 1.) alleges there was a second vehicle involved, following Unit 1 too closely, possibly an older style, dark-colored vehicle, no plate provided, partial or otherwise due to poor lighting and wet weather. Road conditions: Wet and slippery. Unit 1, vehicle extensively damaged, predominantly front and rear. Rear damage? Impact of Unit 2, no evidence from Traffic Accident Investigators to confirm. At this stage, accident ruled as accidental. Unit 1, single occupant, 28 yo female, driver, suffering from traumatic head injuries, transported to University Hospital via QAS. Vehicle recovered, held in compound until further notice. TAIS attended. No further information.

I throw the report down on the table, clutching my forehead, the second car weighing heavily on my mind. The thought of someone forcing me off the road, someone trying to hurt me, or *kill* me, inconceivable, terrifying. I stand, about to head inside, when my cell phone rings.

It's Nick.

"Hello," I answer timidly.

"Hello, beautiful wife. I thought you'd be out in your new car for sure."

"No, not today. Just relaxing around the pool."

"I almost took it to work today instead of the Benz. Did you hear me take it for a strap this morning? Red-lined it all the way up the street."

"*What?*"

He lets out a sharp, devious laugh. "Just kidding. I did take it for a quick spin, though. I'll put it through its paces tonight when I get home."

"You wish."

He laughs harder. "I'm sorry I left without saying goodbye this morning. I know you haven't been getting much sleep, so I didn't wake you."

"Mmmh, thank you."

"Listen, I've got a prospective new client, a *big* prospective new client, coming in at three-thirty. I don't think we'll be wrapped up until five-thirty and if all goes well with the deal, I'll have to do drinks and kiss ass for a couple of hours, so…"

"So I'll either see you at six o'clock or ten o'clock."

"I'm sorry, sweetheart."

"It's fine. I'll be okay."

He pauses. "Are you all right?"

"Yeah, just had another dream, that's all."

"A bad one?"

"You could say that."

"About the accident?"

"Uh, I'll tell you when you get home tonight."

"Tell me now, I've got time," he insists.

"No, it's not something to talk about on the phone."

"Now you've got me worried."

"Don't. We'll talk tonight. Good luck with your client."

"Okay. Thanks. I'll see you later."

"Yep. Bye."

"Bye, beautiful," he says softly, his concern evident.

I hang up, staring down at the phone, my thoughts reverting to Mitch, the accident, the car behind me, him and me, the dream. So many questions and I know who more than likely has the answers. I need to call him. I *have* to call him.

No! I promised Nick I wouldn't see him again. Although I have already seen him. But that wasn't my fault. Surely that doesn't count. Does it?

I groan, then stand and dive into the pool, swimming — no, struggling — to the other end. I promised myself after the accident I'll learn to swim, and though I'm trying, I really wouldn't dignify it by calling it swimming. It's more a hybrid of dog paddling and leg spasms until eventually sinking below the surface then coming up gasping for air. I finally reach the other end, wiping the water from my eyes, but the instant they can see again, they betray me — I stare at the phone.

I hop out of the pool and lie down on the daybed, closing my eyes, enjoying the warmth of the sun on my face. I love the sun, the way I feel after a day around the pool — somehow calmer, clearer, brighter. How my skin looks so brown, exuding a youthful, radiant glow. They say too much sun's no good for us but I'm not so sure. Anything that makes me feel this good can't be all that bad.

Skin cancer? Somehow, that seems so much less important than the things I have weighing on my mind right now. I pick up my book before throwing it right back down. I can't deal with Cathy and her suffering without Heathcliff today. I have enough problems of my own. Again, the phone catches my attention.

That's it.

I snatch it in my hand and jump up, running through the house to the foyer, skidding to a stop in front of the end table. I pull the drawers open, rummaging for Mitch's card. Paperwork and keys spill out everywhere onto the floor, then there it is. I hesitate before picking it up, as if it's a key to a room I'd been warned not to open. A curse or salvation. I wasn't sure. I look down at his name printed on the watermarked white card and walk into the lounge, setting the card down on the coffee table with my phone. I stare at the number, tucking my hands under my legs to stop them from trembling. I need to think this through.

Once I do this, it's done and there's no turning back. This would be *me* making contact. *Me* going against Nick's wishes. *My* fault if anything goes wrong. There are so many reasons not to call him, so many reasons to rip the card up and throw it away, but that won't answer these nagging questions in my head. I can't fight it any longer. I pick up the phone and tap in his number. He answers on the third ring.

"Morgan," he snaps, his voice so stern that I almost hang up.

"Mitch?"

"Yes," he replies, distracted.

"It's Scarlet."

He doesn't respond.

"I need to talk to you." Still silence. "In person. Is that possible at all? Now?"

"Uh…" He hesitates. "Sure. Yeah. I can get away. How about my place, the boatyard, in about twenty minutes?"

"Okay."

"Okay," he replies softly.

I hang up, my head spinning, wondering what the hell I've just done, but there's no time for a postmortem. I have to go. I rush upstairs to the bedroom to get changed, dressing quickly and practically running to the car. I'm nervous. So nervous.

I fly out of the driveway onto the street, narrowly missing a dark-colored car pulling into the cul-de-sac. We're the only driveway in the street so there's not normally any traffic when I pull out. I look back in the rear-vision mirror, wondering if it's going to our house. The car turns around at the end of the street, driving back out. I dismiss it, turning onto the main road, toward the motorway. I drive fast, my mind deep in thought, my heart in my throat as I take his exit.

The boatyard driveway comes into view just ahead. I can't believe I got there so quickly. I barely remember making the trip, changing lanes, turning corners…it's all a blur.

I pull into the lot, searching for his truck. He's not here yet. I glance back at the rearview mirror and notice a dark car driving slowly past the yard. I slam my foot on the brake, looking over my shoulder, wondering if it's the same dark car I saw at the house. *It can't be. I drove too fast.*

I park right at the entrance, looking around anxiously as I step out of the car. The sun is sinking fast, fading to a faint orange glow, the sky bruised in pinks and blues. The boatyard feels more deserted than usual today and I shiver at the touch of the late-afternoon haze settling in all around me. I hear a car approaching and turn around to see Mitch's big black Chevy pulling into the lot, instantly relieving my anxiety. He gets out of the truck, wearing a police uniform. I swallow hard, unable to tear my gaze from him. He waves but doesn't smile, striding quickly toward me.

"Is everything okay?" he asks as he gets closer.

I nod, glancing down briefly, a strange feeling stirring in the pit of my stomach.

He stops just inches in front of me, bowing his head down to mine. "What's going on?" he asks, softly.

He's close, so close.

"I…" I let my gaze drift down the fold of his shirt, to the police badge on his chest, and I falter. "You're in uniform. I thought…" I shake my head. "You said you weren't a police officer anymore."

He looks down, running his hand over his uniform as though he forgot he was wearing it. "Uh, yeah. They offered me Senior Sergeant. Heading up a new squad. It was too good an offer to turn down." He shrugs. "It's been a welcome distraction, actually."

I tuck an errant strand of hair behind my ear.

"Are you okay?" he asks.

"Yeah, I just needed to talk to you for a minute. To ask you a couple of questions."

"Okay. Sure. Do you wanna come inside?" He doesn't wait for me to answer. He turns swiftly, unlocking the door, then steps inside.

I follow him, scanning the room. It's a huge space, but surprisingly warm and inviting with its rustic timber floors and red rum-colored walls. The brick feature wall in the center of the room draws my eye upward and I tilt my head back to see dozens of small wooden boats floating above me, suspended by thick woven ropes from the aged timber rafters overhead.

I gasp. "My God. Are these all boats you've made?"

He throws his keys down on the desk. "Uh, yeah. Except for the mounted boats on the wall. Those my grandfather made."

I look across at him. "Your grandfather taught you to make these?"

"Taught me a lot of things. He was a great man."

"Your dad, did he make boats, too?"

He raises his brow. "No. My dad was a cop, actually. He, uh, died when I was five."

"Oh, I'm sorry. I didn't—"

"It's okay. I don't really remember him, so it's, yeah, it is what it is."

"How did it happen?"

His eyes glaze over, suffused simultaneously with love and pain. "He, uh, drowned, actually." He reaches up, rubbing the back of his neck. "He and my grandfather were out fishing and the weather turned bad and, yeah, my grandfather came home, my father didn't. My grandfather always blamed himself. Made his life's work designing better, stronger boats."

I can't look away. "I'm very sorry about your father."

"Me, too."

"What about your mother?"

He unbuckles his gun belt and puts it down on the desk in front of him.

"My mother died when I was ten. My grandfather raised Matty and me on his own."

"Is your grandfather…?" I pause, unable to say the word.

"No, he died about four years ago now, but I still feel him here." He casts his gaze around the room. "This was his place. I've made a few changes, modernized the front and put in an apartment out back, but it's pretty much how he left it." He touches his finger to the corner of his eye.

I swallow hard, a crushing heaviness in my heart. "Are you okay?"

"Yeah, I'm fine. That's the tradeoff when you lose people you love. Tears on tap." He crinkles his eyes at the corners. "That would have to be the one good thing about losing your memory, to not know loss or grief."

I bow my head. "I'm sorry, that was insensitive."

"No. It's fine. It's just that it's quite the opposite, actually."

"What do you mean?"

I pause before answering. "I just think that, things that really hurt us, stay with us, etched into our skin forever. Memory or no memory, the sadness remains."

He nods. "Memories hurt. Especially the good ones."

We stand there, staring at each other, neither of us speaking. I break the spell, looking at the boats above me.

"So you make these for people?"

"Only for certain people, and only if it's for the right reasons. Mounting boats I don't do, but if they're going to love it and respect it as I would, I build one here and there, for a hefty price. But it's not about that. It's more a hobby than anything. When you start doing what you love for money, you tend to lose the love along the way."

He walks around to my side of the desk, taking off his tie and undoing the top two buttons of his shirt. I watch him, my lips parting, the uniform unnerving, my reaction alarming.

"Have a seat," he says, pulling out a chair from the front

of his desk.

I drift toward him and sit down.

"So, what did you want to know?" he asks, taking a seat beside me. His scent fills my nostrils. A thick, musky manly smell that completely disarms me, leaving me sitting mindlessly in front of him, summoning sense.

"Uh, I've been having dreams. The most recent one, last night, was about Nick. And me."

He leans back in his seat, folding his arms across his chest.

"I fell down on the floor. Nick was standing above me. He was so angry, shouting. I was crying, cowering beneath him. He raised his hand as though he was going to hit me and I screamed and that's it. I woke up."

He glowers at me, not moving, not saying a word. I swallow hard, waiting for something, anything, but he says nothing. He stands abruptly and walks over to the window, staring out at the street.

"I've had others," I continue. "But this is the most confronting."

He turns back to me, his eyes ablaze. "Have you told *him* about this?"

I shake my head.

"But you're telling *me*."

"Because I need to know what you know."

"But you said you didn't *want* to know. You said you were *happy* with him."

My bottom lip begins to quiver, tears pooling in my eyes.

He closes his eyes briefly. "Oh, God. I'm sorry, Scar. Please don't cry."

But I do. I can't stop myself. He strides across the room and resumes his seat beside me.

"It's so hard to see you like this," he says.

I breathe deeper, trying to control my tears. He reaches his hand out to mine then screws it up into a fist and brings it down hard on his knee.

"What do you want to know?" he asks, his voice filled with despair.

"Everything. How we met, how long we were together…"

He exhales loudly then nods. "A friend of mine, Kurt Timmins, used to work for you as a contract bodyguard for one of your political clients. His wife got sick, he resigned to take care of her and recommended me to take over. You called me, asking me to meet you at your office, said you were expanding your security division, searching for someone to head up the department. Looking for someone you could trust."

He leans back in his chair. "I really didn't have the time, or inclination, but you seemed really nice and Kurt's a good friend of mine. I didn't want to let him down, so I gathered a list of interested coworkers and I met with you a couple of weeks later at your office to discuss the terms. Our connection was instant." He shakes his head. "The moment I laid eyes on you, I was lost. You were and always will be the most beautiful woman I've ever known. Smart, sophisticated, but not arrogant, not caught up in all the bullshit, really down to Earth.

"We worked together for around three months, getting the new branch off the ground, meeting up frequently to discuss new clients, contracts, stuff like that. We never spoke about it at the time, but there was definitely something between us. The chemistry was undeniable, but I was seeing someone, you were married—there didn't seem any point in talking about it, but one day, things changed between us."

"Changed?"

He nods. "I came to your office late one afternoon, unannounced, dropping off pay claims. There was hardly anyone there. Your assistant was gone, your door was open and I walked in. You were standing by the window, this incredible sadness in your eyes. I asked you if you were okay and you started crying. I reached my hand out to sweep the hair from your eyes and you flinched. You reacted like every other abuse victim I've ever met, jumpy, anxious, impulsive." He raises his shoulders. "I suspected.

But you were one tough cookie to crack. I started calling to check on you, pressing you about what was going on. Finally, you let me in. Just a little, just enough. He treated you more like a possession than a wife. He controlled you, wouldn't let you do anything you wanted to do, wouldn't let you go out with your friends, always jealous, always suspicious. The only time he let you out of his sight was when you were both at work, and even then…"

My mind recoils, Tayla's words echoing in my ear.

His voice grows deep and low. "We became friends, good friends. The more time I spent with you, the more you opened up to me. You said he'd changed, that he lost his temper a lot, that he had violent mood swings. He was under a lot of pressure at work and you thought he might be taking something to help him cope. You were adamant that he'd never hit you, that you didn't think he was capable of hitting you, but I wasn't so sure." He looks away, his words clearly affecting him.

"The dynamics in our relationship started to change. You began taking time off work, meeting me for coffee, then for lunches. Then one day, you agreed to come out on the boat and one thing led to another. It was an amazing day. A day I'll never forget."

I bow my head, the evil clutches of my transgressions taking hold.

"Our relationship grew stronger and stronger, seeing each other as often as we could over the next three months. It was the best three months of my life, but also the worst. I grew increasingly concerned about Nick's behavior, always worried that he might hurt you. I developed this gut-wrenching desire to protect you from him. To never let things get that far." His eyes grow intense and consuming. "I started developing feelings for you, feelings I'd never felt before. When I was with you, I couldn't get close enough to you. When I wasn't with you, I couldn't think of anything *but* you. Everything else was just noise. Nothing mattered anymore, not work, not the boats, not the girl I was seeing at the time, only you." He rests his hand on mine.

"And I mattered to *you*, Scar."

I glance down at our hands in my lap, feeling my pulse quicken. He shifts in his seat, retracting his hand as though he senses my anxiety.

"You came to me about two weeks before the accident. Told me pretty much what you just told me in your dream, that you'd had a fight, that he'd chased you through the house, he was angry, he threatened you, raised his hand to you."

"Do you know what we were fighting about?"

"You didn't answer your cell, he didn't know where you were. When he finally got a hold of you, you told him you were in your office, but you weren't. You were with me. He was the one in your office."

He straightens his back. "He knew you'd lied to him. He accused you of having an affair, tore the house apart, smashed everything in it. Things weren't the same after that. *You* weren't the same after that. If you came here to ask me if he hit you, I don't know. You would never have told me if he did, because you knew what I would have done to him.

"He was close to finding out about us. I begged you to leave him, to be with me, and finally, you agreed. The night of the accident, you decided to tell him. I wanted to go with you but you said it would only make it worse, so I drove with you to the fiveways near the lake and waited for you to call." He stands abruptly, walking over to the window, his back to me.

"When you called, you were crying, hysterical. I couldn't understand what you were saying, but I could hear your car in the background. I jumped in my truck and drove toward you. That's when I saw your car go off the road into the lake. There was a car right behind you, a dark-colored car, but I didn't get a good look at it, I was too busy trying to get down to the water to get you. Your car was sinking—" He stops abruptly, his words choking him.

He turns back to look at me, his eyes red, his face pale and there, in that one unguarded moment, I see him, for all that he is, for everything that made him the wondrous man standing before me and everything I'd lost.

I stand and walk toward him, taking his hand in mine. "I wouldn't be here if it wasn't for you."

"I'd never let that happen," he murmurs, his wounded eyes stained by the darkness that divided us.

"You think he did this to me, don't you?" He doesn't answer. "But Nick's car is silver."

"Yes, but your estate car, the Lexus, is black."

I close my mouth, his words resonating in my mind. *It can't be Nick. It just can't be. But what if it is?* I'm suddenly angry at him, angry at him raising his hand to me, for every errant look, for every lie.

"There's something I want you to see," Mitch murmurs, his soothing voice surmounting my anger. He leads me to a door at the other end of his office, pausing before opening it. "This is my apartment," he says, letting go of my hand and passing through the doorway.

I hesitate, then drift slowly toward him.

The room opens up to a cozy living space with a timber kitchen and an old-fashioned wood-fired heater in the corner, a basket of logs sitting by its side. A rustic red-brick feature wall lined with guitars sits in the center of the room, dividing the kitchen from the lounge. The exterior windows and doors arch, features in their own right that look out over the boatyard to the river beyond. He stands by the couch to my right, watching, waiting, as I take in the wall in front of me. A wall full of canvases.

Pictures of us. Mitch and I, together.

I step forward, studying each picture closely. He and I aboard his boat, laughing, scuba diving, cuddling on the deck. But there's one that captures my eye, captures my heart.

We're both wearing sunglasses—mine are tipped to my nose, revealing my eyes. My hair's windblown, my face glowing. Mitch stands by my side, kissing my cheek. The sun glistens off the water behind us and bounces off my hair. Something's familiar about it.

He reaches down, taking my hand in his, and I start breathing again. I didn't even realize I'd stopped. I stand there, completely still, staring at the pictures.

"Sometimes if I stare at them long enough, you walk right out of them and into my dreams."

He places my hand on his heart as if it's a scar, a wound that I inflicted and only I can heal.

"We were in love, Scarlet. Crazy love. We were *wild*, like the sea. You don't remember us, but you feel us, I know you do."

I can smell his scent, feel his breath on my face. He touches his lips to mine, just once, then retreats just an inch. Mitch keeps his eyes on mine, enthusiastic but unsure. I don't move. I can't move. He parts his lips just a little, sweeping them against mine again, once, twice. I quiver, so uncertain of what I'm feeling. He rests his forehead against mine, our breathing erratic.

"What do you want?" he whispers.

His words ripple through my body, through my mind, threatening the balance of my entire world. My subconscious steps in, biting hard, its venom stinging, wanting him to kiss me, but knowing it's wrong. I'm married. I took a vow. Whether I remember taking it or not doesn't change anything. It's not right to want him like this.

I press my hands firmly against his chest. Neither of us moves. I let my gaze linger on his neck then slowly rise to his lips.

"Do you have any idea how hard it's been for me to stay away from you?"

My eyes meet his and he responds. He seizes my arms in his hands, bringing his mouth down on mine in a frenzied attack, demanding and determined. He forces his swift, powerful tongue inside my mouth, taking mine prisoner. It's too much. My hands are still on his chest, and I press against him, but he's too strong. He wraps his arms around me, holding me tightly to him, pressing his body against mine.

I turn my face from his, pushing back from him with all my strength. He stares down at me, breathless, his eyes burning into mine.

"Mitch. Let me go."

He ignores me, drifting his gaze slowly down my face, to my chest, watching my breasts rise and fall with each ragged breath. He lowers his mouth to my ear. "You want this as much as I do," he whispers.

"I don't. That's not why I'm here!"

He pulls his head back from mine, studying my face.

"I mean it. Let go of me!"

He glares down at me, then releases me.

"You just don't get it, do you? The girl you're in love with doesn't exist anymore!"

He turns, slamming the chair beside him into the kitchen bench. "You do exist, goddamn it! You're here. Flesh and bone, standing in front of me as beautiful as the morning sun, and I love you. I love you, but I can't touch you. It kills me, Scarlet."

"I can't listen to this." I turn, toward the door and he moves in front of me. "Mitch, don't do this. Just let me go."

"Where are you gonna go, Scarlet? Back to *him*? Back to the man who you're so unsure of that you came running here to me? He's probably watching you right now. He probably knows you're here!"

"Why would you agree to meet me if you thought that? Is that what you want? You want him to see us together? *Why?* Why would you deliberately try to make things harder for me?"

"Harder for *you*? Do you have any idea, any concept at all, how hard this has been for *me*? To face each day without you? To lie in bed at night, thinking that his hands might be on you, that his arms might be around you, that he's inside you?"

I ball my hands up into fists. "What do you want from me? *I don't remember.* Do you think I'm intentionally blocking it out?"

"But you remember something," he interrupts.

Tears bead on my lashes and I hold my stare, knowing if I blink, they'll fall like rain.

"Do you see me in your dreams?" I look away, but he turns my face back to his.

"You see me. I know you do. Do you see me touching you? Making love to you? What do you see?" he whispers, his voice like hands on my body, stripping me of my armor. I part my lips, unable to breathe. He sees me crumbling and moves.

Mitch forces me back against the wall behind me, pressing his body firmly against mine, pinning my wrists. I gasp as he brings his mouth down on my mine, flicking his tongue at my lips, begging me to surrender, but I resist.

He pulls his head back to look at me, his eyes warning, threatening, then attacks, engulfing my mouth, biting down on my bottom lip, tugging hard. I wince, shocked by the intensity of his kiss. He caresses my lip with his tongue, soothing his bite, then forces it inside my mouth, circling mine, cornering it, stealing my will to fight.

He senses my impending surrender and presses his body firmly against mine so I feel his hard, threatening erection between us. My mind ventures to a place I know I shouldn't go. A place with no yesterdays, no tomorrows, only here and now. This moment. Him and me. A jolting spike of adrenaline rushes through me, my knees weak, my thighs damp, my body betraying me. I close my eyes, trembling and needy. I want him.

I return his kiss, moving my lips with his, slipping my tongue inside his mouth. He releases my wrists, clutching me to him, and I wrap my arms around his neck, hungry for more. He groans, gliding his hands down my body, eagerly clutching at my top, tugging it free of my skirt. Mitch draws his mouth down my neck and slides his hand under my shirt, caressing my breasts, tracing the outline of my bra and brushing against my firm, erect nipples. I tilt my head back and close my eyes for him to glide his powerful tongue up and down my throat while caressing my soft skin with his lips.

He lifts my shirt up and I raise my arms willingly as he forces it up over my head and undoes my bra, throwing it to the floor. He stares down at me, his eyes euphoric, glorying in the sight of my nakedness.

"You are the most beautiful thing I've ever seen," he whispers.

He brings his mouth to mine, gliding his hands down my hips. He thrusts against me and my breath hitches in my throat, craving his bare-naked body against mine. I trail my fingers in the fabric of his uniform to the folds of his shirt, undoing his buttons one by one, revealing his broad, toned chest.

He reaches up, tearing the shirt from his body, his hungry mouth lunging at mine and nipping at my lips before he tilts his head and strikes again, wild and wolfish.

He takes my hand in his, rubbing it over his hard, ready shaft straining against his pants, then groans, staring down at me, his eyes glowing. Mitch reaches behind me to my zipper, slipping off my skirt with my panties, pulling me to him as they fall freely to the floor. I unbuckle his belt and undo his zipper, slipping my fingers inside his underwear, taking him in my hand, stroking, marveling at his strength and magnificent size.

This will be interesting.

He watches me, curling his lips up at the corners, relishing my reaction. I tighten my grip around him, pulling hard just once. His breath rushes from his body as he tilts his head back, clutching at my hips.

"Come here."

He lifts me up with his strong arms and I wrap my arms and legs around him, taking my mouth to his, clinging to him, shivering, spellbound by his power, his authority over me. He turns swiftly, carrying me to the bedroom then lowering me to the bed beneath us.

He anchors his arms on either side of my head, pressing his body firmly against mine. He grinds his huge, rigid cock against me and I look up at him, terrified by my lustful desire to feel him inside me. Mitch sweeps his lips against mine, his kiss gentle and tender. He trails his hand down the line of my hips then between my thighs, urging my legs apart while he makes his way down my body with his eager tongue, forcing it inside me, licking me, tasting me, diving deeper and deeper.

"Mmm, you taste incredible," he groans, teasing me with his fingers then plunging them inside me. I gasp, throwing my head back against the pillows. He circles his thumb, flicks his tongue, his fingers multiplying in number with each stroke. He increases the pressure, spreading his fingers apart each time he draws back. I whimper as my skin strains against his hand. I've never experienced anything like it. It hurts, but it feels good at the same time. He watches me intently, his eyes softening.

"I have to do this or you'll never be able to take me inside you," he whispers.

Oh, God.

I tilt my head back, closing my eyes, crying out as he continues working me, stretching my skin. I arch my back, thrusting my hips against his hand, opening my legs to him as he plunges his fingers deeper.

Suddenly, I feel like Little Red Riding Hood inviting the big bad wolf into my home, only this is his home, so I guess that makes me the wolf. My eyes flash open. I bring his face to mine, kissing him with a wild, demonic lust, summoned from the dark side of my soul, wanting him, needing him deep inside me. I flex and tighten around his fingers, moaning into his mouth as the compulsion, the fever, the strength of his power-driven strokes consumes me.

"Oh, Mitch, Oh, my God!" I cry, squeezing my eyes shut and clutching him to me as I come harder and louder than ever before.

"*Scar*," he breathes, his strokes growing slow and deliberate.

I open my eyes. He withdraws his fingers, moving his body on top of mine. He looks down at me, his eyes filled with fire, spreading my legs open wider. I feel him between my thighs, circling the tip of his hard, massive cock against me, warning me, preparing to make me his own. I bite down on my bottom lip, scared but exhilarated as he slowly forces himself inside me. I gasp, my whole being tense, shocked by the tremendous pressure of my body stretching to accommodate him. His eyes fill with concern.

"Are you okay?"

I nod, swallowing hard. He eases back then pushes in deeper, each millimeter of him feeling like a yard. I reach down to the bed beneath me, clutching at the bedsheets, and he draws back, driving himself into me harder. My eyes open wider, my lips parting.

"Oh, God," I cry, tears instantly filling my eyes. It hurts. He weaves his hand into my hair, raising my head and cradling it against his chest.

"I'll take it slowly," he whispers. I wrap my arms around him, clutching him to me as he circles his hips, thrusting deeper inside me. My mouth opens wide, my chest constricting my breaths to short, sharp gasps.

"Mitch," I moan, yielding to his slow, steady torture. He slides his hand down my thigh, pulling my knee up to his hip, spreading my legs wider, diving deep. Oh, God, it hurts, but somehow the pain feeds my pleasure.

I sink my fingers into his skin, my body shuddering, shaking.

"Not hurting you?" he breathes against my ear.

"No," I whisper. I lie.

"Good." He bites my earlobe, and I cry out as he draws in a raw, savage breath, then pulls back, ramming himself into me, over and over with all his strength, touching me deeper than anyone could ever, filling me so completely.

I scream his name, arching my back. He rocks against me, giving me everything he's got. I close my eyes, burying my head back in the pillows, intoxicated. I can feel my pleasure building with every beat of my heart, feel him pulsating inside me, feel every contour of his skin, every vein. He pulls back quickly then touches me there again, deep inside my soul.

"*Mitch!*" I scream, my body vibrating, burning, craving more.

I hold him tighter, digging my fingernails deep into his skin. He winces then rears up, driving himself into me harder, again and again. I never imagined anything could feel so amazing and hurt like hell at the same time. Tears form in my eyes. I gasp for air, teetering on the ledge beyond the edge of reason, when he stops completely.

"Not yet," he breathes.

Every muscle in my body tightens. I flash my eyes up to his, commanding, demanding, but he ignores me, burying himself deep inside me, staying deep, his movements minute and purposeful.

"Oh, God, don't stop," I beg, bucking my hips against him.

He curls up the corners of his mouth in a devilish twist then thrusts hard just once, ensuring my torment. *He's enjoying this.* He withdraws completely, feeding himself slowly back inside me, watching as my face contorts with a heady rush of pleasure and pain, then eases back, falling into a torturous, disciplined, denying rhythm. I clench tightly around him, sinking my fingernails mercilessly into his skin, willing him to thrust faster. He winces again. I like that. His eyes fill with the darkness of a demon, but I fear nothing will make him deviate from his slow, soul-touching punishment. I feel the friction between us building, feel the heat from his skin. I buck wildly against him, begging, pleading. I can't wait a second longer. "Oh, God, Mitch, fuck me!"

"Yeah?" he whispers.

"*Yes!*" I shout, his voice in my ear only adding to my delirium.

He increases his stroke. "Yeah?"

"*Yes! Oh, God!*" I scream, biting my palm. He anchors his feet, spreading my legs wider, slamming his hips against mine. I cry out, lost in his thrusts. I'm so close, I can't stand it. His breathing grows rough and rugged as the pulsating inside me grows insufferable. I clench tightly around him, my breaths coming in ragged gasps as I topple over the edge, falling into his world, and he into mine as we come together, me screaming his name, him screaming mine.

"Holy fuck," he breathes, his body shuddering, his face nuzzling into my neck.

"Oh, Mitch," I murmur against his skin, wrapping my arms and legs around him, so completely fulfilled.

He pulls his head back to look at me, his eyes imprinted with an unparalleled level of intensity as he touches his lips to mine. I feel him twitching and twinging inside me, still so hard and threatening, reminding me how sore I am.

He withdraws slowly, painstakingly, then collapses down onto the bed beside me. I look across at him, admiring his bare chest, glistening with sweat. He flashes me a sexy curled-up smile and I clutch my forehead, so completely at sea.

He turns onto his side to face me, propping his head up on his palm, his eyes electric. "You liked that, huh?"

I decide to mess with him. "It was okay."

He stares at me incredulously. "*Okay?*"

I shrug. "What do you want me to say? It was okay, *thank you?*"

His eyes crinkle at the corners. "Oh, you're gonna get it!" He grabs me, tickling me while I toss and turn wildly, both of us shaking with laughter.

His eyes grow tender and rueful as he watches me laugh. He reaches up to my face, trailing his fingers over the tiny scars near my hairline. I take his hand in mine, stopping him. He looks down at me, laying himself bare.

"Was it always like this between us? So intense?" I ask.

"So much more than intense," he murmurs, slipping his hand between my legs.

I stop breathing. "Mitch."

He clutches the inside of my thigh, spreading my legs, then moves his body on top of mine, pressing the tip of his shaft against me, instantly monstrous and hard.

"Mitch, I can't." I panic, pushing about his chest. I don't know if I can. I'm so sore. My resistance does nothing. He watches me intently, his breath hissing from his lips as he slowly forces inside me.

"Mitch, it hurts," I whimper.

He looks down at me, then stops, wrapping his arms around me and rolling onto his back so that I'm on top of him.

"Ssssh," he whispers. "I just want to be inside you." But neither of us can leave it at that.

He takes my hands in his, clutching them tightly and I beg him with my eyes to take it slow. He moves inside me and my stomach flutters, instantly craving the euphoric pleasure I know he has to give. I close my eyes and breathe deeply through my nose, rising up then slowly descending on his thick, merciless shaft. I gasp, my body sore but still so needy. When I return my eyes to his, they're filled with heat. I lift my hips then drop back down, sinking lower this time. He groans. "Just a little more to go, honey." I look down at him, alarmed.

"More?"

He nods, clutching at my hips and pulling me down hard onto him for him to thrust up, so entirely inside me.

"Mitch! Oh, Jesus Christ!" I pant, tears welling in my eyes.

He rocks me back and forth then lifts my hips, only to lower me down again, watching as I take every inch of him inside my body.

"Oh, Scar, you're unbelievable."

I cry out, involuntarily tightening around him. He glides his hands up my body to my breasts, cupping them, gently pinching my nipples. I whimper and he squeezes harder, the shock wave spreading through my body all the way to my toes. I sink my fingertips into his chest, rising and falling as fast as I can, over and over, exploding around him, moaning so intensely he sits up, clutching me to him to thrust inside me. I cling to him, screaming, crying, just a passenger on his wild ride as he fills me again and again.

"Oh, fuck. *Fuck!*" He groans and comes, his body shaking, shuddering in my arms.

I bury my head in his neck, tears on my lashes, overwrought by the raw, unbridled power of our connection.

He pulls his head back to look at me, the pleasure in his eyes spreading to his lips. "Now, *that* was intense."

"So intense I'm scared to move," I murmur.

"Then don't."

I nod, resting my head on his shoulder, inhaling the sweaty, manly scent of his skin. I close my lips around his throat, gently sucking, my tongue tasting the saltiness of his sweat. He tilts his head, exhaling loudly, and I feel him twitch inside me.

"If you keep doing that, woman, I'm gonna fuck you again."

I stop abruptly. There's no way I could survive another round right now and he knows it. He throws himself back against the bed and I rise slowly, my body tensing as I feel every inch of him withdrawing from inside me, then fall on the bed beside him. I close my eyes, my body reeling with an exquisite blend of pain and pleasure, like Dutch chocolate, strawberries and champagne, and a hangover all at once.

"You're gonna be sore for a couple of days," he says, unable to hide his joy.

"And you're happy about that?"

"You'll think of me every time you move."

I frown, praying to God that Nick doesn't start something in the next few days that I can't finish. He starts to sit up, then groans loudly, clutching at his side, his face screwed up as though he's in pain.

"Are you okay?"

He nods, his brow furrowed tightly. "I'm fine."

"You're not fine. What's wrong?"

"I want more."

"What?"

He leans toward me. "I want more of you."

"Oh, no you don't."

"Oh, yes, I do," he says, pulling me closer.

I put my hand on his chest, pushing him away. "There's no way in the world I'm letting you anywhere near this body."

"Okay, but soon." My eyes open wider at the thought.

He glances across at the clock. "What time do you have to be home?"

"Uh, around six, I guess."

"Great, plenty of time. Get dressed. I'm taking you out on the boat."

Chapter Eleven

A Bump in the Night

It's late when I arrive home, almost seven o'clock, my afternoon on the boat with Mitch opening my eyes to an entirely different world. The saltwater stings my skin and my hair looks as though I've just jumped out of a plane, strands stuck fast to my forehead and each other in clumps, but I don't care. I had the time of my life. I run straight up to the shower to de-boat, so completely exhausted, yet exhilarated after my adventurous afternoon with Mitch.

The warm water streams down my face and I close my eyes, my mind wandering. Remembering the amber glow of the sun dancing in the ripples of the ocean as it stretches across the horizon, reaching up to the heavens above and becoming one. Mitch and I, just the two of us, drifting so freely, cradled in the ocean's palm, only the soothing sound of small, gentle waves lapping against the hull as we sat huddled on the deck, him wrapping his arms tightly around me. I'd never seen such beauty, nor felt such inner peace and comfort, being so far from people, from land, from life. Remembering the pure joy on his face, the excitement of racing the sinking sun into the impending night sky. The same night sky that would tear us apart.

I take my time showering and getting dressed, then call my mother back. I forgot to call her after my neurologist appointment and she's left countless messages. Afterward, I wander downstairs to wait for Nick when the home phone rings. I rush down to the lounge, picking up the cordless phone. It's Nick.

"Hello, wife," he says cheerfully, already a few drinks under his belt by the sound of it. "How are you? Is everything okay?"

"Yeah, I'm fine. I take it things went well with the client?"

"Well, it's not a done deal just yet, but I'm trying. I miss you."

"I miss you, too."

"Okay, well, we'll be wrapping things up here shortly and I'll be home. Just give me about an hour or so."

"Great. I'll see you soon, then."

"Sure will. Bye, baby."

"Bye."

I hang up, scanning the room. The house is eerily quiet tonight. I turn on the TV to drown out the nothingness then lie down on the couch, picking up the book that Mitch bought me. I still haven't finished *Wuthering Heights*. I couldn't bring myself to pick it up again, its tales of heartbreak and revenge stirring feelings inside me I hadn't yet discovered, nor ever want to feel.

I read the first two pages when the home phone rings again. I mute the TV and pick the handset up, assuming Nick's forgotten to tell me something, but there's no one there.

I put the phone down, reading the first chapter of the book when the phone rings again. This time, I'm alarmed. I sit up, staring down at the phone on the coffee table. I reach for the remote, muting the sound, and the phone stops ringing. It's dead quiet now, only the dull hum of the refrigerator emanating from the kitchen. I glance toward the dining room, looking at all the glass panels with the plantation shutters wide open, and wonder why I don't close them at night. There're no neighbors, I know, but that doesn't mean there are no prying eyes.

The phone rings again and I let it ring, leaning back against the couch, pulling my knees up to my chest, suddenly feeling ridiculously naïve being here alone at night. The phone stops ringing and I turn the sound back up on the

TV and sit there quietly, wondering if I'm being a big baby or whether I should call Nick. My eyes grow heavy. I slump down in the chair, putting a cushion over my cold feet, when I hear a loud bang outside. I sit bolt upright and turn off the TV, too afraid to move. My heart starts beating faster than hooves on a racetrack, my whole body wired.

I could really use a dog right now. One of those big, black-and-tan, burly looking ones with the studded collar and drool oozing from its mouth. I hear what sounds like a car outside and jump up, running for the front door. I throw it open and see taillights going down the driveway. The cool night air whirls around me, making the hairs on my arms stand on end, like a whisper in the dark. I slam the door shut and lock it, then run for my cell. It's just after nine. I call Nick, but he doesn't answer, his phone diverting straight to voicemail. I leave a message then call again. Still no answer. I know there's a really simple three-digit phone number for the police but I can't think of it. I decide to call Mitch instead. He answers straight away.

"Hey, you," he says softly.

"Mitch, someone was just here," I blubber.

"What?"

"Someone kept calling the house, then there was a loud bang outside and I saw taillights going down the driveway," I sob into the phone.

"What the hell? Where's Nick?"

"He's at some dinner with a client. I rang, but he's not answering."

"Fuck! Stay inside, lock the door. I'm sending a patrol car over and I'll be on my way."

"What? *No.* You can't come here. Nick might come home."

"I'm coming. I'm worried about you," he says sternly.

"No. Just send a car, please. I'm so scared."

"Hang up. I'll call them and I'll call you straight back, okay?"

"Okay." I hang up, huddling in the corner of the couch, my eyes blurry with tears. A minute later Mitch calls back.

"There's a car on the way. It'll be there real soon, okay. Just stay on the phone and talk to me."

"Uh-huh," I whisper, sniffing back my tears.

"It's okay, honey, I'm sure they're gone. Did you get a look at the car?"

"No, nothing. Just taillights."

"Have you been at home all alone since you left me?"

"Yes."

He groans. "What the fuck is wrong with that guy, leaving you alone out there at night like that? Do you have a gun?"

"*What*? No!"

"I'll get you one and you're going to learn how to shoot it."

"No. Guns scare me."

"Well, I'm getting you a dog. It's crazy to live on all that property and not have either."

"Nick doesn't like dogs."

"Yeah, well, there's a lot to be said about people who don't like dogs. In his case, it definitely applies to him."

I swallow hard, pulling my knees in tighter to my chest.

"Are you okay?"

"Yeah, I'm just scared."

"Do you have any idea who might have come there?"

"No. No one ever comes here late at night. Do you think it's got something to do with my accident?"

"What? Why do you say that?"

"I don't know. We've been getting strange calls here at the house and this afternoon when I was coming to see you, there was this car in the street outside our house. I didn't think much of it at the time, but then I thought I saw it again behind me when I pulled in to the boatyard. Now this."

"*What*? Why didn't you tell me?"

"I didn't really put it all together until now."

"Shit, Scarlet! What kind of car did you see in the street this afternoon?"

"I don't know. It was biggish and a dark-gray or dark-blue color."

"Did you see the license plate?"

"No. I didn't look at the plate." Tears sting my face. "Somebody's after me, aren't they?"

"Hey, hey. Don't think that."

"Well, what else could it be?"

"It could be a lot of things. It doesn't mean it's someone after you. What about Nick? How much do you know about his work?"

"What do you mean?"

"Well, he *is* an international financier." He pauses. "Fuck this, I'm coming over."

"You can't."

"Where exactly is Nick, anyway?"

"I told you, he's at some business dinner with a client."

He huffs. "That's convenient."

"What's convenient?"

"This happening when he's not there."

"What are you saying?" I hear something smash in the background of the call. "Mitch? Are you okay?"

"Yes," he snaps.

"What was that noise?"

"I can't protect you like this, Scarlet. There's no way of knowing when you need me."

I hear police sirens growing louder in the background. "The police are here. I have to go."

"No. Stay on the phone. Give the phone to one of the police officers so I can talk to them."

"Okay."

I hear a loud rapping at the front door and I rush over to answer it. A portly, gray-haired police officer stands in the doorway.

"Mrs. Pierce?" he asks.

"Yes."

"I'm Sergeant Moss from Coomera Police. We received a call about a disturbance here."

"Yes," I reply. My tears disable me and I pass him my cell.

He looks down at the phone curiously, then puts it up to

his ear, watching me. "Hello. Sergeant Moss here." After a moment, he grins. "Oh, g'day buddy, how you doin'?" He shifts his gaze, listening intently as Mitch speaks. "Ah, okay. No. No signs of anyone on the way in but the Dog Squad just booked back on at Hope Island. I'll get them to pop over and give the place a thorough search."

He turns back to me. "Yeah, sure, mate. I'll give ya a bell." He nods. "No worries, I'll put you back on to your friend." He hands me the phone, two small dents appearing in his flushed cheeks. "My partner and I are going to take a look around. We'll come and see you when we're done."

"Thank you," I reply.

I shut the door, putting the phone to my ear.

"Are you there?" I ask.

"Yeah, beautiful, I'm here. I'll stay on the phone with you till Nick gets home."

"Thank you for helping me. I don't know what I'd do without you." I stop. The gravity of those last small eight words sinking in.

"You're welcome. You're safe now."

I glance around the room nervously. "I'm going to be afraid here now, when I'm on my own."

He doesn't answer.

"What's wrong?"

"You're not supposed to be there. You're supposed to be here, with me."

"I'm sorry," I whisper and that's all I can offer. We talk for about ten minutes when I hear knocking at the front door. I open it and put the phone on loudspeaker so Mitch can hear.

"Okay, ma'am, we've done a thorough sweep of the area. You've got a smashed pot on the back terrace and the dog picked up a fresh scent leading from there to about halfway down the driveway, where it stops. That indicates to us that someone got into a car there and drove away."

"Yes, that's about where I saw the taillights."

"Okay, so there's no one here now. We've checked all the

exterior doors and windows. The property appears secure. Do you want us to come in and check inside for you?"

I turn, looking around the room. "Uh, no, it's okay."

"Okay. Keep your door locked and stay inside. Are you here on your own?"

"Yes, my husband will be home soon. He had a late meeting."

He nods. "Senior Sergeant Morgan said you saw a suspect vehicle out the front of your house this afternoon?"

"Uh, yes—"

"Yeah, Mossy," Mitch interrupts. "I've got all the details. I'll file a report about it tomorrow when I get to work, save you going through it all."

"Oh, cheers, that'd be great, thanks, mate," Moss replies.

"Thanks for getting there so quick. I heard the sirens."

"Yeah, no worries, comms code three'd it, but I heard your name mentioned and I thought fuck it, pedal to the metal. Think I got all four wheels off the ground at the fiveways."

They laugh. Moss looks up at me, straightening his stance as though he forgot I was there.

"Okay, well," Moss continues, his voice suddenly charged with authority. "We'll stay around the area for the next half an hour or so, but if you have any problems, ring in and they'll send someone out immediately. Or ring Mitch— they'll get here quicker." Mitch chuckles.

"Okay, thank you very much."

"Thanks, Mossy," Mitch shouts.

"No problem. We'll do some breath testing on the main road for a bit, mate. She'll be right."

"Thanks, buddy."

"Okay, bye."

He tips his hat, turning to leave, and I shut the door and lock it. Mitch stays on the phone, refusing to get off the line until Nick comes home about forty-five minutes later. I hang up from Mitch and hear the front door slam.

"Hey, baby, what's with all the lights?" Nick shouts.

I rush out to the foyer as he turns off the entry lights and spotlights.

"Someone was here," I reply.

He throws his keys down on the end table and looks up at me. He's a mess, his eyes glassy, his shirt hanging out, his hair disheveled. "*What?*"

"Someone was here, out the back of the house. I called the police, they just left."

"What? Are you okay?"

"I tried to call you, but you didn't answer."

"Shit! I must have left my cell on silent. I'm so sorry." He pulls his cell out of his pocket, my missed calls and messages still on the screen. He tosses the phone down on the table and wraps his arms around me. There's alcohol on his breath.

"How did you get home?"

"I caught a cab. I left my car at work. What happened here?"

"I was watching TV and the home phone rang a couple times, but no one was there, then I heard a loud bang outside. Scared me to death. I turned the TV off and I heard a car start up outside and saw taillights going down the driveway."

"Oh, my God."

"The police came. They had a dog with them, they said there was a fresh scent from the back terrace to halfway down the driveway, then it stops. The big pot out by the terrace doors is smashed, apparently, so I'd say that was the bang."

He tightens his arms around me, kissing my forehead. "I can't believe it. I'm so sorry I wasn't here."

I nuzzle into his chest, clutching his shirt, so glad that he's home. "I was so scared."

He rubs his hands across my back. "I know, I know, but I'm here now. You're safe. I won't let anything happen to you. It was probably just some drunk kids messing around."

"What if it's not?"

He pulls his head back, looking down at me. "What do

you mean?"

"What if it's someone after me?"

"*What?* Why would someone be after you?"

"Malaylie's been getting strange calls here at the house and today there was a strange car in the street."

He screws up his face, dropping his arms from around me. "*Damn it*, Scarlet! Why is this the first I'm hearing of this?"

I feel faint. I sit down on the couch, clutching my forehead. "I didn't see a connection until now," I reply with a weary inflection.

"You should have told me! I would never have left you alone here tonight." He sits down on the coffee table in front of me. "What kind of car was out in the street?"

"I don't know. It was biggish, a dark-gray, dark-blue color." His lips twitch at the corners as though he's amused.

"What?" I ask.

"It wasn't your boyfriend, was it?"

"It wasn't him."

"How do you know?"

"Because it wasn't."

"You seem fairly certain about that."

I glower at him, folding my arms theatrically across my chest. "What about you?"

"What about me?"

"Maybe it was someone after *you*."

"Why would someone be after *me*?"

"I don't know. You're a banker. Maybe it's someone after money or something?"

He scoffs. "I don't think so."

We sit there in silence for a moment. Finally, he leans forward, resting his hands on mine.

"I'll have Gabe stay in the guest house for the next couple of weeks, just to be on the safe side, and we'll start using the electric gates on the driveway again. I know they're really slow, but I'll have them looked at, okay, and we can start using the alarm, too."

"I hate that alarm! It goes off at the slightest thing and it's way too loud. It scares me."

"I know, but if it keeps you safe…"

I throw myself back against the couch, folding my arms. "How did it go with the new client?"

"Yeah, it went well. She liked our ideas about going global and she's looking to expand, so we're on the same page. She's playing it cool, though, she hasn't signed yet."

"She?"

He nods just once. "Annabella Van Zant. She owns Van Zant Enterprises. One of the largest clothing and textile companies in the southern hemisphere. She's launched a new sportswear brand that's already selling better than Nike's first year of trade."

"Really? What's she like?"

He shrugs. "She's nice enough."

"How old is she?"

"Too old."

I rub my arms and glance around the room.

"What's wrong?"

"Gee, I don't know. I guess I just don't get it! I'm here alone, late at night and you're out drinking with female clients."

"It's not like that, Scarlet. It wasn't just me. Pete and Steve were there. She's a big client. This account could be worth millions of dollars to us. We have to be on point and we need to have the numbers. I'm a partner in this firm now, Scarlet. I have to pull my weight."

"Why does this company mean so much to you? If it's about money, we have plenty."

"It's not about money."

"Then what is it?"

"I was a washed-up football player, Scarlet. Five years ago, when I met you, I was a no one in that firm. I had no real goals—it was just a job, working for a mate's dad. *You're* the one who made me who I am. I never thought I had a chance with you. You were this successful, confident businesswoman with the world at her feet, and you had money, which only made it worse. I had nothing to offer you. I never thought you'd fall for me so hard. I wanted to be successful for *you*. You were always pushing me to dig deeper, reach higher and I, well, wanted to be man you deserved, with money of my own."

He stares at me, his eyes scarred by life, by others' expectations, by me.

"It doesn't matter to me what you do for a living."

"It did. Before the accident. You're different now."

"And it seems you are, too."

"What do you mean?"

"I had a dream last night. About you and me, and I need to ask you something. You're not going to like the question, but I have to ask it."

"Sounds serious."

"It is."

He pauses. "Okay. Go ahead."

I dip my head, looking up at him through my lashes. "Have you ever hit me?"

"*What?*"

"I dreamed that we were having a fight." He doesn't move. "You were angry. Really angry. I was terrified. I was running from you, you were chasing me. I ran up to the bedroom and I fell. You came in. You were standing over me, shouting, your hand raised as though you were going to hit me."

He hangs his head, looking down at his hands. *The culprits, perhaps?* "I didn't hit you," he says gruffly.

"But I saw —"

"I didn't hit you. I could *never* hit you. I lost my temper. *Once.* We had a terrible fight. I raised my hand to you, but that's all."

He rests his hands on mine. "Your face. The way you looked at me. It killed me. I could never intentionally lay a hand on you, Scarlet. I could *never* hurt you like that." I nod, knowing it's true.

"I have a serious question for you." He takes my hand in his. "Do you love me?"

"I do. But sometimes you scare me."

"*I scare you?*"

I swallow hard, all the things Mitch had said about Nick coming to a head. "Did you chase me in the car that night? I read the police report. It says there was another unidentified vehicle behind me that may have forced me off the road."

"*What?* No!" He jumps to his feet, his eyes intense and forbidding. "You think *I want you dead*? I love you, Scarlet! I was trying to save our marriage—why the hell would I want to hurt you?"

"Well, who else would it be?"

"That's what you think of me? That I'm some violent, road-raging killer?"

I stand, clutching his arms. "No! No, I don't think that. I'm sorry! I love you. I'm just confused. Mitch said some things that made me think—"

"Mitch *wants* you. He would say just about *anything* to destroy me, to destroy our marriage, and *you're* listening to him."

"I'm not. I'm sorry. I know you didn't do it. I'm sorry for what I said. I'm just so confused."

I throw my arms around him, holding him tightly against me, but he keeps his arms hanging limp by his sides. "Please forgive me. I'm sorry. I just have so many questions. I need to know what happened to me, why this happened to me—"

Because I get the feeling that it's not over yet.

I don't dare say it out loud. His body stays tense and unforgiving. He brings his arms up around me slowly, hanging them loosely around me. I feel sick to my stomach. I squeeze him tighter.

"I love you, Nick."

"I love you, too," he murmurs, but I fear the damage is done. He steps back, taking me to arm's length. "I'm gonna go work out for a while, okay?"

I mash my lips together and nod. He turns slowly, heading

toward his gym room. I watch him as he walks away, the house deadly quiet.

What have I done?

* * * *

My cell phone rings the next morning on the bedside table beside me. I open one eye and glance across at it, then look at the clock. Eight-fifteen.

Damn. The one morning I really need to see Nick and he's gone.

I didn't even hear him come to bed last night. His side of the bed doesn't even look as if it's been slept in. Fear creeps in. I reach across for the phone to call him and stop, wincing in pain, a not-so-subtle reminder of Mitch's punishment. Feeling him in my every tightly flexed muscle, places where I didn't even know I had muscles. I make another pass at the phone and it rings. I snatch it off the table, looking down at the name. It's Marcy.

"Hi, Marcy," I answer, trying not to sound as if I just woke up.

"Scarlet, hello, sweetie. Listen, it's just a quick call to say thank you. I don't know how you did it, but Mitchell was just here and has sorted out all our problems with the security portfolio."

I sit up. "He did?"

"Ah-ha! He's been here since seven a.m. in his cute little uniform, mind you. Mmm-hmm, I sure could use a big, tall cup of cop like that every morning with my toast and muffins." She giggles. "I'm just the worst, aren't I? My hormones are on fire at the moment and anything that hijacks hormones is a welcome distraction right now." I can't help but laugh.

"He brought a friend with him. Will. He's going to be taking over from now on as Mitch doesn't have the time anymore and, oh, goodness, he's just gorgeous. Anyhow, I just wanted to say that you needn't worry about that anymore and thank you again for getting this done.

Working with Will is going to be a pleasure, all mine."

"Okay. Thanks for ringing, Marcy."

"Bye now, hun."

I throw the phone down on the bed and bury it. *I've got a crazy woman running my office.*

Still, the revelation doesn't make me any more inclined to get back to work sooner. I haven't given it much of a chance, though, I guess, and what will I do with myself if I don't go back? I lie back among the pillows, staring up at the ceiling. Doing just as Mitch said I would, thinking of him every time I move. Remembering how he felt, how he moved inside me, his taste, the smell of his skin. How Nick said he would do anything to destroy our marriage.

Oh, God! I forgot to ring Nick!

I sit up and reach for my phone when a text comes through from Nick.

Hi. I left early this morning, didn't want to wake you. I've closed the security gates on the driveway. I put the remote in your car. Someone's coming to look at the gates tomorrow. Ring me anytime about anything, suspicious cars, phone calls, I want to know.
Nick.

I sit there, rereading it. It's not his usual love-and-kisses type text. He must be pretty angry with me.

I write back.

Hi, baby. Thank you. Can I ring you now?

He texts back after a couple of minutes.

I'm in a meeting. If it's urgent I can go outside and call you.

It's not urgent, just wanted to say hello and that I love you. xx

I'll call you later, he responds.

Still no kisses. He's definitely mad at me and I have no idea how to fix this. I scroll through my contacts, stopping at Mitch. I sit there staring at the number, then quickly hit Call before I change my mind. He answers almost immediately.

"Scarlet?"

"Hi," I reply.

"I wanted to call or text, but I didn't know if he was with you."

"He's not."

He exhales loudly. "Are you okay? I've been worried about you all night."

"I'm fine, and thank you for everything you did last night."

"You're welcome. I can't stop thinking about you. Yesterday was incredible." I don't answer.

"I just wanted to call and say thank you for sorting things out in the office. Marcy called and told me."

"Uh, yeah. No problem. I got a friend of mine to take over though, if you don't mind. I just don't have the time anymore."

"No, that's good, actually. Nick would never have allowed it, anyway." There's silence for a moment.

"You seem distant. Is everything okay?" he asks.

"Yeah, everything's fine."

"Between us, I mean?"

I draw in a deep breath, not knowing what to say. I want to say yes, to blurt out all the things I'm feeling for him, but my feelings for Nick stop me. I've done wrong by him and there's no way of redeeming myself. My only saving grace would be to end it here and now.

"Can I see you?" he asks softly.

And I want to see him. How on Earth can I possibly save grace when I can't even help myself?

"Uh, I have some charity race-day luncheon with my mother and some friends today so…"

He's quiet. He knows something's wrong.

"I should probably go. I just wanted to say thank you."

"Scarlet, I need to see you. We need to talk about this. Come to the boatyard. I don't leave for work until one-thirty."

"I can't."

"Just think about it."

"I can't. I've got to go." I hang up before he has the chance to talk me into it.

I throw back the covers, glancing across at the time. It's almost nine. I slowly, painstakingly, get out of bed and get dressed to meet with my mother and her rich society friends, with whom I have absolutely nothing in common. Apparently, the dress code is elegant formal, so I put on my jeans and a T-shirt before conforming to the pressure of society and frocking up.

Chapter Twelve

Going, Going

I arrive home late from my mother's charity luncheon at the racecourse. It turned out to be much more fun than I had anticipated and I'm certainly glad I didn't wear my T-shirt and jeans. The over-the-top gowns some of the women wore must have cost their husbands an entire year's salary, at least. Fake tans as far as the eye could see, the fashion parade an onslaught of seasoned ladies, bronzed-up, boobs out, strutting down the runway like overcooked chickens. The stage was more like a walk of shame than a catwalk, but it's all for a good cause. My brother Ari and his partner Nigel turned up later in the afternoon, making the day far more enjoyable.

The house is well lit when Gabe pulls into the driveway. I throw my things down on the floor by the front door, giggling, a little tipsy after all the fresh air on the way home. I head into the kitchen for a drink when I hear the front door slam shut.

"Nick?" I call out.

"Yeah, it's me."

He walks around the corner, taking off his tie.

"Hi," he says flatly as I hurry toward him. "You look amazing. How was the race day?"

"It was a lot of fun!" I fall into his arms, kissing him wildly.

He breaks off the kiss, pulling his head back to look at me. "Had a few drinks, have we?"

"Just a few," I giggle.

He nods, not exactly amused.

I narrow my eyes. "Are you okay?"

"Yeah. I'm fine."

He's not. He loosens his arms around me and I stand straight, dropping my arms from around him.

"Is something wrong?"

"I don't like it when you drink when I'm not with you," he snaps, his mouth angry but his eyes filled with lust.

"Oh. I'm sorry," I reply, though this is news to me.

He reaches up, undoing the top two buttons of his shirt, glaring down at me, and I'm suddenly not sure if he wants to kill me or fuck me.

"We need to talk," he says sternly.

He takes my hand in his and leads me over to the couch, sitting me down. A feeling of dread washes over me.

"I don't know how to put this, so I'm just going to come straight out with it."

"Okay."

His face twists as though he's in pain. "Is there something going on between you and Mitch?"

"Have you been following me?" I snap.

"*God!* No. I wasn't completely sure. Until now, it was more of a feeling. You've been different toward me. You've got reservations about us, I can feel it. I checked your phone this morning. You've been ringing him. You rang him last night. Talked for quite a while, right up until I got home actually. And earlier that day."

"I-I couldn't get you on the phone. I didn't know what else to do."

"Are you sleeping with him?"

"What? *No!*" It's an automatic response. A self-preservation type thing. A lie. His gaze holds mine. I want to look away. I need to look away, but I know if I do he'll read me like a book.

"I thought if I just kept him away from you, we'd be okay, but there's much more to this than that. I couldn't see it before, but I see it now. Last night when you asked me if I'd hit you, if I'd tried to run you off the road, I looked into your eyes and I realized just how lost you are. You're not ready for this."

"Nick—" I start.

He puts his hand up to stop me. "I've given this a lot of thought, and I think we need to take a break."

"*What?*"

"If we're going to get through this, if we're going to be together, it has to be because we both want it. I love you, and I want this marriage to work more than anything in the world, but if you have feelings for Mitch, or if you have questions or you just want to spend time with him, I'm not going to fight it anymore."

I bow my head, suddenly so unsure of our future.

"I've been going about this all wrong. I've treated Mitch with nothing but hatred and contempt, and though that's the way I believe any husband would react to a man trying to steal his wife, I was doing it for the wrong reasons. I was trying to keep the two of you apart, when I should have let you go. It's my nature. I don't like to lose, but I can't make you stay. I shouldn't want to make you stay. If you want to be with him then—"

"But that's not what I want," I blurt out.

"And that's exactly what I hoped you'd say. But right now, you need to go and explore what you had with him, before the accident, because it *was* something. Enough to make you leave me, and we can't move forward until you put him behind you."

His eyes leave me in ruins. "Nick, I—"

"This isn't me giving up on us," he interrupts. "Three years ago, on a warm spring afternoon, under a sinking sun and the sprawling green arms of an oak tree, we took a vow, an oath to be bound together forever, and I will fight for you till my last breath. But right now, the battle lies within your heart, and I can't take my fight there. That war is your own."

I lean forward, tears welling in my eyes. "But I love you."

"And I love you. But you care for him, too. Just be sure of

his motives."

"His *motives*?"

"He's a cop, Scarlet, on a cop's wages. You must have considered the golden ticket you present to him."

"*What the hell?*" I glower at him. "This isn't about money."

"Everything is about money, Scarlet."

"Maybe for you."

"What is *that* supposed to mean?"

We stand there, staring at each other, swallowed by the silence surrounding us.

"I've got a conference in Melbourne," he mutters, breaking the spell. "I was going to send Andrew, the new intern, but I've decided to go instead."

"*No!*"

"It will give us both a chance to step away from this and see things more clearly."

Fear chokes me. "I don't want you to leave. What if you decide you don't want this?"

He touches his hand to my face. "I will always want this. I want it all with you, marriage, children. Lots of children. I can't wait to be a father... And soon."

"But I'm not the woman you married. I'm always going to be a work in progress."

He takes my hand in his, his eyes softer, the lines in his forehead making him look much older than he is. "You *are* the woman I married, and much more than that. Just take this time to think things through. Ask yourself what you really want. I hope that you find your way home to me, but that's out of my hands now, and in yours."

I wince. "When do you leave?"

"My plane flies out at six in the morning, but Gabe will here at four-thirty to take me to the airport."

"When will you be back?"

"Three days. My plane gets in around four on Thursday."

Tears stream down my face. "How can you leave at a time like this? After what happened last night?"

"I'm a mess, Scarlet. I can't stay." He swallows hard.

"I talked to Gabe this morning and he's moving into the guest house on a permanent basis, so you'll always have someone here, and Malaylie is going to sleep here in the house while I'm away. The front security gates are getting fixed in the morning and they're installing a whole new security system. You'll be safe."

I drop my head to my chest, my tears cascading to the floor.

"Hey," he says, taking my face in his hands. "This is for you. This is a good thing. No tears."

I nod and try to smile, failing dismally.

"Have you eaten?" he asks.

"Yes."

He reaches down, taking my hands in his, tugging me forward.

"Come on, let's get to bed. We could both do with an early night."

As we walk through the bedroom door, my cell phone rings. He wanders into the dressing room, taking off his shirt as I hurry over to the bed and pick up the phone. It's my mother. Nick gives me a sideways glare as he goes into the bathroom, closing the door behind him. I throw the phone down on the bed, letting it ring. I can't talk to her right now, not in this mood.

I hear the shower start and I fall down onto the end of the bed, abysmally unhappy, a frightening new reality of life without Nick sinking in.

He's leaving.

The thought churns my stomach. I don't want him to go. My heart beats faster and louder, my body vibrating with anger. I storm into the bathroom, slamming the door back against the wall. He turns to me, surprised, his hair wet and slicked back. I've never seen him look more innocent. Water trickles down his tan, toned body, his skin glistening, his every bulging vein and muscle highlighted under the warm glow of the heat lamp above. I stride toward him, straight into the shower, straight into his big, powerful arms.

I wrap myself around him, clutching him tightly against me, kissing him with the fiercest of fire, conjured from the underworld of my soul, our mouths eager, open wide, our tongues sparring, our teeth clashing, wild with emotion. The warm water washes over me, soaking my skin, making my clothes cling to my body. He glides his strong hands across my skin, slipping down the straps of my dress, stripping me of my clothes until I'm completely naked and breathless, standing before him. He pulls me to him, my nipples hard, straining against his chest. I slide my hand between us, touching him, wrapping my fingers around his hard, wet shaft. He stares down at me, his eyes as dark as my mood.

The thudding, pulsing rhythm of my hunger for him percusses through my body. I reach up, clutching his face with both hands, bringing his lips down to mine, my body feeding from his mouth. He lifts me up, and I wrap my legs around him, a raspy hum echoing in his throat as I clutch at his skin, needing him closer.

Water pools between us, trickling between my legs, intensifying my desire. He steps forward, pinning me to the wall with his body, moving his mouth with mine, savage and besieging, like two predators stalking the same prey.

Nick tightens his hand on my hips, positioning himself beneath me then plunging me down onto him at the same time as he thrusts upward, deep inside my body. I gasp, tipping my head back, my eyes closed, my mouth open, crying out as he drives me hard against the wall, filling my body over and over. He clamps his lips down on my jugular, his teeth scraping my neck, his tongue licking, his mouth sucking hard in a wild, fiery frenzy. I cling to his biceps, rippling with strength as they support my weight with ease, his muscles flexing and tensing with every thrust.

The warm water cascades between us, our body heat increasing, creating a steamy haze all around us. His breathing grows rough and ragged as I tighten around him, rocking my hips back and forth. Nick slides his hands down to my thighs, opening my legs wider, forcing himself deeper and harder inside me, again and again.

"Oh, my God, Nick," I cry out. He groans, slamming his hips violently against mine, giving me everything he's got. I weave my fingers into his hair, tugging hard, and he winces, tilting his head back to relieve the pressure. His strokes grow frantic and aggressive and the thrumming inside me too much to bear. I throw my arms around his neck, thrusting against him, screaming his name and sinking my fingers into his back as I fall apart in his arms.

His eyes glow, laden with a devilish darkness I've never seen before, as a deliciously long, sated growl emits from his lips and resonates through his body.

"Oh, fuck!" he yells, his thrusts slowing as his essence fills my body. "Oh, baby," he groans, lowering his mouth to my neck.

I crush him against me, kissing his forehead, his face, his hair, my body twitching and shivering. He pulls his head back to look at me, his eyes filled with wonder.

"What the fuck?" He shakes his head. "I'm going away more often."

I laugh, but it's a fleeting, hollow moment of happiness. He's still leaving and my heart still hurts.

He withdraws slowly, lowering me to the floor, turning me around to face the glass, wrapping one arm around my waist, and I feel his warm lips on my skin, kissing softly. I rest my hands on the glass, watching the water escape down the drain, deep in thought as he takes the soap in his hands, gliding it over my body.

"What's the matter?" he breathes against my ear.

I don't answer. He turns me around to look at him, his eyes murky and clouded like a storm brewing on the horizon.

"I don't want you to go."

"I have to go, it's too late to change it. It's only a couple of days, baby. We have the rest of our lives together. If you want it."

"I want it!"

His eyes brighten as he briefly lowers his lips to mine. I take the soap in my hands, lathering it over his body, wrapping my fingers around his shaft, feeling it grow hard in my hands. He rests his hands on the glass just above the steamy impression of my hands, the image burning into my mind, a ghostly image that will haunt me tomorrow night when he's gone. He takes me in his arms, kissing me, holding me in that shower as though we may never hold each other again and though it's fulfilling in the moment, the second he lets me go, my heavy heart weighs me down, making it hard to stand.

"Come on." He turns off the shower and reaches for a towel and wraps it around me as we climb into bed, a damp, tangled mess, naked, holding each other tightly. I put my head on his chest and look up at him.

"Why are you doing this?" I ask.

"Doing what?"

"Why would you even want me after I left you?"

"Don't do that."

"But I cheated on you. How can you — ?"

"Because it was my fault. I drove you away," he interrupts.

"What?"

"My head wasn't in the right space back then. I was selfish and jealous and possessive and I didn't let you live your life the way you wanted to. I see that now and I'm trying to change. Since the accident, I've given you your space, I've let do you as you choose. I haven't been calling all the time, checking on you like I used to do. It's been hard for me, but I'm trying to be a better man. I was as much at fault as you were, but I've learnt my lesson. I'll never treat you like that again."

I tighten my arm around him. "I love the man who you are. You don't have to change a thing."

He stares down at me, his eyes grief-stricken.

"I was drunk that night," he murmurs.

"What night?"

"The night of your accident. You ran out of here hysterical.

Crying, screaming at me. You were a mess. I didn't want you to drive like that but I couldn't stop you. You jumped into your car and sped off. I tried to find my keys to come after you, but I couldn't find them and by the time I did, you were long gone. I started drinking when you left. Heavily. When the police came to the door, I could barely stand. That's why I got to the hospital after everyone else."

He clutches his forehead tightly.

"Some wonderful husband, aren't I? Your car was sinking to the bottom of an icy lake and I was sitting at home, drunk out of my mind."

"You *are* a wonderful husband. I love you."

"And I love you. More than you'll ever know."

He closes the gap between us, kissing me softly, caressing my skin. Out of breath, we part, both of us deep in thought, neither of us speaking, as we drift off to sleep, fading into the night. Dreading the daylight that would separate us for three days and two long nights.

* * * *

I feel the bed move and wake up to Nick's face above me, his lips kissing my forehead. His eyes form an endearing smile as he pulls the sheet up around me, covering me. The cool, crisp air is creeping in and I'm still naked.

"Hi," he whispers.

"Hi," I reply, rubbing my eyes.

"Go back to sleep. It's really early. I was just kissing you goodbye."

He's fully dressed with a long traveling coat over the top of his suit, his hair tousled with gel.

He's really leaving.

I glance down at his bags beside the bed and start to sit up.

"No, no. Don't get up. Go back to sleep. It's only four-thirty in the morning." I wince. "I'm just a phone call away if you need me. Remember Gabe and Malaylie are going to sleep here on the property with you while I'm away, so you'll be safe. I'll be home on Thursday. It's only three days. You'll barely have time to miss me."

He smiles, but his eyes can't hide his torment. If I begged him to stay, he would, but he wants this, and, perhaps he has a point. We haven't spent a day apart since he brought me home from the hospital. Maybe this *will* be good for us.

He brushes his soft lips against mine. It feels so natural to kiss him, as if our lips were made for each other, so tender, so right. I wrap my arms around him, returning his kiss with just as much tenderness.

As we drift apart, I open my eyes, catching a glint of panic in his. He doesn't want to go. The alarm on his watch sounds, startling us both. I watch him as he turns it off and glances up at me, a whole new look in his eyes.

"I have to go. I love you."

"I love you, too. Be safe."

He leans forward, scooping up the handles of his bags. "I will. You, too. Ring me about anything. Any time of the day or night."

"I will."

He stands swiftly, turning to leave. I lie there, watching him go, then hear the door shut downstairs and he is gone.

Chapter Thirteen

Roadside Manner

The day is long and weary. Helping Ari and Nigel look for a new house turns out to be a much harder feat than I anticipated. I wonder why I ever agreed to help in the first place — they're far too picky for my liking and nothing is ever right. Too much light, not enough light, bedrooms too big, bedrooms too small, the yard's too much to mow, there's no yard at all.

We end up back at his restaurant, just after five, for a quick bite to eat. The atmosphere is a buzzing ball of energy, the laughter loud and the food to die for, but I can barely eat, my stomach squirming like a pit of slimy snakes. I peer out through the big glass panels that lead to the street. The streetlights are on, the evening haze closing in. My breathing shallows, the thought of driving home in the dusky gloom daunting, though I don't know why. I'm no stranger to darkness.

It's almost six-thirty when I decide to head home. The thought of going back there, knowing Nick's not going to be there, is almost unbearable. I can't believe he's gone. Not even in the same state. So, so far away. I must have really upset him to leave me alone like this, at a time when I need him most. Mitch would never leave me alone and unprotected if he didn't have to. Now I'm just angry.

I hear my phone beep with a text message and reach into my purse for the phone. It's Mitch.

Can you text?

I swallow hard, answering almost immediately.

Yes.

He writes back, *Are you okay? I've been worried about you all day. Didn't know if I should text.*

I'm fine. All is well, I reply.

I have to see you. I can't stop thinking about you.

I text, *I'm with my brother. I'm heading home soon. I'll call you when I get home.*

xx Delete these.

It's just after seven when I leave. I drive home, turning off at my exit and pulling onto the long, windy stretch of road where I had my accident. I slow down as I reach the lake, my headlights illuminating the squiggly gray lines that used to be my thick black tire marks on the road. The lines heading straight toward the water's edge still chill me to the bone. As I near home, the streetlights grow fewer, the road ahead darker.

It's quiet tonight. I haven't passed a single car. I reach across to turn on my stereo when my cell rings on the seat beside me. It's Nick.

"Hey, you," I answer cheerfully.

"Hi," he replies. "How are you?"

"I'm fine. I'm just on my way home from dinner with Ari and Nigel, actually."

"How was it?"

"It was educational."

His laughter spirals through the earpiece. "Did they find a house yet?"

"No! They're worse than two women."

He laughs harder. "I've missed you so much today."

"I've missed you, too. I can't wait till Thursday."

"Me, too," he replies. "So, you're heading home then?"

"Yep, almost there."

"Okay, well, I'm just having dinner with some colleagues, so I'll give you a call a bit later."

"Sounds good."

"You've got an echo. Are you using hands-free?"

"No, I forgot."

"Well, use it, will you?"

"Okay."

"All right, drive carefully."

"I will."

"Talk to you soon."

"Yep, bye."

"Bye, baby." I can't help but smile as I hang up. It's so good to hear him in better spirits.

I toss the phone onto the seat beside me. I know the car has some sort of automatic phone connection, but I don't understand it and I can never get it working, so I just don't bother. I look up at the road ahead and notice headlights, coming up fast behind me. I look back in the rearview mirror, spooked.

All of a sudden, a loud siren blares. Red and blue lights flash behind me, illuminating and reflecting off everything around me. My eyes immediately zoom in on the speedometer. I'm not speeding.

I glance across at my phone on the seat beside me. Maybe they saw me on the phone. I indicate and pull over to the side of the road, looking back in the side mirror. The siren stops, but the lights continue to flash. A tall silhouette emerges from the car, walking slowly toward me.

It has to be Mitch.

What if it's not Mitch?

What if it is?

I lower my window and a bright light shines in my face. I look up, trying to shield my eyes.

"Good evening, miss. You've been pulled over this evening for the purposes of a breath test. Have you had anything to drink tonight?"

A heavy dose of adrenaline rushes through my body. My palms, resting on the wheel, sweating profusely.

"Uh, I had a couple of wines, a lot earlier, though," I reply. I feel sick, images of being arrested and locked away in a jail cell flashing through my mind.

"Can you turn your ignition off and step out of the vehicle please, miss." My legs turn to jelly. Maybe I should tell him I know Mitch — he might be lenient with me.

Again, I look up at him, but the light is too bright in my eyes.

"Miss?" He drifts back, waiting for me to get out of the car. He sounds a little like Mitch, but I'm not completely sure. Regardless, I'm still flustered.

"Mitch?" I ask. He doesn't answer. "Did I do something wrong?"

"Just step out of the vehicle please, miss," he says sternly. I turn off the engine, open the door and step out onto the road. He turns out the light. It *is* Mitch. I clutch at my chest.

"Oh, my God, you scared me."

"That's what I was going for."

I jump into his arms, holding him to me. It surprises me how good it is to see him. All my worries, fears and anxiety disappear the moment he touches my skin, as though he's somehow magically absorbing them.

"How are you? Are you okay?" he asks, tightening his arms around me.

"Yes." I reply. "Much better now."

"That's good."

He buries his head in my hair, inhaling my scent, then snatches my upper arms roughly, pushing me back against the car.

"Turn around," he says sternly.

"What?"

"Turn around," he snaps, his face deadly serious.

He seizes my arm, spinning me around, pushing me up hard against the door. I gasp, a spluttering sound leaving my lips when he presses his body firmly against mine, lowering his mouth to my ear.

"Where's Nick?" he breathes, grazing my earlobe with his teeth.

I whimper, my bottom lip quivering as he brushes the hair from my neck, replacing it with his daring, dominant mouth.

Oh God. What am I doing? I can't do this. I can't do this to Nick.

Mitch lashes his tongue up and down the side of my throat with a mesmerizing fierceness that leaves me wet and wanting. I close my eyes, tilting my head to the side, allowing him better access. "He's at a conference in Melbourne."

He pauses, then slides his hand down my body and between my thighs, touching me, teasing me. "How long is he away for?"

"Three days."

He steps back, pulling my arms behind my back a little too roughly.

I look over my shoulder at him. "What are you doing?"

He tugs his handcuffs from his belt, cuffing my hands tightly behind me. I twist my wrists, struggling against them, but the cold steel bites my skin, forcing me to stop. He lowers his mouth to my ear.

"You're all mine now," he growls.

He grabs my arm, dragging me around to the other side of the car, forcing me up against the front guard and bending me over the hood. I try to stand, but he forces me back down, kicking my feet apart so my legs are spread wide.

"Mitch." I gasp, looking around. Anyone could see us here. He thrusts his hips against mine so I can feel him, harder and larger than life behind me. Again I try to lift my head, but he brings his hand down hard on the back of my neck, holding me in place.

"Stay there!" he orders. His voice, gruff and menacing.

The night air is so cold. The warmth from the engine

radiates through the hood, heating my skin, and I turn my face, resting against it, taking comfort in its warmth.

"What are you going to do?"

He lowers his mouth to my ear. "I'm going to fuck you. Hard. Right here on the side of the road and there's nothing you can do about it."

He lifts my skirt and I look around frantically. "What if someone goes past?"

His hand glides down my back to my hip then snatches the fabric of my underwear, tearing them from my body. I yelp in shock, my breaths coming hard and fast as I lie there, completely at his mercy. He slides his fingers between my legs, working them inside me, stretching me.

"Still sore?" he asks.

I wet my lips. "No."

"You will be," he promises.

He withdraws his fingers suddenly, to yank on his belt and undo his zipper, and I feel him against me, circling the head of his monstrous, needy cock between my legs, threatening me, giving me time to prepare myself. I take a deep breath, though it's all I've been able to think about.

My heart pounds harder than ever before. He tightens his hand around the back of my neck, holding me down. His strength is frightening. He's been so gentle with me, but not tonight. Tonight he's in charge, exerting his authority over me, and he's not playing around. He doesn't hesitate, forcing himself inside me, tearing at my skin, pulling back then pounding deeper inside my body.

My mouth opens, my eyes opening wider. "Mitch! Oh, fuck!" I scream. Nothing could prepare me for his size. My body jolts upward involuntarily from the hood at the sheer shock of him so entirely inside me, only to be slammed back down.

"That's it, scream!" His voice is ruthless. "No one can hear you out here, honey."

He pulls back, driving into me harder, again, and again, groaning as he unleashes his relentless, power-driven assault. My skin burns around him, filling me with simultaneous sensations of pain and pleasure as I scream his name, struggling and writhing beneath him. Suddenly he stops, pulling entirely out of my body. I lie there on the hood, gasping, my thighs open wide, his punished prisoner, absolutely his.

I feel him still between my thighs, teasing me, tormenting me, and I whimper, pushing back against him, needing him, wanting him.

"He doesn't make you feel like this, does he? He doesn't excite you like this."

I don't respond, drawing in deep breaths through my nose. He sinks his fingers into my hips and presses the tip of his waiting shaft against me, circling just once then ramming into me again and again. I cry out as my hips are slammed against the car. It hurts, but I have bigger things to worry about, like his thick, merciless cock buried so deep inside me that tears form in my eyes.

He knots his fingers in my hair, tilting my head back so he can watch me.

"Does he?" he yells, rocking his hips against mine, making sure that I take all of him.

"*No!*" I scream.

He withdraws swiftly before pounding into me faster and harder, over and over. The pain is almost unbearable. His breathing grows frantic and erratic as I buck my hips against him, moaning and panting beneath him. He pushes the cuffs down hard against my back so they tighten, pinching my skin, reminding me that I'm bound, and I thrash against them, the deprivation turning me on.

"Oh, you're so wet," he groans.

My excitement builds. I'm so close. I clench as tight as I can around him, drawing in every inch of him, desperate for air as I push back hard against him, practically jumping up and down as my blood turns to pure pleasure, pulsating thick and fast through my veins. I scream his name, moaning and muttering as I drench his shaft.

He cries out, thrusting wildly, and his warmth fills me as he collapses onto my back. Both of us panting, breathless, red and blue lights flashing, lighting up the landscape all around us.

"Oh, Scar," he breathes, twitching inside me, moving his hips so slightly back and forth.

I close my eyes as I slowly return to my body, my lungs aching from the raspy, cool night air. He withdraws slowly, pulling my skirt down around me. "Are you okay?"

I raise my head and he takes the cuffs off. He zips his pants and turns me around to look at him. His eyes are not what I expect. They're wild and exhilarated, but there's something else there, something tender and bewitching.

"Yeah, I'm just a little shell-shocked. You're wild!"

"What?"

I shake my head, in awe of him. He takes my face in his hands, kissing me, caressing my lips, as our tongues entwine in a slow, sacred dance. He reluctantly releases me, stepping back, tightening his belt and straightening his uniform. My wrists are burning. I bring them up to my chest, rubbing them. He bows his head to mine, his eyes concerned.

"Did I hurt you?"

I shake my head. He takes my wrists in his hands, inspecting them, then rubs them and pulls them around his waist. I close my eyes, listening to his heartbeat and inhaling his scent, so completely fulfilled.

"Are you sure you're okay?" he asks.

I look up at him. "I'm fine. I was so scared someone was going to go past, but it was amazing."

"It was *fucking* amazing!"

I nod, giggling. "So, what are you doing up this way?"

"I'm doing a couple shifts for traffic branch at Coomera. I wanted to make sure you got home okay."

"Thank you."

He drags his gaze from mine to his police radio and turns it on. Stern voices go back and forth, then suddenly a woman's voice speaks loudly above the others.

"VKR to 901. VKR 901, third call, no response."

He rolls his eyes, pressing the button on his mouthpiece.

"901, VKR." he replies, equally as stern.

"901, what's your location?"

He glances up at the road ahead of us. "901, VKR, I'm stationary RBT, Foxwells Road."

"VKR, 901 received. Job details when ready."

"Go ahead, VKR."

I frown at him, no idea what's going on.

"901, job details to you at nineteen-forty, code 3, please proceed to 2124 Aaron Street, Coomera, take up with a Mr. Wilson in relation to a 313. States neighbors are drunk and shouting abuse in the street. No closer cars. Call for backup if required. 245 proceeding from Hope Island ETA twenty minutes. VKR out."

"901 received, proceeding." He turns to me, pressing his lips together. "I'm so sorry, I have to go."

"I hear that. You're going on your own to that? It sounds dangerous."

He nods, taking my hand and walking me around to the driver's door. "Come here."

He pulls me into his arms, lifting me off the ground, closing his lips over mine. I don't want him to go. The connection between us is so strong yet so fragile. I wrap my arms around his neck, putting all I am into the kiss, engulfing his mouth, twirling my tongue around his in searing, powerful strokes. He groans, his arms squeezing me so tightly I can hardly breathe as he slowly lowers me to the ground, touching his lips to mine just once.

"Come to my place. Sleep there tonight. I'll knock off early."

"I can't. Gabe and Malaylie are staying overnight, I have to go home."

"I'll come to your place, then, sneak in through the night, slip between your thighs and steal away before sun comes up. Your house guests will never know I'm there."

"I'd love that, but I just can't."

He touches his palm to the side of my face and I press against it, closing my eyes, craving his touch.

"Okay. I'll see you tomorrow then?"

"Yes."

He kisses my forehead. "I have to go."

"Be careful."

"Always am."

As I drive off, he does a U-turn, speeding off in the opposite direction, taking a passenger with him.

My soul.

Chapter Fourteen

A Moment to Myself

The drive home is long, though it's not that far. As I grow closer to the house, I notice the front lights are on. Nick's car is parked in the driveway along with the estate car. The lights are on in the garage. *Looks as though Gabe and Malaylie are definitely here.* I head inside, glancing down at my watch. Eight o'clock. *Nick will be calling soon.*

"Malaylie?" I call out.

She rushes into the lounge from the kitchen in her pajamas and slippers, her long black hair flowing loosely down her back. I've never seen her like this before.

"Good evening, Mrs. Pierce. I'm all dressed for the slumber party. I've got my two favorite movies here. *While You Were Sleeping* and *Love Actually*."

"Great," I reply, returning her smile.

"Why don't you go get showered and I'll poppa the popcorn?"

"Sounds like a plan!"

A mindless night in front of the TV. Just what I need.

I wander up to the bedroom and turn on the light. The room looks the same as it always does, but tonight the ambience is awful. Knowing Nick isn't coming home tonight, the next two nights in fact, steals the air right out of the room.

I take off my clothes and turn on the shower, slipping under the warm water, consumed with grief and Mitch. I can't get him out of my head and I can't understand it. I love Nick. I miss him so much. My love for him grows stronger and stronger every day. When I'm in his arms, there's nowhere else I want to be. When we make love, the connection between us is so deep and meaningful and mesmerizing. It's everything I want it to be and more, but when Mitch and I are together, it's fire and brimstone, exciting and exhilarating, an insane madness, an insatiable gluttonous greed. My feelings from him happened so suddenly, so intensely, and now he's all I can think about. The way my body charges with electricity when I'm near him. The way my head tells me to run, but something in his eyes makes me stay. Making love with him is like a glimpse of Utopia. A moment of timelessness in a blissful, forbidden nirvana.

Is that what Mitch and I are doing? Making love? Is it possible to love two people, with such intensity, at the same time?

I watch the water running down the drain, washing Mitch's touch from my body. I close my eyes, recapturing the moment he threw me down on the hood and forced himself inside me, reliving the intense pleasure and pain, then glance down at the wedding ring on my finger, so completely torn between them.

If fate isn't inevitable, then how the hell did I end up here?

* * * *

Salty tears stream down my face as the angry black rain pelts against the windscreen, hammering into the glass like silver nails. My hair falls down around my face and I tuck it back behind my ear as I glance in the rear-vision mirror. Bright lights shine behind me, veering erratically from side to side. I can hear the motor, a loud, threatening, throaty roar.

The rain comes down harder, seemingly merciless in its attempt to create a blurry, disorientated chaos. My tears fall like the rain on my window, the heat from my body fogging the glass all around me. I can't see. I turn on the windscreen wipers faster, swiping at the glass with the sleeve of my shirt, but it makes little difference. My phone rings on the seat beside me and I glance across at the name on the screen. Mitch. He's my only hope. I make a reach for the phone, flicking at it with my fingertips, but the seat belt locks, holding me in place, sawing at my skin. I can't reach it. A car horn sounds and I look up into the lights of an oncoming car, blinding me. I swerve off the road, the back wheels churning up the loose gravel on the side of the road before kicking me back onto the soaking tar. I glance down at the phone just as it slides off the seat onto the floor, the screen still alight, still ringing. I'll never reach it now. I'm on my own.

My heart pounds out a frenzied drumming that amplifies and echoes in my ears. The rain is too hard, the road too dark. I have no idea where I am. I slow down just a little, but the car behind is too close. It nudges the back of mine, propelling me forward, the steering wheel making corrections of its own. I scream, doing all that I can to keep the car on the road. I look back in the rearview mirror, filled with fear, panic, dread, terror, so many emotions, but survival is the one that takes over. My only instinct is to try to outrun it and so I accelerate into the darkness, knowing Mitch is somewhere up ahead.

I focus intently on the road, trying to work out where I am, when a yellow road sign lights up. I'm at the lake. I take my foot off the accelerator, slowing down for the sweeping bend that I know lies just ahead, but the car behind me speeds up, clipping the back corner of my car.

The steering wheel rips out of my hands. I slam on the brakes and feel the wheels bite the wet bitumen, then skip across to the wrong side of the road. The car spins out of control. I can't stop it, there's nothing I can do. My lights shine on the guardrail of the shoulder right before I hit it, the sound of twisted metal and glass breaking filling my ears. My head smashes against my window, then suddenly there's complete silence, nothing but black all around me. I feel my body lift off the seat. I'm falling, falling. A tremendous whirlwind of sound swirls through the air, followed by a deafening thud. I scream. My body slams forward against the steering wheel as the windscreen smashes in front of me. Water bursts through the glass onto my body, pouring into the car. The water is so cold. My head hurts. Everything goes black.

It's cold. I'm so cold. I open my eyes, it's dark. There's water all around me. I scream, but there's no sound. My eyelids flutter as my mind struggles to comprehend the air bubbles coming from my mouth. I try to move, to swim, to get out of the car, but I'm strapped into my seat. My hair floats in front of my face, obstructing my view, and I swipe it out of the way, pushing frantically at the seat belt release, but it holds fast. My chest is hurting, my throat burning, my head thumping as though it's about to explode. My body convulses, my lungs completely filled with water. I yank at the seat belt one last time, screaming, my mind scratching at the inside of my skull, trying to free itself from my body, to shed my skin.

I sit up, screaming, clutching at my throat, gasping for air. There's light all around me. I blink, adjusting to the light, scanning the room. I'm in my room, in my bed. I reach across for Nick, but he's not there. I collapse onto his side of the bed, clutching his pillow, tears consuming me.

There was a second car.

I close my eyes, attempting to block out the horror of trying to escape from my own body. The terror of running out of air, knowing I was about to die, feeling my body convulsing violently in shock, knowing that I'd lost the fight. They say a person isn't supposed to see their own death in their dreams and if they do, they're dead. I died in that car. In the cold. In the darkness. All alone.

Though mine was a deathless death, it was still death. Mitch brought me back to life, but I died that night in a watery grave and someone put me there. But why? Why would someone want me dead?

I reach for the phone and call Nick. It's only seven-thirty. He should still be at his hotel. He answers on the first ring.

"Good morning, baby," he answers.

"Nick," I sob.

"What's wrong?"

"I dreamed about the accident. I saw everything."

"What? Oh, God. I'm so sorry I'm not there."

Tears stream down my face. I pant, sucking in deep

breaths.

"It's okay, just breathe. What did you see?"

"It was awful," I sob. "I felt the car go into the water, felt the cold, felt the terror."

"Oh, baby. I'm so sorry."

"There *was* definitely a second car behind me. I saw it. It hit the back of my car. It wasn't an accident. It was chasing me, it forced me off the road."

"What? Did you see who it was?"

"No. It was too dark. It was a dark-colored car, like Mitch said. That's all I could make out."

"Call the police, tell them what you saw."

"It's a dream, Nick. They're not going to investigate anything based on a dream."

"But we have to do something. Do you realize what this means? What if someone's still after you, like you said? I'm coming home. I shouldn't have left you there alone."

"I'm not alone. Gabe and Malaylie are here. Finish your business. It's just a dream."

"It's *not* just a dream. I don't know what I was thinking coming down here. I've been so caught up in all this Mitch bullshit. I can't believe I was so blind."

"Nick, I'm fine. I have Malaylie and Gabe. You'll be home in two days. Finish your business."

He doesn't answer.

I glance across at the clock. "Ari and Nigel will be here soon to pick me up. I'd better get dressed."

"Scarlet," he says, panicked.

"I'll be okay. I'm with the boys all day today. Ring me when you get back to the hotel this afternoon."

"Oh, I'll be ringing you before then. You stay safe."

"Yep. Bye."

"Bye, baby." The doorbell rings.

Shit! They're early.

I jump out of bed and get dressed, then rush down to greet them. They're in the kitchen, busy talking to Malaylie. Ari spots me first, rushing over for one of his customary bear hugs, flanked by Nigel, his face glowing brighter than the sun.

"Good morning, sleepyhead. Sorry we're early. We thought we'd come for one of Malaylie's legendary brews before we head off."

"No, it's fine. I was just getting up when I heard the door."

"I think we've found it," Ari gushes. "Four bedrooms, for sleep-overs, three bathrooms, a private terrace and in-ground whirlpool bath. Ooooh, I'm so excited. I'm *sure* this is the one!"

"Sounds great!" I feign a smile and glance out toward the pool, distracted, my dream lurking around in the back of my mind. I'm so not in the mood for house hunting, but I'm glad of the company and it might keep my fears at bay, at least for a while. We drink our coffees and head off, hopeful of finding 'the one' when my phone beeps with a text message. It's Mitch.

Hi baby. How are you? Can't wait to see you. xx

My heart beats faster and I feel instantly brighter. I start to write back to him, but Ari interrupts me, handing me the brochure of the house listing, and I put the phone down, not remembering to write back until much later.

Later in the day, I write, *Hi, sorry I didn't get back to you sooner. Been busy.*

He replies almost immediately. *Is everything okay?*

Yes and no. Had a nightmare about the accident. Saw the whole thing. You were right, there was a second car behind me. It forced me off the road.

Oh, Scar! Are you okay? Did you see the other car or who was driving?

No. It was raining too hard, but the car looked dark, like you said.

He texts, *Can I ring you? Where are you? Come to me, it's not safe.*

I'm in the car with my brother and Nigel at the moment, can't talk. I'm fine, I text.

I start work at 2. Ring me and I'll amend the police report and reopen the investigation. I'm worried about you. Why didn't you call me?

I reply, *The boys picked me up early. I didn't have time. I'll call you later, okay.*

You better. I'll be waiting. xx

* * * *

Ari drops me home late in the afternoon. It's almost five. He's pestered me all day long about what's wrong, but I can't tell him. He would only tell Mom, who, in turn, would tell everyone she knows, after which no one would leave me alone.

Gabe and Malaylie are talking in the kitchen when I walk in. I say hello quickly and hurry up to the bedroom. The day's been far too long and my feet are killing me. Helping Nigel and Ari pick a house has been a way bigger ordeal than I anticipated. I'm just glad they finally found what they were looking for. I feel as though I've seen the entire city from the inside out. It's been a welcome distraction, though. I've barely had any time to think about someone following me or to torture myself over my feelings for the two men in my life.

I put my phone on the bedside table and lie down on the bed, exhausted. The minute I put my head on the pillow, my phone rings loudly, vibrating across the bedside table. I grab it just before it topples over the edge. It's Tash.

"S'me," she shouts, way-too-cheerfully, in my ear.

"Hi, Tash."

"Oh, Lordy, I hope you're on your way, woman. You're going to be late. You're supposed to be at the art gallery by five-forty-five. Remember? The gallery opening?"

"Oh, crap! I thought that was tomorrow night. I just got home. I've been with Nigel and Ari all day, looking at houses. I'm exhausted."

"Didn't hear that. Get dressed, you're coming," she insists.

"Tash, I—"

"Get dressed. *Now!*"

I exhale loudly. "Okay, okay. I may be fashionably late, but I'll be there."

"Good. See you soon."

I throw down the phone and jump into the shower—just the thing to get me going again. I search through the dressing room for something to wear, finally slipping into my favorite red silk designer Dinnigan, leaving my hair hanging freely down my back. I do my makeup quickly then rush downstairs to find Gabe waiting for me. Evidently *he* didn't forget about the gallery opening.

Nick rings when I'm almost there, checking in. He's so worried about me. It's odd to hear him so nervous.

It's still early when I arrive at the gallery. People still lining the stairs and talking in the street, waiting for friends to arrive, so I can't be too late. I walk up the stairs and spot Tash at the front door, going over the guest list with the doorman. She looks up at me, waving me over and telling the big blond penguin at the door to let me pass. A cool chill in the air breezes over my shoulders and I shudder, regretting my choice of dress already. My long, flowing backless gown provides no warmth whatsoever and in my haste to leave, I left my jacket on the bed.

I hug Tash carefully, trying not to wrinkle her in her elegant empire-wasted dark-gray gown. She ushers me inside, pointing out Tayla in the back corner of the gallery. Tayla's eagerly scanning the room, no doubt searching for tonight's take-home prize. I glance around. The gallery's an enormous upmarket space with raised ceilings, the room divided only by suspended red and blue banners. The soft background opera-style music mixed with guests' voices and laughter electrifies the atmosphere, and the turnout is impressive. Tash has done a great job. The artists are a young, hip, up-and-coming couple and the artwork on the walls is interesting to say the least. Very bright and looks to me like splotches of paint thrown on canvases by a bunch of two-year-olds, but then what do I know about art? Nothing. I feel like a fish out of water.

I take a glass of champagne from a passing waitress and walk across the room toward Tayla. She spots me at the last minute, an infectious smile spreading across her face.

"Darling," she gushes, as though she's the richest woman in the room. I gaze along the length of her long black evening dress.

"What's with the dress?"

She looks down then rolls her eyes. "Ugh, Tash insisted I wear an evening gown. Is it hideous? I feel hideous."

"No, it's not hideous. It's just not like you to wear anything below the—"

"Thigh?"

We laugh. "I was gonna say knee."

She gazes at where her gown sweeps the floor. "Oh, I know, it's so mummyish, isn't it? I feel as if I should have a baby strapped to my boob or something."

I take a sip of champagne, trying to mask my amusement.

"I've got these ridiculous suck-your-gut-in granny pants on underneath here, too. I went to Mom's for an early dinner before I came and she cooked that damn pasta dish I love. I had to eat it, but now I've got this ridiculous pasta bloat." She points to her belly as if she's giving me directions and I look down.

"There's nothing there."

"Well, not *now*, I've got these gut suckers on!" We giggle loudly.

"So, what are you doing over here on your own, or shouldn't I ask?"

"I'm just doing a quick talent scout, but there's an abundance of tuna here tonight. Where are all the rich, good-looking men?"

"Ew, Tayla! That's horrible, and the good-looking men are at home with their good-looking wives."

"Hmmm. How's the house-hunting going with the boys? Did they find something yet?"

"Don't ask!"

"Okay, I won't. How's things with that big muscle-bound spunk of yours?"

I look up at her, eyeing the drink in her hand. "How many of those have you had? You never have anything nice to say about Nick."

"Too many, but I wouldn't exactly say I was being nice. I don't like muscles, or spunk, really, it tastes funny."

Again, we can't contain ourselves.

"Oooh. Ring-a-ding-ding. Fire in the hole." She motions toward a tall, much younger man smiling at her from the pop-up bar. She bats her eyelashes, flashing her most obvious come-hither smile, and he winks back at her.

"Well, that's my cue. I must leave you. Firemen's poles to slide down and all that."

I raise an eyebrow, amused, watching her as she struts toward him, swinging her hips to and fro. He takes two glasses of champagne from the bar, holding them up to her as he walks toward her, grinning like an idiot.

I steal a glance around the room, taking generous gulps of my champagne to settle my nerves. There really is an abundance of 'tuna' or whatever disgusting name Tayla calls it, and way too many couples for my liking, cuddling and kissing. Thoughts of Mitch immediately come to mind *and* the fact that I forgot to call him back.

I take my phone out of my purse and send him a text, typing in ten different things before finally sending, *Thinking of you. x*

A text comes back almost immediately.

Where are you?

"Drink, ma'am?" a waitress interrupts.

I look up at her and smile, drinking down the dregs in my glass and taking another before writing back, *An art gallery opening at Southbank with the girls.*

I'm close. Is it Mathieson's on Main?

I reread his words. He's close. *What?* He's coming here? I glance across at Tayla then Tash, standing at the entrance. I don't feel up to going over my relationship issues with them. It will only complicate things.

I text, *I don't think that's a good idea.*

His message comes through instantly. *I'm here.*

The panicked rhythm of my heart vibrates through my body. I can't breathe. I can't believe he's here. I slip my phone inside my purse, take a generous gulp of champagne to calm my nerves and glance across at Tash at the door. Thankfully, Tayla is on the other side of the room now, staring at an obscure piece of art in a dark corner with Mr. Encouragable. The music and clinking of glasses seem to grow louder, or maybe I'm just more aware of them.

I glance anxiously across toward the doorway, and there he is, filling the space with his grandiose presence. His uniform clinging to his tall, toned frame. His arms projecting out from his broad shoulders to clear his gun, sitting proud on his hip. His dark hair sitting up at the front, accentuating his even darker eyes. I've never seen him look more handsome. I tremble. A heady dose of desire courses through my veins, burning me up from the inside out.

I can't believe just laying eyes on him can do such things to my body. Everything stops. Everyone in the room turns to look at him, men consumed by him, women besotted, but his eyes are on me. He speaks to Tash momentarily, then strides across the room toward me. My face burns like molten lead. Tash comes into view behind him, pulling 'WTF?' faces at me. I have no idea what I'm going to say to her, or Tayla, who by now has surely noticed him. Who can miss him? He stops just in front of me and nothing but that matters now.

"Hi," he murmurs, swallowing hard, ravaging my body with his eyes.

"Hi."

He curls his lips up into a devilish grin and I smile back, fighting every urge in my body to jump into his arms and smother him in kisses so that everyone can see he's mine. His hands twitch at his sides and I know he feels the same way. "God, it's good to see you."

"You, too."

We keep our eyes locked on each other, saying things with them our mouths can't. I glance around the room — people still staring at us. I feel so self-conscious, as though my desire for him is written all over my body and everyone can see what he did to me last night. He drifts his gaze down my neck to my breasts, lingering there, then continuing down my dress.

"Is that dress backless?"

I nod, wetting my lips, then tilt my shoulders just a little so he can see. He presses his fist to his mouth, trying to conceal his jubilant grin. I bite my bottom lip, letting my gaze drift down his body to his chest, afraid to roam any farther in case there's something on display there that shouldn't be.

"Oh. My God," I hear a voice from behind me, and I know immediately whose it is. "*Mitch?*"

We both turn around to see Tayla well on her way over. Mitch feigns a smile.

"What the—? You're a cop? I thought you built tugboats or something."

He dips his head, doing his best not to laugh. "I do both," he replies.

"Wow," she gushes, quickly swinging around to meet with Tash's eagle-eyed stare. "So what are you doing here?"

"Uh, I was just checking on a car crew that weren't responding and I saw Scarlet through the window," he lies.

"Right," Tayla responds, still checking him out.

He glances toward the door again, casually flicking his fingertips against his neck. I've seen him do that before. He's nervous about something.

I follow his gaze toward the door as a tall, dark-haired female police officer walks in. The same female officer I saw at the mall, the same woman I saw at the boatyard a few days ago. I find my gaze lingers on her, as does that of everyone else in the room. She's quite striking, actually, her hair pulled back in a bun, her skin the softest china-doll shade of white. She strides toward us, exuding confidence, fixing her hard eyes on me, assessing me, completely unashamed to stare. I shift on my feet awkwardly, growing more and more self-conscious under her gaze.

She stops beside Mitch. "Mitch, we should get going. The squad's on its way. Looks as if that car belongs to Reyus."

"Really? Any sign of him?"

She shakes her head sternly.

Tayla excuses herself, rushing over to Tash as a male voice talks on the police radio on Mitch's shoulder. He turns it off. I feel Jade's eyes on me, but I ignore her, focusing my attention on Mitch. I glance down at his uniform. Something's different. A police emblem now where his stripes used to be and his name badge reads *Senior Sergeant Morgan* instead of *Sergeant*. He looks back up at me and I glance across at his partner.

"Uh, sorry, Scarlet, this is Jade, Jade, Scarlet," he mumbles.

"Oh, hi." I smile at her. "Nice to meet you."

Jade sneers back at me, not extending me the same courtesy. *Wow! Friendly.*

Mitch clears his throat and I focus my attention on him,

Jade's silhouette quickly fading into the background along with everyone else's. There's only him and me. A female's voice speaks loudly on the police radio on Jade's shoulder and she turns away, responding.

Mitch takes a deep breath as she sashays off. "So. A gallery opening, huh? I didn't really think art was your thing."

"It's not, really. Tash is a friend of the owner and they asked her to host the opening. It's more of a numbers-type thing, though I'm not sure that's an issue. There's quite a turnout."

He nods.

Jade walks back toward us, taking Mitch's arm in her hand, moving in close to his ear. I watch her slide her hand up and down his arm slowly, caressing him as she speaks. My stomach turns, my jaw clenching involuntarily. I don't like it. She stops talking as a voice speaks on the radio again. Mitch reaches over, leaning in close to her ear, talking on her radio. I glance down at Jade's shirt. Only one stripe. I guess that means she's far less senior than Mitch. He had three stripes last time I saw him in uniform, before it was upgraded to the emblem.

She rests her hand on Mitch's back, tugging me from my thoughts, then glares over her shoulder at me, blatantly sliding her hand across his body, claiming him, warning me off. I can't hide my feelings. Seeing Mitch so close to her like that boils my blood. I frown, filled with a sudden urge to strangle her until she turns blue. Luckily for her, Mitch speaks loudly into the radio, breaking our stare.

"VKR, this is 102. We've had confirmation of that suspect at that location. Can you send 211 and 212 to Fifth and North, 213 and 214 to Seventh and North then advise to switch to channel 32 and await further instructions. 102 out."

"VKR received," a commanding male voice replies.

Mitch turns back to me. "Sorry about that."

Jade steps forward, touching his hand. "Mitch, we should get going," she says, her voice charged with authority.

"It's fine. The squad's at least fifteen minutes away." He hands her the car keys. "I'll be out in just a minute."

She glowers at him then snatches the keys from his hand, turning abruptly and storming toward the door. Definitely not the way anyone would respond to their boss. There's something between them, I can feel it. His brow creases as he turns in my direction, scanning the room.

"Could you come with me for just a minute?" he asks.

"Uh, yeah. Sure." I step forward, leading him toward the bathrooms. As we walk down the corridor, he tries the doorknob of the utilities room. The door opens. He looks around quickly then pushes me inside. The room is dark, a small red light on the alarm panel on the wall beside the door giving the room a dull blood-red glow. The door's barely shut when he pulls me into his arms, his eager lips on mine, his tongue inside my mouth, his hands everywhere.

He presses himself against me so that I feel what he has to give, tilting his head to find just the right angle to devour my mouth. A wolfish growl rumbles in his throat and I moan into his mouth, relishing its hot, wet heat, sharing his warmth, while he clutches at the exposed skin of my back.

Out of breath, we part, "Do you have any idea how stunning you are? Every man in this place was looking at you out there," he whispers against my ear.

"And every woman was looking at you."

"Let them look. All I want is you."

I whimper, his voice in my ear making my whole body quiver. He swoops his mouth down on my neck. Mitch snatches at my dress, hitching it up, then glides between my thighs, stopping abruptly when he realizes I'm not wearing underwear. "What the fuck?" He touches me there again. "Is that for me?"

"Yes," I whisper.

He draws in a deep breath, grabbing me roughly and pushing me back against a table beside the door. I slide my hand down his body, over his gun to the tremendous bulge threatening to burst out of his pants.

"Yeah?" he breathes.

I moan against his ear and he tightens his grip on my arms, spinning me around and bending me over the table. I hear his zipper and I reach back, feeling him, taking him hot and throbbing in my hand, guiding him toward me. He clutches at my hips, holding me steady as I rub him against my soft, damp lips, feeding him slowly inside me. I whimper and throw back my head, pushing against him, the thought of him entirely inside me the only one on my mind. He leans forward, wrapping his arm around my waist, pulling me back hard against him, forcing himself deep inside me, putting his hand over my mouth just in time to stifle my cries.

He eases back then drives himself into me deeper and harder, filling me with his monstrous, rock-hard cock again and again, stifling cries of his own. I tighten around him, flexing my hips up and down, whimpering as he grows harder and harder to take. I clench tightly around him, breathless, lost in the wilds of his savage strokes. I tense my calves, rising to my toes as I scream into his cupped hand, thudding nosily into the abyss of my subconscious, floating in a weightless realm. He groans, tightening his grip on my mouth, the feeling of his hand depriving me of air so erotic that it prolongs my orgasm. He pounds his hips against mine, unleashing a release of his own. He lets go of my mouth and I collapse, gasping for air, lying limp over the desk.

"*Oh, Scar,*" he pants, lowering his chest to my back and kissing my neck.

"Again," I breathe.

He chuckles, withdrawing slowly, pulling my dress down around me. "I'd love to, but I've got bad guys to catch, remember."

I hear his zipper and belt dinging and stand slowly, turning to face him.

He presses the light on his watch, checking the time. "Oh God, I really, really have to go," he says, his voice filled with humor.

"I know. Go."

He adjusts his uniform, taking my face in his hands, kissing me hard and fast.

"I'm so sorry. I'll see you tomorrow?"

"Yes. Go!" I giggle.

He opens the door, chuckling as he leaves, leaving me smiling into the dim, red glow of the room like the devil's daughter.

Chapter Fifteen

Fear and Love

The next morning, I wake up to my phone ringing. It's Nick, calling to check how I am, but I'm too tired to talk. I splutter out a few incoherent words and he tells me to go back to sleep. I put the phone down, drifting off, then wake shortly after to the sound of my phone beeping with a text message. I look across at the clock. It's eight. I'm way too tired and my head hurts way too much.

Another headache.

A friendly reminder of my brain injury, though this one is not so friendly. I open my drawer and take out a new bottle of painkillers, my only defense against the rock concert that insists on playing in my head. I roll over and try to go back to sleep, but a couple of minutes later another text comes through. This time I make the effort.

Two texts from Mitch. The first one reads, *Hi Beautiful. I'm going out of my mind thinking about you. xx*

The second text reads, *Can't stand another minute without you in my arms. xxxx*

I stare down at the message, feeling exactly the same way, wishing more than anything I was lying in his arms right now. I can't believe the way I've come to feel about him. I feel *bad* about the way I've come to feel about him. Wretched. I know in my heart this affair, this addiction, these feelings, they can't go on. The lies, the betrayal, a testament to my human frailty that will eventually scar us all, but I can't give him up. I don't want to give him up. I can't believe that girl last night with her paws all over him. I didn't like it last night and I really don't like it this morning.

I write back, *Me neither. x*

I need to see you. I need to be inside you…

A stab of desire hits me hard. I text, *I'm touching where you were inside me. x*

Holy fuck. Thanks a lot. I'm sitting in the dayroom, surrounded by a room full of coppers and I've got a boner.

I laugh.

He sends another, *I finish work at 2pm. Meet me at my place?*

I read the words over and over, consumed with thoughts of what he'll do to me when I get there.

And what will happen if I do?

I'll blow…your mind.

I may blow yours… See you at 2.

Well I'm off to the bathroom…Can't wait to see you. xxxxx

I laugh harder, dropping the phone and throwing myself back among the pillows.
What am I doing? This isn't just playing with fire, it's conjuring a nuclear holocaust.
There's no hope for me. I'm completely besotted with him. Last night, when I saw him walk into that room, he was all I wanted, all I could ever need, but in the light of day, as I glance across at Nick's side of the bed, empty, I'd

give anything to have Nick here with me. I roll over into his pillows, inhaling the faint scent of his cologne, then exhale loudly. I'm in big trouble. I'm supposed to be sorting out my feelings and all I'm doing is complicating them.

I lie there looking at the ceiling, my moral compass haywire, my mind south of sane. Somewhere I took a wrong turn, just as I did before the accident that led me to where I am. The devil's playground. A dark, twisted place of chaos and anarchy without horizons or borderlines to define us. I glance across at the picture of Nick and me on our wedding day. We look so incredibly happy. So in love. Everyone tells me it was a wonderful day. An outdoor wedding, under the biggest oak tree in our yard. We drank vino all day and danced all night under the colored lanterns intricately strung through the branches of the tree overhead. I wish I could remember it.

Ever since the dreams started, I've spent many a night falling asleep looking at that picture, hoping that I'll dream of it. So far, nothing, but there is always hope. I stare right into Nick's Van Gogh-style blue eyes. I love him. I want to believe he's the loving, devoted husband that I think he is, but every now and then I catch a glimpse of someone else. An oppressive, monopolizing version of himself that fills me with fear. The kind of fear that a person backs away from slowly because they're too afraid to take their eyes off whatever it is they think they see.

He's gone away, insisting that I explore my feelings. Explore what I had with Mitch before the accident. It didn't make sense for him to be so rational about this when he'd been doing everything he could to keep us apart. If he knew what was happening between Mitch and me, he'd be devastated. Yet he said this is what he wanted. He wanted me to spend time with Mitch. He had to consider the possibility of him and me sleeping together. He definitely had to consider that. The question that worries me most is, why? I shake off the thought then roll over and jump out of bed. Lots to do before two.

I get dressed and leave early, driving into town to run errands before heading over to Mitch's just before two p.m. I pull into the boatyard carpark, glancing down at the clock on the dash. Two-twelve. A flurry of butterflies arrive, fluttering in my stomach just at the mere thought of seeing Mitch again. And there he is. Standing at the tailgate of his Chevy, taking a duffel bag out of the back. He glances up at me, a smile spreading across his lips, his sunglasses dipped to the edge of his nose. I park just down from him and he walks toward me. He's not in uniform today. He's in a black collared shirt and black tailored pants, his gun holster strapped across his broad shoulders and a badge on his hip. I shiver just looking at him, then get out of the car and rush toward him.

He takes off his glasses and snatches me up in his arms, lifting me into the air then lowering me down slowly until his lips touch mine. I giggle. Seeing him again is even better than I imagined.

"Oh, God, it's good to hold you," he murmurs. He presses his lips to mine one more time then lowers me to the ground, our eyes locked on each other, knowing if there was nothing more than this, it would be enough. He picks up his bag then turns, leading me toward the office.

"How was your day?" I ask.

He groans. "Terrible. I couldn't stop thinking about you. Almost got myself killed a couple of times."

"What?"

He opens the front door, leading me inside, then drops his bag, locking the door behind us.

"Come here."

He pulls me into his arms, his mouth instantly on mine. I throw my arms around his neck and he lifts me up, carrying me through to his apartment, then setting me down on the kitchen bench. He kisses my eyes, my cheeks, my nose then pulls his head back to look at me.

"You look incredible as usual. Would you like a drink?"

"Yeah, a water would be nice."

"A water it is."

He walks over to the fridge, taking out a beer and a bottle of water. I watch him, admiring his body, my eyes feeding my insatiable hunger for him.

"So, how come you're dressed like this today?"

"Uh, I'm on an undercover operation this week. Doing surveillance on a drug trafficking ring for CIB." He shakes his head, amused.

"What?" I ask.

"I can't believe you sent me that message this morning. I had the biggest boner thinking about you touching yourself. I look up and all the morning staff start gathering around me doing handover. I couldn't move. I had to just sit there until it went down." We laugh.

"Do you do that often? Touch yourself?" he asks, twisting the top off his beer and taking a sip.

I shrug, biting my bottom lip as I slide down off the bench and take a seat on the stool below it. He raises his eyebrow, exhaling loudly, clearly aroused.

"You must have started early today?"

"Yep, six a.m.," he replies, taking another sip of beer.

"What time did you finish last night?"

"Well, I was supposed to finish at ten, but I had an arrest right on knock-off, so I was stuck at the watchhouse till midnight."

"Wow. Not much of a break between shifts."

"You get used to it."

"And do you always work with that girl you were with last night?" I can't bring myself to say her name. He squares his shoulders, then puts his beer up to his mouth, drinking slowly, seemingly not prepared to talk about her. I watch him, waiting.

"I work with her a bit, yeah."

"She had her paws all over you."

He perches on the stool beside me. "Really?" he asks curiously, curling his lips up at the corners. "Jealous, are we?"

I don't answer. He pulls my chair around to face him, slides my knees between his and rests his hands on my legs.

"Hmmm?" He brings his face closer to mine, waiting for my answer.

"Have you slept with her?"

He breathes in sharply, his forehead creasing.

He has.

"Not lately," he replies, touching his lips to mine. He cups a hand around the back of my neck, holding me to him, but I pull back, breaking off the kiss.

"Will you be serious?" I snap.

"About what?" he murmurs, inching toward me.

I push him back and he lets go of me, leaning back in his seat.

"What's wrong?"

"That policewoman last night. She had her hands all over you and you were completely comfortable with it. She deliberately looked at me when she touched you. She wanted me to see. And I saw you with her at the pub that day. You had your arm around her, laughing and whispering into her ear."

He takes a hard swallow of his beer.

"Have you slept with her?" I ask again, annoyed with his avoidance of the question.

"Do you really wanna do this?"

"Do what?"

"This!"

"Why can't you just answer the question?"

He exhales loudly, his voice stern. "Because you might not like the answer."

I drop my gaze, staring down at his hand on my leg, not wanting it there.

"Don't do this, Scar."

"Don't do what?"

"Don't be like this. You've got no right to be jealous. You've been sleeping with Nick. How do you think *I* feel? Thinking about him making love to you, looking into your eyes, wondering if he sees what I see. It did my head in, Scarlet. It broke me. I'm a shadow of the man I used to be. Jealousy's a dark, dark place. You can lose yourself there."

"I know about dark places."

He frowns into the palpable silence, then reaches up and tucks my hair behind my ear. I jerk my head away and he drops his hands onto his lap with weary resignation. "If I seemed comfortable with her touching me, it's because there's history there. That's all. It's over."

"Not for her. You said you were seeing someone when you met me. Is she the girl you were seeing?"

He pauses before answering. "Yes."

"Did she know we were seeing each other?"

"I don't think so. Why do you ask?"

I shake my head, not really knowing where I'm going with this, let alone able to explain it to him. "Are there other women? I mean, I saw the way they were looking at you at the art gallery last night. It was overwhelming."

He screws up his face. "No. There aren't *other women*. I don't sleep around, if that's what you're asking. You're the only woman I've ever slept with in my life without a condom. I haven't slept with Jade for months, nor anyone else. There's only you, and, yes, women throw themselves at me, but if you can't see how obsessed I am with you, woman, then we've got bigger problems."

He pulls me into his arms, looking down at me sincerely. "There's something else going here. What's *really* bothering you?"

"It's nothing."

"Tell me," he says softly. "You used to tell me everything."

I shake my head. "It's just something Nick said."

He drops his arms from around me. "Huh, this should be interesting! What did *Nick* say?"

I stand and walk across to the window, rubbing my arms. "It's hard for me to say."

He walks over to me, blocking my view. "What did he say?"

"He said that your only interest in me is money, that being a cop doesn't pay very well."

"And what do *you* think?"

I don't answer.

"Wow!" He steps back from me, throwing up his hands in the air. "Look around you, Scarlet. I own this place, I own this entire boatyard, this entire block. I don't need money from you. I'm not a cop because of the pay, I'm a cop because my dad was a cop. I do it out of a sense of responsibility, to him, to my mother, to others. Of late, it's been to take my mind off you. It's never been about money!"

"I know that. I told him that. We fought over it. I'm sorry."

I turn away from him and he grabs my wrist, turning me back to face him.

"I love you, Scarlet. There's only you and me in this, nothing shiny, nothing to gain, but I'll give you the world if you let me."

I arch an eyebrow. "Well, you've certainly got a lot to offer a girl."

Light slowly creeps into his dark, serious eyes. "Is that so?"

"Yeah, that's so."

"Come here." He takes me into his arms, kissing me, softly, tenderly, but I'm in no mood for tenderness. I slide my hand down his body to the front of his pants, gliding it over his huge, swollen erection. His eyes light up. "Or I could just give you that?"

I take his hand, leading him into the bedroom, reaching eagerly for his face, pulling his lips down to mine, groaning as I slide my hands down the fabric of his uniform to his hips. I snatch at his belt buckle, loosening it, then slide his gun holster and easily unbuttoned shirt off his shoulders. I glance up at him, his eyes glowing with anticipation, as hungry as mine.

I push him backward to the bed and he falls, a wicked grin forming on his lips as he raises his head, propping himself up on his elbows, so he can watch me. I flash him a dirty-martini look of desire, undoing the buttons of my blouse, one by one, to reveal my white lacy bra. He swallows hard as I take it off, revealing my supple, tan breasts and hard nipples. I unzip my skirt, letting it fall to the ground with my underwear, standing before him completely naked, all his. Mitch parts his lips, taking in more air as he ravages my body with his eyes.

"Get over here, woman," he growls.

I walk across to the bed slowly, seductively, kneeling down in front of him. He pulls me against him, bringing his mouth down hard on mine, and I bite his lip, just like he bit mine, warning him to back off. He winces in shock and I use the opportunity to push him back down.

"I'm in control here," I warn.

He raises his eyebrow as I unzip his pants, chuckling at my determination as I tug them eagerly from his body then free him from his underwear. I take him in my hand, stroking him gently, glorying in his impressive size. He groans, tilting his head back as I glide my fingertips lightly over his balls, tickling and teasing.

He raises his head, watching me, his eyes glistening with exultation as I bring my mouth down on him, twirling my tongue around the tip of his throbbing head then slowly descending down his thick, rigid shaft.

"Oh, Scar." He clutches his forehead in ecstasy as I pull up, sucking hard, then slide back down. His body tenses beneath me as I suck harder, increase the pace then stop.

He rises to his elbows, his bare chest surging and constricting with the ebb and flow of his labored breaths. He watches intently, his lips parting as I slowly, seductively lower my mouth to the inside of his thighs, licking his entire length from the base of his balls to the tip of his cock, then slide slowly down, taking him as deep into my throat as I can.

"Oh, my God," he gasps, throwing himself back down against the bed. I pull back, running my tongue up his length, then engulf him in long, languid strokes. His breathing grows rapid and raw as I wrap my hand around him, pulling up and down, faster and faster, my lips in hot pursuit of my hand. He bucks his hips, slamming his hands down on the bed by his sides, clutching the sheets beneath him.

"Oh, that's incredible. Don't stop."

I increase my stroke, licking and sucking as hard as I can, my saliva drenching my hand, my other hand between his legs, stroking and teasing. He groans loudly. He's close. He thrusts into my mouth as I slide my hand up and down in a wild, erratic rhythm. My arm is shaking, about to give out. His body shudders.

"Oh, Christ." Mitch reaches for me, knotting his fingers in my hair to thrust wildly into my mouth, gasping as he climaxes hot and hard, deep down my throat.

"Oh, fuck, fuck!" he cries, his chest heaving, his body jerking and twitching beneath me. He looks down at me, watching in awe as I swallow all he has to give. I stand slowly, falling down beside him, resting my head on his chest, listening to his heart racing in my ear.

"You're sensational," he pants, wrapping his arm around me.

A light sheen of sweat covers his body, making his skin glisten in the mellow golden glow of light from the window. I love that I did that to him, made him come, made him sweat. I follow the light trail of hair down his stomach to his red-hot cock, still so spirited and ready, amazed by my ability to handle his size.

"That was phenomenal. My legs are shaking so bad."

I laugh. "So's my arm."

He chuckles. I jump up and head into the kitchen.

"Like a drink?" I yell.

"Uh-huh," he calls back.

I take a bottle of water from the fridge, gulp some down, then walk back into the bedroom. As I step inside the doorway, I feel him behind me. He grabs my arms, pulling them behind my back. The water bottle falls to the floor and I yelp in surprise as something cold and hard brushes against my back. I hear a familiar clicking sound and feel something cold and heavy around one wrist.

He spins me around and throws me back on the bed, sitting astride me. He snatches at my wrists, pulling them up over my head to weave the cuff through the slats of his timber bedhead, then attaches the other cuff to my wrist.

"Mitch, what are you —?"

I stop talking, struggling against the cold, hard steel, but my hands are locked firmly in place. I look up at him, anxious, not knowing what to expect. He reaches across to the chair beside the bed, taking his tie in his hand and holding it against my lips.

"Open," he says gruffly.

"What are you going to do to me?"

"*Open*," he demands, his eyes sharp as claws.

I tentatively part my lips and he slips the tie into my mouth, fastening it tightly behind my head. I bite down on the material and meet his gaze. His eyes burn with fire.

He stares down at me, shaking his head, so completely aroused by the sight of my incarceration.

"I could keep you like this forever. Fuck you every day and every night, over and over. No one would ever find you."

I open my eyes wide at the thought. He slides his hands down my body, caressing me, teasing me, and I wriggle beneath him, tugging at the cuffs, realizing there's no escape.

He lowers his mouth to my ear. "I'm gonna make you scream harder than you've ever screamed before," he breathes, squeezing my nipple then closing his mouth around my earlobe, biting hard. I cry out, my teeth clamping down hard on the tie that muffles my howl. I feel his tongue on my neck, gliding down to my collarbone, slowly, leisurely down to my breasts. Mitch closes his lips around my nipple, scraping his teeth against my skin, threatening me, warning me, then he bites. My whole body responds. I whimper and arch my back, sinking my teeth into the gag. He bites again harder and I cry out, consumed by a thunderous, pulsating sensation deep inside my body. My hands ball up into fists, tugging hard against the cold steel as it nips at my skin. A heady vortex of pleasure and pain swirls inside me. He watches me, his eyes drenched in desire, enjoying every second of my torment.

He moves his mouth down my stomach, continuing south to my hips as he snatches at my legs, tearing them apart. His chest vibrates with a bloodthirsty growl and he lowers his mouth to the inside of my thighs, driving his masterful tongue deep inside me, exploring me, tasting me, darting in and out of my mound, trembling body with determination and insistence.

I moan, lifting and sinking my hips in quick succession as Mitch replaces his tongue with his fingers, plunging deep, his tongue complementing his dedicated fingers as they build up to a fierce, ever-increasing rhythm.

I bury my head back in the pillows, whimpering, my body on fire. I lose my mind, wrapping my legs around his neck, thrusting into his mouth, biting down on the gag and tugging at the cuffs, crying out as I ride my wagon of pleasure through town with no regard for others. He groans, withdrawing his fingers, exchanging them for his tongue, licking deep inside me, drinking from me. He watches me, equally invested in my pleasure, reveling in my return from my mindless, reckless rampage.

"Oh, Scar," he moans.

I close my eyes, drawing in deep breaths through my nose, the tie restricting my air and adding to my ecstasy. I feel his mouth on my stomach and I open my eyes, watching him slowly lick his way up my body, nipping at my stomach, my nipples, my neck. I can't stand another minute of his denial. I want him. I want to touch him, run my fingers through his hair, something, anything.

I twist my head, struggling to get my mouth free of the gag, and he pulls it down onto my chin.

"Please," I pant, flexing my hips against him.

"Please what?" he whispers against my ear, squeezing my inner thigh. I spread my legs for him and feel his huge, threatening shaft pressing against me, circling, sharking. He brushes the hair from my face, his eyes locked with mine.

"Please, I need you," I beg.

Mitch clenches his jaw, applying the slightest, sweetest taste of pressure, and I whimper for more. "What do you need?" he murmurs.

"I need your big, hard cock inside me, now!"

He groans, sinking back onto his knees, pushing my legs up so that my thighs are wide open for him. He puts the gag back into my mouth and forces the head of his cock inside me just a little, circling his hips, warning me of what's to come. "Is this what you need?"

"Oh God, yes!" I cry through the gag.

"Look at me," he says sternly and I do as he says.

He clutches at my ankles, placing them on his shoulders, raising my hips to his for him to ram himself deep inside me. I scream out, tightening my hands into fists, clenching tightly around him. He groans, his eyes enraptured, and he pulls back, thrusting harder, burying himself deep. Tears instantly fill my eyes. *Oh God, it hurts.* His eyes flicker with joy as he feeds every last inch of himself inside me, rocking his hips against mine, making sure every bit of him disappears. He stares down at me, shaking his head, perhaps in awe of my ability to take him.

"Oh, good girl. Are you okay?"

I nod, closing my eyes, harnessing my pleasure until it overrides the pain. He circles his hips, then pulls back swiftly, driving into me deep and hard, over and over. The raw power of his strokes forces incomprehensible cries from my mouth as he fills my ravenous body. I buck my hips against his and he tightens his jaw, reaching for the bedhead, pulling himself toward me, grunting and driving into me as hard as possible. My head thrashes violently from side to side as I scream louder than I ever have, just like he said I would. My skin is stinging around him, my body weak, tense, clinging, hanging then plummeting, plunging, descending deep into my undoing. His thrusts grow wild and frantic, a deep, depraved rumble escaping his lips as he fills my body with his hot, wet cum. He lowers my legs to the bed, moving slowly inside me as I lie limp, exhausted among the pillows beneath him.

"Fuck, you're insatiable," he pants, kissing my neck and face. He withdraws slowly, unfastening the tie from my mouth and uncuffing me.

"Oh God," I breathe.

"Are you all right?"

I nod, drawing in deep breaths, rubbing my wrists as he throws himself down onto the bed beside me, breathless. I put my arm around his waist, snuggling against him.

"Good?"

I nod, squeezing him tightly. "It just gets better every time."

He winces, but I don't pay attention. He tucks his arm behind his head and I rest my face on his chest, gliding my fingers across his skin, tracing down the line of his stomach across to his side. He stops breathing. His hand comes down on mine abruptly, clutching my fingers tightly. I lift my head up to look at him.

"Did I hurt you?" I ask.

His brow creases. "No. It still hurts there sometimes. Where I got shot."

I sit up, my eyes zooming in on his side. There's a scar there. I can't believe I hadn't noticed it. I gasp and put my hand over my mouth.

"What's wrong?"

I hold my hand up, sifting through my dreams, remembering what I saw. A flash of blood, a dark crimson red, all over my hands and soaking the bandage on his side. I feel the horror, but this time I see his face. I pull back my head, sucking in a deep breath.

"Scarlet?" He puts his hand on my back and I flinch.

"Hey, hey. It's me. What did you see?"

He sits up, groaning and clutching his side.

"Scarlet, you're really worrying me."

I look up at him and for some reason I giggle. Uncontrollably.

"What's so funny?"

"It was you." My eyes flood with tears of mixed emotions.

"What was me?"

"It was you, in my dream. I saw you, only I didn't know it was you, until just now. We were making love. You stopped suddenly. You were doubled over in pain, there was blood everywhere. It was all over you, all over me. It was horrible. You had a bandage on your side and it was soaked through with blood. You started peeling it off and that's when I woke up. I never saw your face."

He hugs me tightly. "That's amazing."

"That really happened?"

"Pretty much, yeah. I got shot about three weeks after we first started seeing each other. You were a mess. They couldn't get all of the bullet out. I had to have another surgery. It did some pretty extensive muscle damage but no major organ damage. I was lucky. A few inches to the right and it would have hit my stomach, and the odds of surviving that are pretty low."

"Oh, my God."

"I was in the hospital for about three weeks. It hurt like hell to move. You were upset because you couldn't be with me as much as you wanted. You'd visit me as often as you could and we'd fool around a little, but sex was pretty much out of the question. You brought me home from the hospital. They told me I shouldn't do any physical exercise for at least six weeks, which was ridiculous. We couldn't wait a day. You did all the work for weeks, but one afternoon I had to have it my way. We took it really slowly, but I must have been bleeding for a while because there was blood everywhere. I got an infection. It was awful, but it was worth it. So you're dreaming your memories, huh?"

"I guess so."

He leans back against the pillows and winces. I look down at the scar. "How did it happen?"

He exhales loudly. "I, uh, walked in on a kid robbing a service station late one Friday night." He shrugs. "I underestimated him."

I rise to my hands and knees, very carefully sitting astride him, resting my hand over the scar, feeling the warmth there. "Did they catch him?" I whisper.

He looks down at my hand on his scar, letting his gaze linger between my legs before slowly moving up my body to my face.

"Yeah." He pauses, distracted. "I managed to get a shot off before I lost consciousness. I hit him in the leg when he was running out."

I move against him, wet, wanting him inside me. "Uh-huh," I murmur, swallowing hard as he slides his hands leisurely up my legs to my hips.

"Slowed him down," he continues, clutching at my hips, lifting me up then lowering me onto his rigid, waiting cock. My mouth opens, whimpering as I slide down him. "They caught up with him a couple blocks away."

"Oh," I reply, interlocking our fingers and clutching his hands in mine to rise slowly then lower myself back down. He lifts his hips, thrusting up inside me then winces, gritting his teeth in pain.

"Don't move," I murmur, ascending again, dropping down harder. He groans, his hands tightening around mine as I bring my mouth down to his ear. "So you've been off work ever since?" I whisper, lowering my mouth to his neck and sucking hard.

"Uh-huh," he breathes.

I lean back, rocking against him, slowly lifting my hips and sinking down. He wets his lips, closing his eyes briefly.

"So, that's why you said you weren't a cop anymore." I rise then descend hard and fast. He groans, thrusting against me. "Don't move!"

He stills, staring up at me. "I didn't think I'd ever go back, either, but you changed that."

"Me?" I breathe, moving my hips back and forth, clenching tightly around him.

"Being stripped of your reason for living tends to bring out a person's reckless side." He thrusts up inside me again.

"Oh?" I whimper. He lets go of my hands, trailing his fingers across my breasts as I rise and fall harder and faster. "I thought it was the promotion that lured you back to work."

"Oh, the promotion. That's right. I forgot." He squeezes my nipples hard and I shudder, a ripple of pleasure and pain flowing through me.

"And I thought *I* was the forgetful one."

He chuckles softly, thrusting up hard inside me, then he cries out, clutching at his side, his brow furrowed tightly with pain. I stop and move off him. He tries to stop me but he's too late.

"Don't stop," he protests.

I look down at him, wrapping the top sheet from the bed around me. "Mitch, something's really wrong."

"No. It's not. I'm fine. It just pinches sometimes, when I run or overdo it. I chased that suspect through a car park last night before I made the arrest. I must have agitated it and this has made it worse."

"I'm so sorry. I shouldn't have—"

"I'm fine."

"Does it hurt every time you have sex?"

He nods. "But not this bad."

"Oh, my God, you were carrying me before and you've been fighting with Nick. He hit you in the stomach a couple of times. I saw it."

"And I deserved it. I'm fucking his wife. I deserve whatever I get. But I won't give you up. I tried that already. It didn't work."

"Don't say that."

"Say what?"

"You don't deserve this. You don't deserve any of this. It's me who deserves what I get. I'm married and look at me, in another man's bed. What kind of person does that make me?"

"Stop that. You can't keep putting this all on you. You left him — you were getting a divorce. We were going to sail around the world, get married, have as many children as the boat could handle before it sank, but somebody rocked the boat and you fell out. We were robbed. That's the facts. This isn't your fault and it's not my intention to badmouth Nick, but he treated you badly. He's not exactly an innocent in all of this. Don't beat yourself up because you found happiness."

I swallow hard, searching his face.

"Tell me about the dream you had of the accident. What did you see?"

"I saw everything. It was terrifying. A car was chasing me. It hit the back of my car twice. I couldn't see anything. It was too dark and the windscreen was covered in rain, but at one point, when my car was spinning, my lights shone on it. It was definitely a dark-colored car, but that's all I can tell you." Tears build up in my eyes, spilling down my cheeks. "Someone wanted me dead, Mitch. I died in that car. I saw it. I saw my own death."

He sits up, not making a sound though I know it must have hurt him, holding me against his chest. "You're alive, Scar. You're here with me, where you're supposed to be."

My cell phone rings out on the kitchen bench. We both look toward the doorway, knowing exactly who it is. He exhales loudly. I swipe at my tears, pulling out of his arms, standing swiftly. He grabs my wrist at the last second.

"Leave it."

"I can't." I pull my hand from his and rush out to the kitchen, picking up the phone. It's Nick. If I don't answer, he'll keep ringing then he'll be suspicious.

"Hello," I answer softly.

"Hi," he replies, his voice low and weary. "How are you?"

"I'm okay."

"You don't sound okay. What's wrong?"

I make another pass at my eyes, drying my tears. "Nothing. I'm fine. How are you?"

"Not great." He sounds terrible. "I want to come home to you. I tried to get an earlier flight, but I can't get another one until tomorrow afternoon."

"It's okay. Finish what you have to do. It's just one more day."

"It's not okay, I'm worried about you. I'm thinking about chartering a private jet."

"Nick, I'm fine. Catch your flight tomorrow. You sound tired," I reply, changing the subject.

"I am, it's been pretty full on here and I'm not getting much sleep."

"Well, you should try. You need your sleep."

He's quiet for a moment. "I can't stop thinking about you."

"Me, too," I reply.

"I made a mistake coming here," he murmurs.

"A mistake?"

"Have you seen Mitch?"

I look up at the pictures of Mitch and me, on the wall in front of me and hesitate. He exhales loudly. "I'll take that as a yes. I don't want you to."

"What?"

"I don't want you to see him."

"But you told me—"

"I know what I told you," he interrupts. "But I don't want you to see him. Please don't see him. I don't want you anywhere near him. I don't know what I was thinking." I don't answer.

"Have I lost you?"

"What? *No*."

He pauses. "I love you, Scarlet."

"I love you, too," I reply, peering nervously through the bedroom door to Mitch. He's still lying on the bed, not

248

moving. "When does your plane get in?" I ask, digressing from the mushy stuff.

"Five-thirty, so I'll be home around six-thirty." He sounds so deflated. I've never heard him like this.

"Great," I reply, trying to sound cheerful.

"Where are you? I called the house but there was no answer."

"No. I'm at Tash's," I reply hastily.

"How did the gallery opening go?"

My thoughts immediately turn to Mitch, his eyes on me, walking toward me at the gallery in his uniform. "It was really good. Yeah, I had a good time," I answer, racked with guilt.

Mitch walks out of the bedroom to the kitchen, glowering at me.

"What about you? How's everything going down there?"

"Yeah, everything's going well. I just can't wait to get home to you."

"Me, neither," I answer, watching Mitch as he pours himself a glass of milk and gulps it down.

"Will you be there when I get home?"

"Yes, I'll be there. Of course I'll be there," I reply.

He exhales loudly. "That's good. I miss you so much."

I hesitate, knowing that Mitch isn't going to like this. "I miss you, too."

Mitch purposely drops his cup into the sink, making a clatter. I look up at him. He glowers then turns and walks into the bedroom.

"What was that?" Nick asks.

"Uh, I dropped a cup in the sink." I hear a loud voice in the background making an announcement.

"They're calling the next intake. I have to go. I love you, baby."

"I love you, too. Call me later and I'll see you tomorrow." I hang up and cringe, looking toward the bedroom. I can't see him but I can feel his anger from here. I put the phone down on the bench, clenching my jaw.

This is going to be fun.

He's standing at the window when I enter the bedroom, staring out toward the water, his jeans hanging loosely around his hips, his arms folded across his bare chest. I stand beside him, staring out at his yacht that holds such wonderful new memories for me, watching as it bobs gently in its mooring, under the wind's hand.

"Two 'I love you' and an 'I'll see you tomorrow'." He looks across at me. "What happens tomorrow, Scarlet? You go home to him and what happened between us just gets written off as a bad dream?"

"What?"

He shakes his head. "I can't lose you again. It would destroy me." I rest my hand on the back of his head, stroking his hair. I don't know what to say to him. He turns to me, his eyes red. "You can't seriously be going home to him tomorrow, after everything that's happened between us."

"He's my husband, I can't just—"

He steps back out of my clutches, furious.

"So, what, that's *it*? You love me, I know you do. I see the way you look at me. I see it in your eyes, just as you feel it in your soul. I've never felt this way about anyone, and neither have you. You told me over and over before the accident that I'm the love of your life. You can't take that away from me, Scarlet—you can't just dismiss this. It's coming back to you. *It will come back to you.*" He stares down at me, reaching beyond my eyes to the girl trapped behind them, fighting to find her way out. I feel faint. I sit down on the bed, clutching my forehead.

"What are you thinking? Just say it," he snaps.

"Okay. I'm thinking it doesn't change the fact that I'm married. Don't you see? I don't have a choice."

He strides toward me, standing me up and clutching my shoulders. "You do have a choice. I'm standing right here in front you. I love you. I want you. I'm asking you to choose me."

"Mitch, it's not that simple."

He drops his hands from my shoulders, his eyes like open wounds. It's not what he wants to hear, but I'm so confused and that's all I have to offer him right now. He's right. I do love him. Seeing the hurt and sadness in his eyes brings nothing but hurt and sadness to me. The connection between us is stronger than I thought. The prospect of not being able to see him again is unbearable. I don't know how I will ever stop wanting him, stop needing him, but I love Nick and I have to give this marriage everything I've got—that means setting Mitch free. I don't want to hurt him. I don't want to hurt either of them, though the fact of the matter is, I have, and I'm not done yet.

"I'm going home, at least for now. I need time. My head's a mess. You don't want me like this."

"You're really doing this then? You're really going home to play happy families?"

"Mitch…"

"Go then! Go now. I'll make this easy for you," he snaps.

"You don't mean that."

His eyes bear down on me, bitter and forbidding. "I do."

"You're just angry, Mitch. Don't do this."

He grabs my arm and forces me toward the bedroom door. "I've got Jade, right? I'll call her the minute you're gone. I'll fuck her until I forget you."

I pull my arm from his grasp and slap him across the face, hard, the sound ricocheting around the room. He snatches my forearm, never before angrier.

"*Is that right?*" he shouts. He seizes both my wrists together in his hand, wrapping his other arm around me, squeezing me against him. His strength is terrifying. I look up at him, panicked, my fear fueling the fire. He crashes his mouth down on mine, driven with a poisonous mixture of anger and passion, and I return his kiss.

Mitch moves his lips with mine, forceful and determined, our heads tilting, our tongues fighting, our teeth clashing. He releases my wrists, sliding his hands up to my throat, holding me to him in a way that there can be no illusions about his power over me. I close my eyes, feeling his fingers tighten around my throat, feeling him hard and throbbing against me. I tilt my head back, a soft moan escaping my lips.

He rips the sheet from my body and throws me back onto the bed, breathless. I watch him stride toward me. He doesn't speak. I fixate on his bare, heaving chest as he lowers his body to mine, his eyes aflame. He slides his hand down my body, snatching at my thighs, spreading my legs. He unzips his jeans, forcing himself inside me without a second's thought. I'm not prepared for him at all. It hurts. I cry out, gasping, tears forming in my eyes, not knowing what to think or feel as I lie beneath him, enduring his bittersweet symphony of pleasure and pain.

He draws back, sinking himself as deep as he can inside me, then pushing harder, tearing at my skin, his face devoid of expression. I whimper, my body tense, my bottom lip quivering. He knows he's hurting me, but his words hurt me more.

"Look at me," he demands. "This may be our last time together."

Tears trickle down my face, their salt stinging my skin.

"Look at me!"

I clench my jaw. He has no right to make me feel like this. I look up at him, see him pushing my legs open wider, plunging forcefully inside me. It hurts so much. He sees my eyes, sees the hurt in my eyes, sees that he's the one hurting me, but his eyes stay hard. He wants it to hurt. He's punishing me, wanting me to look at my punisher while he punishes me, the way my leaving will punish him.

I look up at him through my tender tears. "You're killing me," I sob.

He lowers his mouth to my ear. "I'm loving you," he whispers.

My whole body shudders.

"Do you want me to stop?" he murmurs.

"No," I whimper. He closes his eyes briefly as if savoring

my image, then draws back swiftly, driving himself into me as hard as he can, over and over. Both of us lost, hiding deep in the darkness of each other's soul.

"Don't cry. You're too beautiful to cry," he whispers, hurting me with his body yet loving me so completely with his eyes.

He draws back, squeezing his eyes closed, then groans loudly, clutching his side.

"Oh, Christ," he hisses through gritted teeth.

"Mitch, stop!"

He opens his eyes, looking down at me. "No. I want it to hurt me, too."

I swallow hard. He thrusts again slowly, his jaw clenched tightly, trying to hide his pain. He reaches his hands down, clutching each of mine, interlocking our fingers and sliding them up beside my head, tightening and loosening his grip with his thrusts. The intensity of our connection is so strong, so fulfilling, that in that moment, I don't think I can give him up.

He plunges deep into the incandescent depths of my body, his eyes drenched in pain, increasing with every stroke. His body moves with mine, so in rhythm, so in sync, our pleasure building so equally.

"Don't make me live without you," he breathes against my ear.

"I can't stay," I whisper softly, not knowing if he heard me.

He lunges faster, stronger and we cry out, coming together, our bodies shaking, shuddering. He clutches my head tightly to his chest, nuzzling his face into my hair then kissing my forehead. I feel his body grow tense as he withdraws, falling down onto the bed beside me, his hand on his side.

"Mitch, you're hurting. Why didn't you stop?" He doesn't answer. I prop myself up on my elbow to look at him.

"Mitch?"

He lies there, his face contorted with pain, pushing the

scar into his skin. He doesn't look at me. "You should go," he snaps.

"What?"

His eyes flash to mine as red as blood. "Just go. Please. I can't say goodbye to you again, Scarlet. Just leave."

His words are like a bullet to the heart. I've never been shot before, that I know of, but this is probably how it feels. That moment where the bullet sinks beneath your skin, you feel the pain and you're faced with a choice. You can either embrace death or embrace the bullet, hoping that it passes right through because you don't need that heart anymore anyway. But pain would be nothing right now, compared to the anguish in my heart and so I embrace the bullet.

"Mitch," I whisper through my tears.

He doesn't answer. I can't breathe. I swallow hard and force myself out of his bed, dressing quickly and collecting my things. He doesn't move. I walk to the bedroom door and turn back to look at him. He doesn't look at me. I turn, pulling the door closed behind me and walk out of his life forever.

Chapter Sixteen

Jaded

I glance across at the clock. Four o'clock. Nick will be home soon. It's been a very, very, long day, here at home, alone with my thoughts. Thoughts of Nick, my feelings for him so strong, his love for me, confounding, unshakable. Then there's Mitch. His last words haunt me. His pain, the way he looked at me, the way it ended, will leave a scar in my heart forever. I look at the clock again. It's been almost twenty-four hours since I saw him.

Mitch. My heartbeat quickens if I just think his name. When I close my eyes, he's all I see. His dark, hungry eyes above me, our bodies one. I feel the pull of my desire, pulsating in my core, once, twice. I bite my bottom lip and shift in my seat. I'm wet, trembling. I clutch the arms of the chair in a feeble attempt to curb my energy, scared, terrified by my desperate, suffocating desire to see him.

I steal a glimpse at the clock again. Four-ten. I take a deep breath, jump out of the chair and rush to the door. I have to see him.

I run to the garage and jump into the car, roaring out of the driveway, flashes of our most intimate moments replaying in my head. I drive faster, faster, not fast enough, accelerating into the sweeping bend where my car went into the water, no longer scared of the repercussions. I pass through the fiveways, merging onto the motorway. It's not far now. I tighten my hands on the steering wheel, my palms sweating. Luckily the traffic is light today and I make it there in record time.

The boatyard driveway comes into view just ahead, rendering my mind nothing but a frenzy of disconnected thoughts. I slow down and pull into the lot, my breathing shallow. His car's the first thing I see. I park beside it, rushing to the front entrance of the office. I have to see him. I *need* to see him. The front door's unlocked. I slide it open and step inside, hurrying to his apartment door. It's ajar.

I hear voices. A woman. I stop. Listening. Her laughter echoes down the hall. I hear him say her name, "Jade," and it forces every last ounce of air from my body. His voice is soft and low. I can't hear what he's saying. I step forward to the doorway, peering carefully through the opening.

He's sitting on a chair, facing me. Jade, sitting astride him, her thin arms draped around his neck, her long, messy dark hair dangling just above a tattoo on the small of her back. He's grinning up at her. I gasp.

His dog, Blue, barks from inside the apartment and I stumble backward. My shirt catches on the door handle, pulling it open, making a loud creaking sound. Mitch looks up at me, startled.

"Scarlet?" He snatches Jade's arms from around his neck and jumps up.

"Mitch!" she shouts at him.

"Why did you come here, Jade?" he shouts back, but I'm gone. I burst through the front door and run toward the car, pressing the remote twice in my panic. The car opens then locks again.

"Scarlet!" he shouts from behind me.

I press the remote again frantically, but it's too late. He tightens a hand around my arm. I fight forward, reaching for the door handle, but he's too strong.

"Stop, just stop!" he yells, spinning me around to face him. "Look at me!" He grabs my other arm, holding me to him.

"No! Don't touch me." I push against him, trying to break free, my body rigid and tense.

"Listen to me. There's nothing between Jade and me."

I glare up at him. "You didn't waste much time. You're a man of your word, I'll give you that."

"She came here unannounced! I love *you*, Scarlet. I'm in love with *you*."

I shake my head, turning away. He lets go of my arm, turning my face back to his.

"I love you. There's only you. There's only ever been you."

Tears pool in my eyes, threatening to fall, but I fight them off, standing my ground. I see Jade over his shoulder, her hands on her hips, her face enraged. I jerk my head out of his clutches.

"I was wrong to come here."

"Why *did* you come here, Scarlet? You walk in and out of my life as if it's your office. You dismissed my love as if it was a pebble in your shoe. Now you see someone else showing interest and you're angry? You've got no right to be."

I bring my fists up between us, pushing against his chest. "Let me go, Mitch," I snarl.

He ignores me, holding me tighter, his face pained. "Not until you tell me why you came."

"I don't know why I came!" I shout, struggling against him.

"Stop fighting me, Scarlet! Talk to me."

"No. Let me go. I can't trust you!"

"You can trust me." He wraps his arms around me, pressing his body against mine, and I want him as much as I want him to let me go. He looks into my eyes and he knows it. He lowers his face to mine.

"We've found each other again. We're meant to be together."

I feel my resistance to him failing. His lips inch closer, almost on mine.

"No. I'll never kiss you again!" I push against him, but his grip is firmer than ever.

"*Mitch!*" Jade yells from behind us.

He stops in his tracks, blinking as if he's suddenly remembered she's there. He steps back, releasing me, and I unlock the car and jump in, reversing from the park as fast as I can. He folds his hands behind his head, watching helplessly as I accelerate out of the lot, not looking back.

I pull out onto the street, my tears falling with the wrath of the winter rain. The sun is almost down. I head for the motorway, racing the darkness as it closes in around me, settling on the hills beyond home. The traffic is surprisingly light for this time of day and I speed up, wanting to put as much distance as possible between Mitch and me. I merge between two cars, switching on my headlights as I turn off the motorway onto my exit, consumed by thoughts of him. I can still see his eyes, hear his voice, feel his hands on my arms. I look down at my hands on the wheel, shaking uncontrollably. *How could I have been so naïve?* I swallow hard, choking back my anger. At least I know who he is now.

He told me he was going to fuck Jade until he forgot me and I'm sure that if I hadn't interrupted, he would have. A light shimmers in my rear-vision mirror and I look back, noticing headlights behind me, coming up fast. I don't remember seeing anyone turn off at the exit behind me. The lights grow brighter, closer. Too close. My frantic heartbeat pulses through my body, the terror from my dreams reasserting itself as reality.

The car speeds up behind me, its horn sounding and its headlights flashing. I glance up at the road ahead then back in the rear-vision mirror and the car is gone. I spin my head around, searching for it. *It's beside me.* It swerves toward me and I scream, veering to the side of the road and stomping on the brake. My tires bear down, kicking up gravel like an Arabian dust storm, the wheels sliding, the car finally coming to a rest beside the guardrail on the shoulder.

I sit there, dazed, crying, slumped over the steering wheel, when I notice bright lights coming right at me. I scream, bracing for the smash, but the car stops just short of me, its lights shining in my face. I hear footsteps in the gravel and my car door swings open. I put my arm up, trying to shield my eyes from the light, but I can't see who it is. I feel a heavy weight on my chest as cool hands tighten around my throat, then a woman's voice.

"One man not enough for you, you fucking bitch, you have to take mine as well?" I recognize her voice immediately.

Jade.

"I won't let you. I won't let you take him away from me again."

Her hands tighten around my throat, her body weight constricting my chest. I gasp for air, scratching at her hands, but she's too strong.

"Jade, please," I splutter, pounding my fists against her forearms.

"Stay the fuck away from him, do you hear me? Or next time, I'll make sure you *stay* at the bottom of that watery grave I sent you to last time."

She tightens her grip, shaking me violently, and I sink my fingernails into her arms, screaming at her to stop. She squeals, the volume decreasing rapidly as my hearing fades out. I close my eyes, praying for Nick, wishing that I could see him one last time as the dark salvation in my eyelids turns white. All of a sudden, she yelps and the pressure is gone. I open my eyes, gasping, choking, spluttering as the cool night air overfills my lungs.

I hear Mitch's voice. "*You?*" he shouts, in horror. "*You did this?*"

I straighten in my seat, clutching at my burning throat. I still can't see him, Jade's headlights shining brightly in my eyes. Mitch steps in front of me, blocking their sheen, and I look up him, wheezing. He reaches into the car, pulling my hands away from my neck.

"Are you okay? Can you breathe?" he asks, checking my chest and throat.

I nod, drawing in a deep, agonizing breath.

"I'll call you an ambulance."

I put my hand on his. "I'm okay."

He helps me out of the car. "Are you sure?"

"Yes."

His brow creases. He leans me against the car and turns on Jade. I see her now, on the ground in front of me, Mitch towering over her.

"How could you do this?" he shouts, his hands clenched tightly into fists. She shrinks under the gaze of his hateful glare, scrambling backward over the stones. He follows her, lowering his face to hers.

"*Why?*" he shouts.

"Mitch, please," she cries out. "I didn't mean to hurt her."

"*Don't lie to me!* I heard you. I heard what you said to her."

She bows her head, tears streaming down her face.

"*Why did you do it?*"

"I never set out to hurt her. I drove to her house that night to confront her. To tell her husband what she was doing to him, to us, but when I got to the door, they were having a terrible argument. She was screaming out that it was over between them. She came tearing out of the house and got in her car and I knew she was gonna run to you. Into your arms, into your bed. I jumped in the car and chased after her. I had to stop her."

I cup my hand over my mouth, a heavy dose of reality sinking in. She did this. She really did this to me. I rest my hands on the car, steadying myself, my knees weak with the knowledge.

"*Stop her?* You *killed* her! She died in that car!" Mitch shouts.

"I did it because I love you, Mitch," she cries, cowering beneath him.

"Well, I don't love you, you crazy bitch! It's over between us—it was over long ago!"

She jumps to her feet. "How can you say that to me? We were talking about getting married before you let *her* come between us. She wrecked our lives, Mitch!" she screams.

I glance across at Mitch. "Married?"

She spins around to me, her eyes burning like the sun. "That's right. *Married.* Before you came along and fucked it all up."

"Just stop it, Jade!" Mitch growls, his voice dark and menacing.

"No! She should know what you really are. A walking textbook—The Fickle Male 101. Promising me the world, while he's busy giving it to you." She takes a step toward me, her hands twitching at her sides, and I can see she'd like nothing more than to pick up where she left off.

Mitch moves in front of me, putting his arm out protectively.

She shrugs as though she's amused. "What, did you think I didn't know?"

"*I don't care that you know!*" he shouts.

His words are like a slap across the face and have the same effect. She stands there staring at him, a broken-down ghost of her former self.

"It's not her fault, Jade. It's mine. *I* started the relationship with her. *I* fell in love with her. *I'm* the bad guy here. There's nothing to be done. I can't help how I feel about her. It's not a matter of choosing her over you. I did love you. Without question. We did talk about marriage, but things changed and I can't change them back."

His voice grows softer. "I wasn't fair to you, but I *can* be honest with you. If you want someone to blame, or worse still, here I am. Do your worst! But sending the woman I love to the bottom of an icy lake isn't going to make me love you again."

She drops to her knees, hanging her face in her hands, her sobbing relentless. He glares down at her, his face stony and expressionless, as though he doesn't see her tears. For some strange reason, I feel sorry for her. Mitch reaches down, snatching at her arm.

"Stand up!" he says sternly. "Put your hands behind your back. I'm taking you in."

Jade lifts her head, glowering at him. She's an absolute mess and Mitch is wrong. It's not his fault. It's mine. I was weak to let this happen in the first place and I'd have to be out of my mind to let it happen again. Finally, I see this for what it is.

I'm the homewrecker here. She was marrying this man. She planned to spend the rest of her life with him and I ruined that. Twice. She'd taken my life in some respects and twenty-eight years of memories, but right now I feel nothing but regret and remorse. For the decisions I've made, for the life I've led and for Jade.

Mitch pulls her to her feet and I stride toward them.

"Mitch. Let her go."

"*What?*"

"Let her go."

He shakes his head. "I can't do that."

"Mitch, please—"

"Have you forgotten what she did to you?"

I press my lips together firmly, shaking my head. "No."

"You want me to let this go?"

I look Jade directly in the eyes with all the sincerity I can muster. "Yes."

Mitch creases his brow as though he doesn't understand, and maybe he never will. He glowers at Jade then lets go of her arm, his gaze filled with contempt.

"This ends here and now. Do you understand me? If you come anywhere near her again, I'll kill you myself," he hisses. "Get a transfer, somewhere far, far away from here. I never want to see you again. Do you hear me?"

She nods, reaching up and snatching the salty water from her eyes.

He tilts his head toward her car. "Now, get the fuck out of here before I do something I'll regret."

She makes a loud spluttering sound, sniffing back her tears. "I'm sorry, Mitch," she mutters. "I love you."

He looks away. She glances at me briefly then turns, stumbling back to her car, reversing and speeding away, her tires skipping and kicking up rocks as she leaves.

Mitch rushes over to me, pulling me into his arms, holding my head against his chest. "Are you okay?" he asks softly.

"Yes."

He clasps my chin, frantically checking my face and neck for marks. "Did she hurt you?"

"A little, but I'm all right."

"I'm so sorry. This is all my fault, Scarlet. I should have known. I considered the possibility of it being Jade, the dark car, the way she keeps hanging around, the constant niggly remarks, but I guess I just didn't want to believe it. I was so sure it was Nick. I had no idea she could be capable of doing something so awful. I convinced myself it wasn't her, but I watched her chase after you when you left this afternoon and I got a terrible feeling that I'd misjudged her."

I twist out of his arms and look up at him. "Tell me something honestly. If I hadn't come there today, would you have slept with her?"

"What?"

"You told me you were going to."

"You told *me* you were going back to your husband, that you didn't want anything to do with me!"

"So, you called her?"

"No, I didn't call her. I told you, she showed up unannounced. I had no intention of sleeping with her."

"She was sitting on your lap. You looked plenty intent to me."

"It's not like that." He reaches out for my hand, his touch desperate. "I was heartbroken after your accident. When I dragged you from that car and swam you back to the shore, I thought I'd lost you forever. I knew you hadn't taken a breath for so long. You were so cold. Your lips were blue. You had no pulse. Every breath you didn't take was one you took from me."

His tormented eyes stare straight into mine. I can't look away. My tears spill out onto my lashes one by one, freefalling to the ground. He's never told me any of that.

"I did everything I could to save you. To get your heart going, to keep you warm. I begged you to stay with me. The ambulance came and took you away and I waited and waited for you to open your eyes, but when you finally did, you didn't know me. I came to see you at the hospital a couple of times, but you looked right through me. It was as if you'd died. I mourned you. There was no graveside to visit, no coffin to bury—you were just gone, torn from my arms, ripped from my life and in the arms of another. Can you imagine what that's like? To look into the eyes of the woman you love, that you planned to spend the rest of your life with and she doesn't even recognize you. It's like someone showing you paradise then burning it down."

He stares at me, not moving. "It was so hard, for so long." He shrugs. "Jade, well, Jade was there."

"She loves you, Mitch. You were marrying her and I came between you."

"No! You *didn't* come between us."

"But I did. Twice. You loved her. Things may have worked out for you both, if I—"

"I didn't want to work things out with her. I didn't feel anything for her. It was just comfort sex."

"Wow!"

He pulls his head back, making a choking sound. "Oh! You're judging *me*? That's incredible. The woman ran you off the road, *twice*, cost you a lifetime of memories and you're judging *me*. That's— Yeah, that's great."

"I'm not judging you."

"Yes, she's been there for me and she probably deserved better, but how can I help it that I don't see her? I only see you. The sun rises and sets with you, Scarlet. I can't change that. God knows I've tried."

He rests his hands on my shoulders. "Your vow to him means nothing to me. I will fight for you. Openly, honestly. I'm not going away."

I shake my head, not doubting his words for a second. "I think we both just need some time."

"Oh, yeah! Great! More time! Time heals, right? Well, here I am, standing before you, a product of time. Look at me! Time has done nothing but tear me to shreds. Time is the devil and every minute without you is hell." He takes my hands in his. "I love you, Scarlet. I want you to be with me. I want you to choose me."

I stand there staring at him, his bleeding heart in my hands. I love him. I don't want to hurt him. I want to end his pain and I suddenly know what I have to do. I pull my hands from his, drifting back from him.

"I'm not the woman you fell in love with, Mitch. I'm the shell of the woman you love. How could I possibly give myself to you when I don't even know who I am?" His lips part, but he doesn't speak. *He knows I'm right.*

"I have to go."

He blocks my path, his face so close to mine. "Don't do this."

He stares down at me, waiting for the slightest hint of reservation to touch my eyes. If I blink, it will be the end of me. "I'm going home, Mitch. I can't see you anymore. You're an amazing man and an incredible lover. I love you. I'm not afraid to say it. I love you, but I love Nick, too. I'm *married* to him and I need to, but more than that, I want to try to make my marriage work."

He tilts his head back, running his hands through his hair as I turn, hurrying back to my car.

"*Scarlet!*"

The sorrow in his voice breaks my heart, but I don't stop. I know what I want and I know where to find him.

I jump into my car and start the engine, driving away as fast as I can, not looking back, my heart hollow, yet driven with determination to set things right with Nick. I look down at the clock on the dash. Five-fifteen. I've got time to get to the airport if I hurry. I speed out onto the motorway, high on adrenaline, never more sure of myself than I am right now. I need to see him. To tell him I love him, that I'm committed to our marriage. That I'm his, and only his, now and forever.

I accelerate, flying down the motorway, overtaking car after car when an outline of a plane comes into view on the exit sign above the bypass ahead. I merge between two cars, exiting onto Kingsford Smith Drive. I'm almost there.

I tighten my hands around the wheel, my head thumping, my racing heartbeat charging my body with electricity. I take the second exit to the domestic terminal and park in the pickup zone, rushing in to the front entrance. I run to the flight information board, searching for the flights out of Tullamarine. There's one at Gate 7 exiting now. I kick off my shoes then snatch them up, running as fast as I can, dodging people and jumping over suitcases, because all that matters now is finding Nick.

I reach the corridor to Gate 7 and hurtle down to the terminal as people start to emerge through the gate. I slip my shoes back on and stand on my tiptoes, peering through the crowd, finally catching a glimpse of him. The man I'm about to start forever with. He looks up at me and it's like seeing everything I've ever wanted, hoped and wished for all at once. His eyes light up like the night sky on the Fourth of July, leaving me breathless and speechless and lost.

He drops his bags, holding out his arms, and I run to him, jumping into his embrace, wrapping my arms and legs around him, tears of joy streaming down my face.

"I love you, I love you," I sob, kissing his eyes, his nose, his cheeks.

His mouth nuzzles into my neck. "Oh, baby, I missed you so much."

I weave my hands into his hair and his mouth is instantly on mine, kissing me wildly, fiercely, his fingers squeezing my thighs, not caring who's watching, like two giddy teenagers in love. Out of breath, he pulls his head back to look at me and there in his glistening eyes, in a moment of infinite clarity, I see my past, my present and my future. Our future. Nick tightens his arms around me.

"I'm never leaving you again."

"I'll never let you go."

He touches his lips to mine, then leans down, picking up his bags. He doesn't put me down and I wouldn't let him even if he tried.

"Let's go home," he whispers against my ear.

I tighten my arms around his neck, replacing the air in my lungs with his scent.

"I'm already there."

And filled with a love once forgotten.

More books from
Totally Bound Publishing

Book four in the Deadly Intent series

Fury, Fear, Fate.

Book one in the Strike Force series

Had he found her again only to lose her to a stalker?

Book one in the Brass Ring Sorority series

Think archeology is just dead bones? Think again

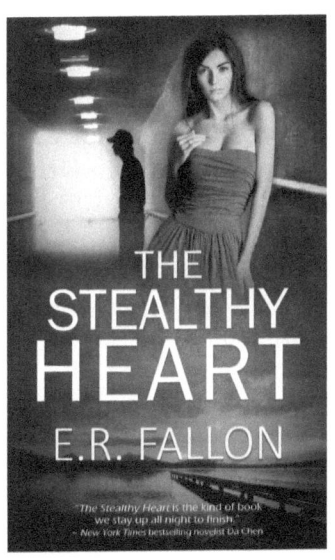

THE
STEALTHY
HEART

E.R. FALLON

"The Stealthy Heart is the kind of book
we stay up all night to finish."
~ New York Times bestselling novelist Da Chen

A magical romance saga spanning two generations of
women and the men who love them. Love on Blackthorn
Island is as complex as its enchanted secrets…

About the Author

Julianna Zacleese

Julianna Zacleese is an author and songwriter from the small country town of Childers in Queensland, Australia. Her love of literature and writing began at an early age and developed into a deep-seated passion for all things written.

While her decade-long career with the Police Service inspires the suspense element in her writing, it was her love of writing media releases and freelance articles for the local newspaper that led to her return to writing and success as a published author.

An entrant in the 2016 Cannes Screenplay Contest and 2017 Page International Screenwriting Awards, Julianna one day aspires to write for the big screen.

Julianna Zacleese loves to hear from readers. You can find contact information, website details and an author profile page at https://www.totallybound.com/

www.ingramcontent.com/pod-product-compliance
Lightning Source LLC
Chambersburg PA
CBHW021520240626
47154CB00002B/717